Hounds and Whippoorwills

By: RG Heinsohn Jr.

RG Heinsohn Jr. Books are available for order through Ingram
Press Catalogues

RG Heinsohn Jr.

Visit my website at www.gilsstories.com

Printed in the United States of America
First Printing: November 2015
Published by Sojourn Publishing, LLC

ISBN: 978-1-62747-169-5
Ebook ISBN: 978-1-62747-170-1

Introduction

People's personalities are formed through a blend of their conscious thoughts, their subconscious thoughts, their life experiences, and their dreams. It also has a little bit to do with how they are wired to begin with at birth. We define ourselves through our actions. But a person's actions are often controlled by various forces colliding within the soul. Mixed into this are our learned and instinctive behaviors. Sex may be instinctive, but it takes years to get any good at it.

This story starts with a young man growing up in the South. He matures and moves from adolescent behavior into the demands of adulthood. During his life, he witnesses the changes in East Tennessee while living in various small cities and mountain towns in Appalachia. Some of these towns struggle as they try to grow from rural hunting, fishing, and farming communities into upscale tourist and retirement destinations.

Hounds and Whippoorwills is about growth. It is about how we all need to grow out of our younger years and replace them with something meaningful. How we need to grow out of bad behavior and replace it with good behavior. It is about the conflicts between those who are growing, and those who wish to fight any intrusion into the present pattern of their lifestyles. The dream sequences that this young man experiences bring a warning of a future change, along with a much deeper philosophical understanding of the moment at hand. Some people may just enjoy reading this story, while others will find themselves regularly pausing to try to determine if, in fact, they fully understand why people behave as they do.

Dedication

This work is dedicated to my God, who has protected me and saved my soul.

To my family: in particular my wife, Penni, who I could always be sure of, and my children, Nathaniel, Madison, and Brooke, who have blessed me with great joy.

Contents

Psalm of the Citico

As the morning sun rises I can feel in the air; Lord God will deliver me with his kind care. With his kind care.

God please deliver me from the pain of my stress; my body is so tired my mind needs some rest.

As I sit in the forest watching the birds and the crows; my hands shake, my vision is blurred, how my age shows.

As the morning sun rises I can feel in the air; Lord God will deliver me with his kind care. With his kind care.

The leaves have now fallen; the air crisp and dry; I have enjoyed my stay on Earth, but for what and for why?

For years I was so driven, felt so strong and so known; now all that matters is that I may enter your throne.

As the morning sun rises I can feel in the air; Lord God will deliver me with his kind care. With his kind care.

From the time I was born you kept me warm and safe; you guided me the right way, put me in the right place.

You delivered me a wife who has stood strong by my side; then three beautiful children; what a wonderful ride.

As the morning sun rises I can feel in the air; Lord God will deliver me with his kind care. With his kind care.

My soul is now ready, I lay in the ground; I wait for my journey from this soft earthen mound.

Time will go on, many more generations will be born; Lord God please let me watch it with you from your throne.

As the morning sun rises I can feel in the air; Lord God will deliver me with his kind care. With his kind care.

Vocals and audio recording of Psalm of the Citico by Steve Boyce, Cantor from St. John's Cathedral, Knoxville, TN

Chapter 1
How did this start?

****Last night I dreamed of a beautiful morning. The sun's rays were filtering into the deep forest. The warmth of the sun flowed and ebbed like the tides as I sat looking into a mountain creek. I watched the bits of twigs and leaves and the insects float by on the stream's surface, glued there by the waters viscous: the very catalyst of life. The insects on the surface floated into a deeper section of water. As the current changed, it tossed them into a small trough within the stream. For an instant they paused on the water's surface. Just as the insects were about to enter a wider expansion of calm water, free from the currents and undertow, they were sucked off the surface by a large trout. The trout carefully determined the difference between the particles of vegetation and the helpless insects. The efficiency of the trout's movement was amazing. I then awoke.****

I blinked my eyes several times to make sure I was awake. There was some sticky matter on the eyelashes of my left eye, making it difficult to open it fully. The light from the moon bled into the room from the window over my desk. I moved my foot in an effort to stretch my right calf muscle, as it seemed to be on the verge of a cramp. Slowly I drew my knees toward my chest to flex my back, while removing the pillow from between my knees. I smirked at my slow, deliberate moves, thinking I must look like a reptile trying to re-emerge after a long winter hibernation. I flexed my hands to reboot my sense of touch. I propped my six-foot, 180-pound body up in bed and rubbed my eyes. I felt so nervous and mentally alert, yet somewhat scared to get out of bed. Where were these feelings coming from? My nervousness caused my body to start pumping so many hormones that I found myself challenged and ready to fight the fear. The fear of all intangible, uncontrollable thoughts in a dream would be a strong opponent. Was this just a beautiful dream about sitting by a trout stream – or was it something more meaningful? Did it have something to do with my stream of life drifting by? I know I have been losing it for some time. Isn't it true we are all slipping a little? My dreams often seemed more like reality than what may be actually happening. In fact, this may have become the core of my problem – or the very essence of my survival.

I sat there pondering for a moment while I stared at the quilt covering my knees. This quilt had been given to me over seven decades ago by my grandmother. She had asked me what my favorite bedtime stories were when I was but a child. Each night I would watch her add one stitch after another to see what image she would depict. As the summer turned to fall, the quilt filled with images from my favorite childhood memories, stories told to me by my mother at bedtime. That Christmas the quilt, complete with all my most favorite childhood images, awaited me under the tree, wrapped with a large bow. Now it covered my arthritic knees, and with my advanced age it somehow eased the pain. I was saddened for a moment, as I had always intended to give the quilt one day to a young man I'd met decades ago. He would give it to his children after he died, and it would always have a good home. I have a wonderful daughter I would have liked to give it to, but circumstances don't allow for this option.

What was this dream about? The insects seemed to be enjoying the ride through the woods on the water's surface, at least until they arrived at the trout's lair. They were all so different, having just hatched on the stream's bottom. As they advanced up the column of water toward the surface of the stream, their wings unfolded, and their bodies pulsed from the energy of the currents. Now on the stream's surface, their colors – red, neon blue and hunter green – reflected the dim light of the dense forest. All similar, but each unique, they floated through the lottery of life. Some were to be consumed by a greater force, while others would snag the stream's banks and crawl into the gleeful air to enter the next phase of their life. The trout was letting the stream of life flow by while benefitting greatly by the bounty of insects the stream produced. Why not relax and enjoy the big stream of life? We are all born. Most of us are blessed with good parents, who strive to make our life better than theirs. We compete; we win and lose. We are happy and sad. While we love and are loved we mature, while history is recorded all around us and about us and then it ends. So why do some of us try so hard, and put so much effort into our lives? In America everyone gets a chance. But who or what determines who will be a trout, and who will be a fly? And will the stream be big enough? Who or what determines if you are able to move at will about the stream of life, and control your own destiny? Is any of this important any longer to most people? Live for today. There will always be a tomorrow. Everyone is given time in equal increments. A minute is a minute. A moment is a moment. Does it really matter to anyone who is in control? To me, whatever control of this moment the trout seemed to have was all-important. I rolled onto my side, stared at the wall, and drifted back to sleep.

I grew up in a small town called Cleveland, Tennessee. By the time I was eighteen years old, I couldn't wait to get away from this town. We were just close enough to the Bowater's paper mill plant to smell the discharge from the manufacturing process when the wind was blowing from the southeast. When this happened, the whole town smelled like a big fart. Your house smelled like your neighbor's hound dog that had never had a bath. Your car smelled like you just hit a skunk in the road. Cleveland only had a few thousand residents and was located "off the beaten path." The larger cities in Tennessee all matured because they were located on navigable waterways. Other small towns matured because the railroads offered them a catalyst for commerce. More recently, interstate highways were built, and state routes connected the small towns scattered through the rural areas. But when I grew up in Cleveland, there was a textile mill that employed half the town, and everyone else farmed or took care of the service needs of those employed at the mill. The mill and the farms only produced so many dollars of income from their products. That meant there were only so many dollars for the townspeople to use to trade amongst themselves. As long as the mill and the farmers survived, the town could exist. Almost every child who grew up in Cleveland wanted to leave and go to Chattanooga, Knoxville, or Nashville to start their adult lives. No one wanted to go to Memphis. I wondered why anyone would want to go to Memphis. At birth I was given a strong Southern name: Grey Louise Carlton. My family had a strong family tree, with deep roots in the South. I was a direct descendant of Captain George Grey, who formed his own militia to help defeat the British during the Revolutionary War. Most of the Revolutionary War may have been fought in the North, but there was quite a lot of fighting going on in South Carolina, Georgia, and the Appalachian Mountains. The point is: when you are fighting for your country and your liberty, there is no second place. There are no do-overs. No mulligans. No practice shots. You are all in, and there is nowhere to hide. Like the events in my life, these memories – so important to our country – have become dull and forgotten. Time erases how important these moments really were to the people who were actually experiencing them. No one really cares anymore that our forefathers had to risk everything to give us the country we have today. It used to matter a lot if you were a direct descendant of those who fought to gain our freedom from England. To be able to say you were a son or daughter of someone who fought in the American Revolution was to get instant respect from your peers. Now, these old bones of courage won't feed the new pack of civilization. People no longer care, and some people don't know who their relatives are. Heritage seems to have been replaced with shiny cars and name-brand clothes. The Carltons were all known as Southern gentlemen. Louise was my middle name from my mother's side of the family. Many strong Southern men have girly middle names to respect their moms.

In review of our family's past, all was going well with our family tree until my father was born. There is an old Southern expression, "The acorn doesn't fall far from the tree." In the case of my father, the acorn fell very far from the tree. Something went very wrong. Maybe a crow ate his "genetic acorn" and shit it out while flying over some lower holler. I don't think my father really appreciated his heritage. Our ancestors were known for hard work, fairness, honesty, and socially acceptable behavior. My father was known for his ability to drink and fight, and for those stupid tattoos on his fingers. On one hand, each finger had a capital letter that spelled "LOVE." On the other hand, each finger had a capital letter that spelled "HATE." He really was not a badass; he just really wanted everyone to think he was tougher than he really was. What was even more noticeable, though; neither hand ever accomplished much or showed any signs of hard labor. Because my grandfather and grandmother were so well respected in the community, my father thought he deserved the same respect. This is where he was confused. Heritage is granted from the previous generation; respect must be earned.

I loved my parents, but our household was always in turmoil. Most of the turmoil started at the end of each month when the bills were due. We never had enough money. My father always assumed his parents were going to give him their house when they died. This was his excuse for renting, and never trying to save for our own house. When his parents died I was fourteen years old, and they gave everything to the church and left a little money in my name for college. This instantly caused my father to hate both me and the church. Somehow the church and I were now responsible for all our financial problems. Dad immediately started charging me rent to live at home, and within three years, I no longer had any money left for college. Mom just kept making me study, and refused to address the issue. My mother was strong, but my dad disrespected her regularly. The truth is that my mom had to marry my father. When she was fifteen years old, my dad was the "bad boy" of the school. Many young, pubescent girls want to date the bad boys, and from this lack of judgment, she soon became pregnant. My grandparents made my sixteen-year-old father "do the right thing," and they were married. He never loved her, and she no longer even liked him. After my birth, Mom stopped having sex with my father. For some reason, Dad never strayed, but this forced abstinence caused him to become short-tempered and angry with her all the time. Eventually, Mom got a good job, and as Dad never worked and never had any money, he just kept getting madder at my Mom. My father was always trying to put my mother down. He was so angry; he thought that by putting her down, he was somehow elevating himself.

We attended a small Pentecostal county church not far from our house. There was always a lot of shouting, and everyone was going to hell. That is not really a fair statement, as the people who attended this church were some of the nicest, and most honorable, decent, forgiving and truly religious people I have ever met. By my sixteenth birthday, I had read the entire Bible. I soon learned the difference between acting nice and true grace. The people in this small Pentecostal church taught me the difference. The Bible tells us, in a little over sixty stories, how life began and how it is going to end. I had a student Bible that carefully explained each chapter, and the history of what was going on at the moment. In my later years I found myself gravitating toward the doctrine, structure, and pageantry of the Episcopal Church. Their sermons seemed to follow the religious calendar, and speak to how it pertains to today's issues, with more clarity. If a church has a congregation of knowledgeable Christians, they already know how the story began, and how it is going to end. This makes it very hard to keep people interested in the story of Christ. It takes very strong leadership to keep things interesting. It is like reading the same book over and over again. Eventually you get the message, and start comparing it to what is happening at the moment in your life.

Take the Old and New Testament as an example. If you really step back from all the text and take a broad overview, it is not that hard to understand or believe what was really happening. First of all, whoever could claim ownership of the real estate, and have the will to fight to continue owning the ground, had a lot to do with how well things were going to go for the future generations of that group. A lot of the decisions that were made by the men of the time had to be made. Should you fight that impending force on the horizon, welcome them into your town, and hope for the best – or flee and try to live for another day? These were serious decisions, and often you didn't have the luxury of time, so you always have to make carefully vetted choices. Sometimes you have to break a few eggs to make an omelet, and likewise, sometimes you just have to go with your gut feelings. These moments were a fertile ground for the beginning of faith as we know it today. At the time, they were also fertile moments for a Holy Spirit to guide you, and help you make a decision that would determine your survival. Those who prayed to God had an uncanny amount of success – and those who did not became small specks on the timeline of history. It is so unfortunate that our society hasn't studied the small specks of history, as we are soon about to become one ourselves. Just look at history – do you *really* think that we, in our era, are going to be a very noticeable speck in the total story of history?

Of course, by the time we get to the New Testament, a lot of the real-estate boundaries were more established, and people gravitated more toward representation than war. It is a lot less messy, and it leaves you a lot more time to do meaningful things that move society forward at a faster pace. First of all, someone had to be in charge. As an example, how is this new Christian group of people going to be able to talk out their differences with the Roman government without a spokesman? Only through debate can people gain a perspective that may lead to compromise. But sometimes one's ideas threaten other people. Understanding why the government was concerned over the growth of Christianity would be half the battle. The Roman Emperor could not have his authority challenged without risking civil disorder. So the Christians created some divine positions within their ranks to negotiate with the government. Possibly it was divinity at work, and out of that were created the positions of divinity. One could argue how it happened, but at the end of the day it really doesn't matter how it came about; it just matters that it did. Either way, there was a lot of work to be done. If you are going to take on the huge responsibility of straightening out a large religious movement, you need to dress the part. Some really nice robes and one pimping hat would set these important religious leaders apart from the crowd. Now, dressed like styling Italians steeped in divinity, the first thing that these religious leaders needed to do was to get the message correct. It was first decided that only four of the Gospels about Jesus were to be taught in the church. Eventually, over time, the New Testament would swell to twenty-seven or so books, but for now we just needed to get along with the Roman Government. It was important to stop inflaming the strained relationship between the government and the church. After all, there were "Christian storytellers" wandering the countryside, and each storyteller was personalizing the story; thus giving slightly different versions of the Gospels. Some versions of these Gospels were very different, and they were causing a lot of trouble. Remember that Rome had an Emperor then, and he had to be the coolest guy on the block.

As the man in charge, the Emperor needed some "issues" in order to have something to rule over. There always has to be a bad guy so everyone can blame their miserable lives on him. For a period of time the Roman rulers were hung up on using Christians as their centerpiece of torture and hate crimes, to entertain the masses of stupid Roman people. If the populace could take all their anger out on the Christians, then why would anyone be mad at the government?

The rulers had franchised the populace into hating Christians for various "issues" that they felt were not in Rome's best interest. It really didn't matter that none of these "issues" were true. What the heck, everyone was following the Government's lead, and that is what rulers want. They want the people to feel that they are in charge, when in fact they have lost all control. Whether or not Rome was doing a bad job of governing was too subjective. After all, what were you going to compare them to?

I know this is not necessarily how history records religion, but in my mind I can see things happening like this. Other people in past history, who might be slipping even more than I am, may have written some of this stuff; so are we really sure it is exactly correct? I do know one thing for sure: I did not follow all the teachings in the books of the Bible, and I am certain I shall pay a penance for my misdeeds. As the song goes, "Jesus loves me this I know, for the Bible tells me so." I hope he is feeling a lot of love the day I am judged.

In my mind, it seems very obvious that the Roman Government did have serious concerns over the content and subject matter of some of the Gospels. The Gospel according to Mark was all too empowering for women. What was going to be the end result if women started cruising around the country with men who seemed as important as the rulers of Rome? What message was being sent to and received by women? Was it really true that you didn't have to cook, stay home, and feed the goats? It appeared that a woman could hang out with a man and tour the world, and that man might someday even become a God. Who in the Roman government would think that this was a good idea to promote? This concept did nothing to make the Emperor the coolest guy in town.

This same perception seemed to prevail in America in the 1960s. Mary traveled on foot and on a donkey. Liberated women of the 1960s hitchhiked and traveled in VW vans. In Mary's time, the sign of a fish was quite popular. In the 1960s there was an inverted dove's foot in a circle that tattooed that group of descendants. For a time in the early A.D.s (shortly after Jesus' death), there was a need to stop women from behaving like Mary.

In the 1960s, the American establishment started titling peace-loving hippy women "sluts." This was really history doing that repeat thing, as the religious establishment in the early A.D.s had decided to make Mary Magdalene a whore. It may not be true – but prove she isn't! Yes, Mary, that whore who was bonking Jesus, doesn't need to be in our official Bible. What father or mother would want their daughter reading a Gospel according to Mary? Just say no to Mary! The church and government controlled the podium. They still control the agenda. By doing so, they control the direction of the conversation. Let's marginalize Mary, and then who will care what Mary says? Often people can underestimate a belief culture, and this was the case with the Roman government. Their first mistake was to confuse behavior with faith. Rome's second mistake was in believing their own propaganda – and not realizing the power of God.

Then, of course, there was the Gospel according to Judas. This Gospel didn't do a thing for anyone, yet it created a fantastic opportunity for the government. Compromise can often be what carries the moment, and keeps the dialogue moving forward. First of all, Judas was a Jew; a people of lesser standing in Rome. But so was Jesus, prior to creating his Holy Catholic and Apostolic Church. To some it is obvious that Judas may have been a favorite of Jesus. The government needed a scapegoat every once in a while, to show that they were carefully monitoring any dissident behavior to protect the populace in Rome. Who could argue that the destruction of a Jew's character wasn't in Rome's best interest? They made Judas appear to be an inside operative, so that the populace would think the government was really on their game. It is also possible that those Christian leaders needed to show a little backbone every once in a while, to prove they were the right men for the job when it came to representing Christianity. The heck with this gospel. We can get rid of Judas by saying he betrayed Jesus; sold him out. Got him crucified. Damn the Jews! You can't trust a Jew; look how they treat each other! Certainly you can trust the government more than this group of misfits. Say no to Judas! Judas's Gospel is out!

Of course, no one at the time had any way of knowing that at some time, approximately twenty centuries later, a smarmy black-market antiquities dealer would sell someone an original copy of the Gospel according to Judas. The problem was that it wasn't readable, until some clever person learned that with certain spectrums of light, you could read the faded text on these old goatskins. Then who would guess that the silver and copper scrolls would ever be found? In fact, it appears that Judas was in perfect lockstep in helping Jesus fulfill his prophesy. Without a crucifixion, how do you have a resurrection and ascension, and then sit on the right side of God? To get this storyline rolling, someone who really loved Jesus was going to have to step up and take one for the team. Someone had to get the plan in motion. We needed a crucifixion and a plan to get the process started. I am not suggesting God the father wasn't calling all the shots; I am just saying that someone down here on Earth had to get the plan underway. As I believe God the father was in control the whole time, I feel he decided to start the events by using Judas. This plan appears to have been perfect in accomplishing the goal of a crucifixion, and you can't blame the government and so-called Christian leaders for falling right into place. Remember, this was God's plan. After all, it was a hard job for Rome to govern the masses, especially when you are operating from a platform of fear instead of from a platform of faith. As I have already stated, I freely admit I think I am on the cusp of losing it; whatever that is supposed to mean. But for today, I think this is how I believed things happened – and I feel the scribes have given Judas an unfair shake in the storyline of history.

Yet some of this stuff still just doesn't seem to be lining up in my mind. In my mind, as warped as it may be, I feel there was one particular Gospel that was directly responsible for getting most of the Christians killed: the Gospel according to Artemidorus. I think this is another one of those little specks in history that is no longer taught. I am not sure if this was really the proper name for this gospel, or if my mind made this name up completely on its own. After all it is just a name, and that is not what is important. For the moment, let's just call it the gospel according to Artemidorus. The name really doesn't really matter, but the effect that this gospel had is what is important. This Gospel was the crux of the problem between the Roman government and the Christians. The Roman rulers felt that this Gospel must be buried in time, and never be spoken of again. For this, they had a very good reason.

Who was Artemidorus? He was the cook. Every entourage needs a cook. You can't roam the land for three and a half years with a group of apostles and not eat. That might draw a little too much attention. Yes, people were very gracious in inviting Jesus and his friends to meals on a regular basis. But sometimes you just have to cook your own food. Picture this: you entered a village, then performed a miracle or two, and someone hands you a sack of grain and a bag of goat eyeballs. Someone in your group has to be responsible for turning it into a meal. After all, where do you think the bread for the Last Supper came from? We know Mary didn't cook; she was liberated.

Although no original copy of the Gospel of Artemidorus has ever surfaced, the Gospel has remained quite alive. It didn't need to surface, as it has been with us through all of religious history. It had been passed down from one generation to the next, sung as Psalms in various versions. Some of these Psalms are still being sung in our churches today. This Gospel was the roadmap to the whole system of right versus wrong, good versus evil, and to the way this system worked. The Psalms each had their own lyrical cadence and were easy to remember. These songs were sung in prayer, at family gatherings, or by individuals just trying to pass the day. When people sang these songs they were speaking the truth, and everyone enjoyed hearing them. Think how easy it is to say our alphabet to a rhyme. There were thousands of years between the development of papyrus, or what we know as paper, and the Psalms about David. Which would be easier, to carry large chunks of rock with hieroglyphics on them, or to remember the words to a psalm?

It was this Gospel according to Artemidorus that threatened the entire Roman government. It spelled out in clear form, in ways even the populace could understand, as to how they could interpret their future – and likewise mold their future. People actually had a choice in their destiny, and the choice was simple: Do you want to be good or evil? But much more threatening to the Roman government was that there was proof. There was a clear proof within each individual that this gospel was true. There was proof that every slave, peasant, commoner, or King undisputedly knew existed. This proof was that they dreamed, and their dreams clearly had a purpose. All their dreams were important and had clear meanings. The meanings and interpretations of those dreams were clearly defined in the Gospel of Artemidorus. A dream was a direct message from God. The Emperor of Rome could not control their dreams. The religious leaders could not control their dreams. Their dreams came from Heaven and were delivered by Angels. The Emperor knew he could not fight what he couldn't see. The masses would fight for what they could feel, for what they knew, for what they could understand, and for what their spirit spoke. Deep in their souls, the masses knew that God was more powerful than Rome.

This Gospel was very direct. Unlike the other Gospels that left a lot of room for interpretation, this Gospel was quite exact – and it spelled out one's future, with no room for artistic interpretation by those who told the story. It was your roadmap to your life here on Earth, and your roadmap to your afterlife. It defined you today and defined where you would be tomorrow. It told you, plain and simple, whether you were going to Heaven or Hell. It was an absolute gauge that could be applied to every person to determine if they were good or evil. It didn't care what your rank in society was, your sex or skin color – if you were evil, you were evil. Just think how hard it would be to govern for the Roman Empire if everyone could agree that the government was evil.

But at this point, that is not the story that I really want to tell you. I have a story, the story of my life. Everyone has one. What makes my story interesting is that it is not really about me, but about the people who were around me. I just observe and survive. Play the cards I am dealt and survive. React to the conditions and try to define myself. But God did give me a great gift. He lets me dream, and I pay a lot of attention to these dreams. They are coming from somewhere. They don't just happen. Is it ESP from another person looking after me? Guardian angels? Angels from God?

My subconscious? Another person lurking within my mortal soul? Or am I just completely losing it? But there is no doubt these dreams are real. They are very real, and I pay great attention to them. Are they warnings, or are they paths of opportunity in front of me? After decades of pondering, I have come to realize that they were carefully crafted and indexed. Every one of them has a very clear meaning and purpose. They are indexed from a great force that exists in the vast space above all of us. They are not here by happenstance, but are purposeful; and when I take the time to ponder them, they guide me.

When you read the Bible, do you notice how everyone is following someone, and they are all trying to figure out what is going to happen next? This story of life hasn't changed at all, as we do the same thing today. Once something happens, everyone is trying to understand the meaning of it. In the Bible, it appears that the prophets have some way of predicting or anticipating the future, and everyone can't wait to see if they are going to be correct. But we all approach religion and life differently. Some follow religion like a bug follows a light: blindly, because it is so beautiful! Some stare at their religious future like a dark cave in the mountain; scared of what may lurk in the shadows, but unable to keep from approaching the entrance. But then there are those who are guided by their spirituality. Those people appear to be represented in all religions, and they appear to be very comfortable in their beliefs.

Where are the legitimate prophets or spiritual leaders of today getting their information? How are they more right than wrong? How are they often beating the odds? What guides them, and what are they following? Could it be their dreams? Have they figured out how to apply their spirituality when interpreting their dreams? Have these prophets and spiritual leaders also figured out that something far more powerful than what they can understand is intentionally sending them these dreams? The prophets and true spiritual leaders of our time seem to be less interested in trying to convert their knowledge of the moment into religious doctrine. Instead, the clergy who appear to be pure of heart act as if they are obediently following their spirituality without question or reserve. This is what I tried to do with my life, but I failed. I compromised, and justified my failed moments, as if someone else was always to blame.

This spirituality is happening all around us every day, yet few of us take the time to notice. It was through carefully paying attention to the spirituality instead of the characters within my dreams, which allowed me to develop a better understanding of their purpose. By trying to interpret my dreams, and acting on my interpretations, I often found myself altering the life of many around me. I never discounted the importance of my dreams by blindly following them, nor did I leave any dark caves unexplored. I respected that they were happening for a reason, and I applied what knowledge I had to the messages within. As I pondered the moment, thinking about my spirituality, I grew tired and drifted back into another deep sleep.

As I began to doze, I felt as though I was about to start a journey. I was sure nothing could get by me, and all I needed to experience was in front of me. As I entered the living room, it was at this moment in this dark room that I again understood I only needed to be reacting to the spiritual moment being presented to me in my dreams; not to the characters in my dreams. The characters in this dream were of my own creation, yet the spirit in which they were being delivered was part of a great force. I needed to get control of these thoughts and decide why I was experiencing them. There had to be a greater structure. I again awoke with a sudden jerk of fear. My pillow was wet with the sweat from my neck. My eyes darted around the room to see if there had been an intrusion. I slowly slid my hand down till I found the .45-caliber Glock pistol that I

slept with next to my knees. Slowly, as if I were still asleep, I rolled onto my other side, and then quickly pulled the firearm free of the blankets. With my gun in the ready position, I started sweeping the room for the intruder. I could feel the presence of a being – yet no one was there. I got up, and began the process of first checking the closet, then under the bed, and then the adjoining room, all the time creating meaning for all these dreams. The presence of an indefinable spiritual force is what I was experiencing – yet I had no idea why.

But I started out to tell you a story about how all of this affected my life. The problem is that I am getting old now, and my thoughts now come to me in brief segments, no longer in complete stories or thoughts. Dreams are now piecemeal: disorganized flash cards of seemingly unrelated yet powerful moments. Chasing these thoughts is now overwhelming me. I am now becoming scared, and feeling lost, as I no longer can make sense of my life – yet I feel the strength of these dreams still within my soul. Am I being warned of an upcoming event, possibly a positive or negative encounter?

It is these dreams and thoughts during my conscious and unconscious moments that I have experienced in the last few years, which I have chosen to try to organize. I must organize them before it is too late. The inability to understand or control them has haunted me too long, and trying to index these dreams based only on spirituality is a very risky proposition. For some reason, I feel my only chance for mental stability will be if I can remember and write down my past, carefully review what has happened, and then attempt to understand how I have arrived at this point in my life in this condition. Only a pure understanding of history would allow one to comprehend why this must be done. After all, if you can't remember everything at one time, all at the same moment, then you don't have all of your information in front of you. Without all of the information to analyze your understanding of the moment, one can only be proportionally accurate. If you don't know exactly how you arrived in your present moment, your present state of affairs, then how can you possibly really know what direction you need to go? Once you have decided your direction, how are you going to get there? If you could somehow remove prayer and spirituality from one's past appreciation of an event, and then review what forces in life caused that past event to develop, then possibly one could move forward in a calculated manner. The ability to move forward with such a controlled and calculated plan would clearly demonstrate something that I did need to know. I needed to know the answer to two questions. The first question: Are we able to choose a direction in life without outside spiritual influence? If not, then prayer seems to be way more important than a lot of people realize. If we can choose a direction without spiritual guidance, then is the problem that we may not be in charge of what choices will be made available for us to choose from? Is this simply determined by chance? If not, then who or what is making the choices?

Chapter 2
Why is this Happening?

****I dreamed of a ship. At first, the ship was on a lake. But after I walked to the bridge of the ship and looked back, the ship seemed too small for the large lake. All the sails were up, but we didn't seem to be able to steer away from an island in front of us. Soon the ship wrecked into the island, and on that island stood three men in dark suits. On their chests were large numbers. The first man had the number 7, the second had the number 15 and the third was wearing the number 4. There was a large hive of wasps over their heads. They stood there waiting for me to come before them. I again awoke in a cold sweat.****

I continued to lie there wide awake, yet unable to move. The sweat continued to roll off my forehead and sting my eyes. The pillow under my neck just kept getting wetter from my sweat. The dream was so clear; I lay there pondering the moment while I relaxed my clenched left fist. I put the pistol on the mattress, next to my knees.

Obviously there are those who think dreams are just a hodgepodge blend of crazy flashbacks and unrelated pictures in our mind's eye. What is the chance that they really mean anything? Are there parallel universes existing in time, with spiritual mentors attempting to communicate with us? Is this what Christianity really is, us responding to our other, parallel, spiritual self?

Most people excuse these dreams as random firing of neurons that means nothing. In fact, this is an excuse for ignorance. A mathematical formula looks like a hodgepodge string of numbers to a person who is ignorant in math. The hieroglyphics on the pyramid walls are not just a bunch of pictures. They are a language. Just because a person can't speak Spanish or French it doesn't mean that other people aren't communicating when they speak to each other in Spanish or French. Why would you think that dreams are not a language of their own? What is the chance that there is a parallel universe that is based on God's will, that is there for us to understand if we could just interpret the language? How could a person not entertain the thought that there is at least a chance that their dreams can be interpreted?

To really analyze a dream, you must first take a step back and ask yourself, do you believe in chance? Do dreams serve a specific purpose, or are they just a random combination of unrelated thoughts? What if all the information you needed to ascertain a fact from a dream was really in front of you, just like people speaking a language you don't know? It is there; you are hearing them; but you can't interpret what they are saying. What if, by studying dreams, you were able to start identifying a pattern that would lead to a complete understanding of what was going to be happening to you?

It makes me wonder: what if, like written language or a mathematical algorithm, you could ascertain the meaning of a dream, and know that it was a certainty? I know I am now in my elder years, and I am having some problems confusing my dreams with my day-to-day events – but could this be possible?

But before we try to understand dreams through mathematical analysis, let's first look for proof through research. Let's look back in history, and see if we can find an example of a certain time when chance became not an indefinable moment, but a life-saving discovery. After all, if we can prove it has already happened once, then obviously it can happen again.

Let's pick a speck of history that they still teach in our society. Years ago, in France, a man named Louis

Pasteur was involved in the mundane task of vaccinating some chickens.

Pasteur went on to make many discoveries, including how to "pasteurize" milk and cheese. Most noteworthy was the risky injection of a nine-year-old boy named Joseph Meister, on July 6, 1885, with his rabies vaccine. Never before had a child been used in a lab experiment, and Pasteur was not a physician. The risk that Pasteur took in administering this hypothetical treatment was incredible. If Pasteur had failed, he would have been aggressively prosecuted by the French government. The boy had been mauled by a rabid dog. Sometimes someone just needs to take the bull by the horns and get something done. The boy lived – and now civilization has a vaccine for rabies. Did faith in his beliefs, or random chance, play into this discovery – or was Pasteur just one very lucky scientist?

In 1854, Louis Pasteur was named dean of a new facility for science at Lille University. It was in his acceptance speech that he made the following remark: "Dans les champs de l'observation, le hasard ne favorise que les esprits préparés." When translated, this means, "In the field of observation, chance favors the prepared mind."

Once he realized he could inject a killed virus to make people immune from a disease, modern medicine took a huge leap forward.

Was this discovery purely by chance? If so, then how would you define chance?

In other words, the information was always in front of him. It was in fact his observation of the information, and his faith in his knowledge and beliefs, that made the discovery: not just chance. So is chance more accurately defined as the action taken by someone acting on their knowledge and beliefs?

Later in my life, I had a friend who was balancing his checkbook and reconciling his account against his monthly bank statement. My friend has kept an account at his lending institution for decades, and he was up to check number 12,584. When he checked the balance of his checkbook, at the time he wrote the check, it was $12,584. That caused him to pause and take notice. Something was happening. The odds of these two numbers lining up were astronomical.

That week he was going to purchase a mega-million lottery ticket using those numbers, but he never got around to purchasing the ticket. At the end of the week, he was reading the newspaper, when he noticed that the winner of the $250 million lottery won it on the numbers 12584.

Was it by chance that these numbers appeared in front of my friend earlier that week? Obviously, it was an unprepared mind that failed to act on the information in front of him, and failed to buy a lottery ticket. Don't get me wrong: this man is the smartest person I know. He just wasn't prepared to win the lottery.

All of us have experienced those moments when we pause while thinking about or observing something. It is that pause when something causes us to have a thought that helps us discover something, or figure something out. Could these pauses be spiritual moments? Is it by discovering a pattern or principle that makes chance somewhat definable and controllable? Where does that pause come from? What force or power are we temporarily experiencing during that pause? Or, more likely, what force is it from those realms or dimensions that is momentarily guiding our minds? Like an adolescent child, we fail to listen and recognize what is clearly in front of us. Thus, a mature, prepared mind is favored by chance, as it is willing to accept that there is a force greater than us, and that this force is obviously trying to guide us.

The most obvious question for me becomes: "For what purpose are we being guided?"

But that is what people fail to realize when they fail to seek an interpretation to their dreams. They focus on the storyline of the characters instead of the spiritual message within the story. Often people engage their dream, like someone mining for some precious gem that is slightly out of one's reach or a stone that is hidden under just one more layer of dirt. Smart people search for all of the messages that lie within their dreams, and it is the smart people in life who have helped us up the evolutionary ladder.

The Bible clearly tells us that the Holy Spirit sent an angel to Joseph in his dreams, to tell him that his wife had become pregnant by an Immaculate Conception. Joseph never doubted or challenged this dream. Obviously, the people of this time actually figured out who was guiding them through their dreams, and they were paying a lot of attention to what was expected of them. Does it not become clear from these prepared minds that Christianity was allowed to be born in a manger in Bethlehem? If so, why are we not carefully analyzing our dreams by preparing our minds to realize that our dreams, like chance, is always there; and that we just are not taking the time to understand them?

That is what is going to make the story I am about to tell you, this little speck of history, so important – as I have figured out where my dreams come from, and why they are being sent.

Chapter 3
Think it through

...That evening I dreamed about a man building a large building. It may have been a large bank; it was being built as if to protect something of value.

Each entrance had a large stone built into a wall that jutted out far enough to create a flat roof over the entrance. Over these large, protruding flat rocks were Roman arches. There was a main entrance, with a smaller entrance on the left, and one on the right.

The masons were placing a keystone in the apex of the middle of the Roman arch, when one of the masons asked me to find him another keystone.

When I returned with the keystone for the arch on the right, the mason set it only reluctantly, as he felt it was too ornate. I went looking for another keystone, and found one that had flakes of gold on its surface. It was so full of gold that it almost radiated in the sun. I asked them to remove the keystone that they had just laid in the center, so that they could place the golden one there. They did this, and then placed the one they had removed over the

right-hand arch. I then noticed that there was no keystone for the left arch, and no matter how long I looked, I could not find one...

I have to pull myself back and get it together before it is too late. If I am to tell my story, it needs to happen now. The dreams are overtaking my memories, and soon my memories will lose the battle. To know of these dreams is to fully understand my story. By the time I had graduated from high school, I knew there were big plans ahead for me. I didn't know what they were, but I knew they would be big. I had always been kind of a geek in school. It didn't bother me, and in fact I was proud of it – because I knew I was smarter than anyone in the class. My mother made me study constantly (or at least she thought I was studying, while I enjoyed the most recent issues of Playboy). I always made almost-perfect grades, as my high school subject matter was so stupid and shallow. I was learning so little, I wondered how the students making average grades were ever going to be able to make a living once they graduated. I received a scholarship to the University of Tennessee from some unheard of "think tank" for math. The only requirement was that I take certain math courses. These courses turned out to be really challenging, and I found myself fully consumed in the subject matter. It was only after my sophomore year that I figured out what was going on with this alleged "think tank."

I had driven out to a small park at the end of Cherokee Boulevard, in an upscale neighborhood called Sequoyah Hills. As I sat on the grass, I watched the debris float by on the Tennessee River. Having just completed my probability course, I found myself wondering why I was given a chance to study math at UT. It just didn't add up, and it went against everything I had just learned in my probability course. There were lots of other, clearly smarter students in my classes, who had better math skills. All of a sudden, it didn't make any sense that I would be given a math scholarship at UT. Was I just lucky to get the chance to attend UT on a math scholarship? The high school I attended in Cleveland could hardly teach the students how to add and subtract. Because of the odor from the Bowater's paper plant, the students in the high school knew more about the wind direction than they knew about math. After my spring break, I decided I would carefully research the activities of everyone in an authoritative position who had anything to do with my existence in this math think tank. Who were these people? On what street did they live? What did they do when they were not teaching me or funding my existence?

Following a person can be quite difficult, and it takes a lot of time. My first attempt to follow my math teacher ended up in an awkward moment in the men's bathroom. I got better with time, once I realized it was all right if you lost your "target" every once in a while. Oh, yay –,I was now developing my own slang for my new-found spy hobby. Over the next several months I collected a lot of information. The files kept getting larger, but not interesting. No real association or coincidence was developing between the different parties. I was beginning to wonder if I was developing some new psychotic personality that had not yet been named. Maybe I could write a paper on it for my upcoming physiology class, and get to name my own weird condition. One of the only patterns developing by my "targets" was that they almost all shopped at Kroger and Walmart. That didn't seem unusual, as Kroger and Walmart are somewhat an institution in the Southeast.

I was growing quite weary of following everyone around and writing down everything I observed. It crossed my mind that if anyone found out about what I was up to I might lose my scholarship. I was just about to stop this obsessive project, but then something surfaced. There appeared to be one coincidence that just couldn't be explained. Remember, I was at college on a math scholarship. I loved statistics and probability courses. Like I said earlier, I was an over-focused geek in high school – but one of my favorite hobbies was performance cars. I noticed that every one of the people who were involved with the think tank that gave me the scholarship at UT drove a General Motors car. Not just *a* General Motors car, but the *same* General Motors car: a Chevrolet Caprice. They were different colors, but they were the same car. Every one of these cars had a factory-installed decal, indicating a large-block 454-cubic-inch engine. This was the General Motors' performance package for this particular car, and people would wait months to get it.

I paused with this revelation. What were the odds of that? Sweat started beading on my forehead. I reached over, grabbed a shirt off the bed, and wiped my face. I stupidly scratched my nose with one of the buttons, and I had to get up to see in the mirror if it was bleeding. I turned on the faucet and splashed some cold water on my face. I tried to organize my thoughts, but they were all coming at me at once. I decided to lie down and try to put some order into the thought process. There was no mathematical chance that all of these old and middle-aged people happened to like the same hopped-up performance car. I was now fully challenged to find out what the real story was behind this math "think tank," and what purpose it served.

41

My research shifted aggressively to finding out where these cars were made, by whom, and for whom. It was time to step up the game and find out what was going on, and who was behind this plan to give me a math scholarship. It had slowly crept into my mind that someone was grooming me for something. That summer, I decided to spend my time off in Detroit, and I applied for a job at the Downriver General Motors assembly plant. When I arrived in Westhaven, Michigan, the first thing I realized was that Michigan was full of rednecks. I was from Cleveland, Tennesse, so that presented no problem. The second thing I soon realized was that these factory jobs were coveted, and that it was a slow process to get hired.

During the forties, fifties, and sixties, every good old boy from the South who could not find a job in his hometown moved to Michigan to build cars. I think 90 percent of the people in Michigan have relatives in the South. I also think they all meet every summer in Gatlinburg or Pigeon Forge to catch up with one another.

As I said earlier, getting a job in a GM plant is not that easy. It takes years, and I only had that one summer. So I settled for the next best thing: I landed a job at the local watering hole. From this location, I could find out everything I needed to know about this model of car. The owner gave me the nickname "Bubba," because I was from the South. The summer was hot and humid, and I missed the cool breezes of the Smoky Mountains. Everyone in Michigan smokes when they drink, and I had a sinus headache the entire summer. The average factory worker in Michigan is hopelessly out of shape: a total nicotine, beer, and drug addict who really could never keep their job if it wasn't for the union. It was all too obvious that it was a matter of time before the factories would soon move to where the workers gave a shit, and where they weren't so blessed with entitlements they had neither earned nor deserved.

My research soon revealed that there were lots of people who owned one of these cars. The only thing odd was that the federal government had purchased the car for all of them. Most had been bought by the Pentagon, presumably for the CIA. Yes, the Central Intelligence Agency. There were lots of these cars sold to the FBI. Yes, the Federal Bureau of Investigation. Various branches of federal law enforcement purchased fleets of these cars. The difference in the regular performance cars sold to the public, and these beasts driven by law enforcement, was a special performance package for the federal government, available directly from the factory and sold only to the feds. Why in the hell would any of my professors at the University of Tennessee be driving one of these cars?

When I returned to Tennessee for the beginning of the next semester, I applied for a job as a mechanic's helper at the local Chevy dealership. I still had a few weeks of summer left. I had noticed that all of the "think tank" Chevy owners used this dealer for their cars' scheduled maintenance and oil change. The stickers in their driver's side windshield said "next oil change" along with the mileage and the local dealer's logo.

I was hired for fifty cents over minimum wage to change oil. What a shit job changing oil is. I really don't know how they find anyone to do this job. You often get burned from the oil. It gets all over you, including your mouth and eyes. There is no doubt you are going to develop some type of skin cancer, but I knew it was now just a matter of time before I would be able to carefully inspect one of these cars.

Finally the day arrived, only one week before I was to start fall semester. For the last two weeks, I had been allowed to work unsupervised, changing oil. But this particular oil change, for some reason, required a head mechanic. After he popped the hood open, I knew why. There sat a 454-cubic-inch motor, with a full-blown turbo charger bolted to the intake manifold. It wasn't just a manifold, it was an Edelbrock manifold. It wasn't a stock carburetor, it was a Holley Double Pumper. The exhaust manifold wasn't stock. It looked like custom-made headers with two mufflers to quiet it down. This car was a sleeper. Only the dual exhaust gave it away. There was no way to keep this beast from breathing. It was built to run. Front and back sway bars. It was designed to handle at high speeds in curves. This was not the car of an old fart who evaluated kids for math scholarships at the University of Tennessee.

Fall semester started. I quit my oil-changing job and focused on my studies. I decided to take a few pre-law electives. Don't know why; just wanted to. I was getting bored, and I felt I needed more challenge than the math courses I was taking. I also started feeling as though it might be important for me to learn something about the law.

Everything was settling into place with my schedule. After my morning lecture, I went to the lunchroom. Part of my scholarship provided free food, along with free housing. The food wasn't great but it was free. At some point, everyone should realize that in life there is nothing, and better than nothing. I think that is one of the big problems in our society. When a person is graced with a helping hand, they start expecting it, as if they are due some type of entitlement. Society can only go downhill from here. Well, all I can say is that I sure appreciated my free food and education. After returning to my room to study, I noticed that the file box I had stored for my private covert research project was slightly forward on the shelf above my bed. It was as if someone who was short had put it back, and in doing so, was unable to push it all the way against the wall on the back shelf. Or maybe they were standing on their toes and shoved it, causing it to bounce off the back wall to the front part of the shelf.

My roommate was fairly tall. He could have easily placed the box on the shelf. Someone else had been through these files. The thought of someone going through my files made me nauseous, and I got a drink of water and lay down on the bed. Now someone knew what I was doing, and it caused me to feel very uncomfortable. After some thought, I figured I would start putting some fake entries into the file box to make it look as if I was completely off course in my investigation. This might buy me some time to formulate a plan to get myself out of whatever it was that I had gotten myself into.

The next Tuesday, I met him at lunch. He seemed a little out of place, dressed like a student, but clearly in his forties. Athletic build, alert, blue-grey eyes, with measured emotions. He sat down at my table, although many other tables were available in the lunchroom. I stared at him and said nothing. He stared back and said nothing. I started eating my food while staring at him. He started eating his. For some reason I wasn't scared or nervous, but neither was he. He swallowed his food, took a sip of his tea, and then he asked me "What are you going to do after you graduate?"

Without hesitation I replied, "Get a job." His cold, wolf-looking eyes stared at me and calmly said, "I don't think GM is hiring, and Michigan is a very cold place to bartend in the winter. Are you counting on using your math skills to help the local car dealer calculate how much oil goes into a Chevrolet Caprice?"

I froze. I stared at this man, and tried to disguise my inability to swallow the food in my mouth. He then said, "I would like you to meet me at the North Shore Tower, Building Two, Suite 400, this Saturday at 9:00 am. You will need clearance to enter this office, so bring your student I.D. By the way, this is not a request, but an instruction. You are not in any trouble, or in harm's way – but do not fail to arrive."

I tried to collect myself, and appear as though I was not nervous and still in control. "Will we be through in time for the kickoff?" I asked.

He smiled a pleasant smile and said, "No one in Tennessee misses the season-opening kickoff. By the way, keep this between us." With this, he picked up his tray, dumped his lunch into the trashcan, and casually strolled out of the lunchroom. I returned to Hess Hall and went to my room.

At first I wasn't scared. I was very intrigued, excited, and enjoyably nervous. This guy had been watching my every step. I could feel he knew me and liked me. I looked forward to our upcoming meeting. All I wanted was to know what he knew, and how he knew it. Slowly, over the next few hours, my excitement slipped into paranoia. My nervousness was no longer enjoyable. What had I gotten myself into? This guy was obviously working for the government. Doing what? Inspecting the food quality of the UT cafeteria? This was very doubtful. When he smiled at me, it was clear that he felt he was the mentor I had not yet met. Was he a mentor I wanted, and did I have any choice in the matter? I felt sick, and I lay down on my dorm room floor. The concrete was cold as I fell into a worried sleep, as if trying to escape the history of my last hour. The sweat was running from my hairline, and puddling where my neck touched the cold concrete floor.

Chapter 4
Big Brother is watching

****A great urgency was upon me as I dreamed. I was trying to pack my belongings from being on a long trip. My trunk was located in a dark room, surrounded by young men sleeping under wool blankets on small beds. As I loaded my gear, I came upon a white plastic bag, full of meat from a grocery store. It was individually packaged, but the edges were turning brown and it was no longer cold. Another male, possibly my son or brother, inspected the meat with me. He said it was good meat, and he wanted to grill the steaks for everyone. I felt that the meat was going bad, and I wanted to throw it out. I couldn't decide what to do. I knew there was a great moment in front of me that was going to bring joy or danger.****

I entered the offices at the North Shore Tower, and showed my student I.D. to the receptionist. She looked very athletic, really buff. Her arms were clearly defined, as if she were a gymnast or a sprinter on the track team. I noticed a long scar on the right side of her face. She noticed me noticing, and stared me down all the way back to the only seat in the office. This was the first time I actually believed I could be beaten up by a woman. I acted as though I was reading the magazine I'd picked up from the end table, and tried to get another glance at this woman's legs or maybe even part of her ass. She caught me dead to rights and began glaring at me. This time, I started reading the magazine for real, out of fear she was going to come over and shove it up my ass.

My mentor arrived about ten seconds after I sat down. We walked down a hall into a large office. The only thing in the office, other than the desk, was the American flag in the corner. No pictures, nothing on the desk, no other furniture in the office. At first I thought this must be a typical government office, until I noticed the quality of the desk. I had taken a class in wood carving while in high school. They did do a good job at our high school in teaching the blue-collar trades. Out of boredom in high school, I did extensive research on different styles of joinery. Square-cut, mortise-and-tenon, hand-coped joints were all displayed on this balsawood furniture. This furniture must have come from Southeast Asia, probably Laos or Cambodia. This craftsman's technique is considered a lost art, with the only known remaining artisans living there. I looked up at my mentor, who had been watching my eyes. "We have our own jets," he said. "What did you say?" I asked. "We have our own jets. This is how this piece of furniture got here." "Oh, I see. And why would you be flying Cambodian furniture to Knoxville to furnish this office?" I asked.

He smiled. "Have you thought about your answer to my question?" he asked. "Yes," I answered. "And what did you conclude?" "I decided that when I feel I can really trust you, I will answer your question. But first, I have a question of my own. Why have you been observing me over the last six months?"

"Can you keep a secret?" he asked. "Yes, I can." "Good, because if you don't keep everything I say and do completely confidential, the man observing both of us right now may kill you. Do you understand?" "Yes," I said, as boldly as possible, trying to act unchallenged and not scared. My mentor smirked. He could tell I was about to puke.

"The think tank that funded your scholarship was created by the CIA in an attempt to pre-qualify future resources for the agency for specific tasks. We are putting together a group for an assignment that I will lead, to Vietnam – and possibly Cambodia. We are looking for highly intelligent persons whom we feel we can train for this mission. We placed two "baits" that an overly curious, highly intelligent person would choose to pursue. "Baits" that would be obviously too coincidental, mathematically impossible. You hit on one, the cars. It was what you did afterward that qualifies you for recruitment. It was your over-curious mind: your ability to partially uncover the identity of the owners. Even more impressive was your decision to stop further research before you were discovered. Most people would not know when to back off. These people always end up dead, and most of the good information they acquire dies with them. It becomes a complete waste of time and effort. Do you want me to call you by your birth name, or your nickname?" he asked. "You can call me by my nickname." "Bubba, you would be an excellent undercover man – and we want you to work for us."

"What are you trying to catch, drug dealers?" I asked. "No. We are trying to catch people stealing from America." "So I would be working for the IRS? "No, you would be working for me, and me only. No paperwork, no forms, only the schedule I set and the tasks that I decide we take." "How much do I get paid?" "What do you want for a year's work?" he asked. I thought a moment: now would be the time to flush this guy out, and really find out what I would be doing.

I decided to set a high bar. You know, start high and let them talk you down. "I think $100,000 would be a fair amount for a year of my life." He smiled. "You know that is twice what the average upper-level management makes in Knoxville?" I just stared at him. I always remembered what my grandfather told me, "Once you make a request for money or a closing statement, never say another word. The one who talks next, loses."

My mentor said, "We will pay you two hundred thousand for your first mission. It will take less than a year. Five thousand dollars for you to go and party, get drunk, and whore around for the next week. Tell all your friends you won the football parlay on last week's exhibition game between Alabama and Notre Dame. The other $195,000 is now in an account that I will place in your name in the Cayman Islands. On the way to our mission, we will check in so you can verify that the money is there. You may want to send your mom some of it. She is having a hard time making ends meet since your dad died."

Two days later, we flew out of a small private airport in Knoxville called Island Home. About five hours later, we arrived in the Cayman Islands. I could not believe how beautiful the place was. The air smelled so clean, and the ocean was so clear. After a short drive, we arrived at the bank. It was made out of coral, cut from large blocks that were stacked in a manner that made it look like a fortress. With my mentor's help I sent my mom some money, telling her that an insurance company had contacted me about my dad's death. I told her he'd had an annuity, and that the bank would pay her a little every month. My mentor helped me set it up so that $1000 each month would be sent from my Cayman Islands account to my mother, on a bank draft titled "American Life Insurance Company."

My mentor finally identified himself. "My name is Dave Sadowski; you can call me Dave." I looked over at him across the small café table. "My name is Grey Carlton, but you can call me Bubba," I said. I then realized how stupid that was to say. "Let's go for a walk by the ocean," he said. I followed Dave as he headed to the shoreline.

"All right, Bubba, listen carefully. Our mission is for you to infiltrate the military as a soldier, be transferred to the front lines on the Vietnam DMZ, and find out who on the other end is involved with Senator Kennedy in illegal war contracts. We have to bring back facts with enough information to convict him in a war tribunal court martial. These contracts are all with large companies like Chrysler, for personnel carriers; General Electric, for tens of thousands of double-door refrigerator/freezers; Hughes Aircraft for helicopters –

the list goes on. Someone on the other end is helping them get rid of all this material. As an example, four thousand double-door refrigerators were traced to a rice paddy, where they were dumped. This was over 200 miles from any known Forward Operating Base, or electrical source, that could power them. Bubba, good men are dying in Vietnam for only one reason: to keep the economy in America rolling. War creates jobs. President Johnson is so stupid, he really thinks he is fighting a force called Communism. President Kennedy got us into this war to help keep Chrysler from going bankrupt. He did this to get the AFL-CIO union voting support during the Presidential election. Since his assassination and Johnson's inauguration, things have gotten much worse. President Kennedy's brothers Robert and Edward have taken the program to an art form. Bobby works out of the Attorney General's office, and Ted is a senator. Every company who wants to get a war contract has to bring two things to the table: political support and money. We have verified, through our successful infiltration of the Cayman Islands, that the money taken by these two people alone is over two billion dollars. These politicians are ruining our country, and killing our young men. These young men are the sons of good, hard-working Americans. Their scheme is almost perfect. The stupid populace keeps supporting them and voting them into office.

People don't vote by what is best for their country anymore. They vote for what is best for their pocketbook. History is showing us that this is the beginning of what is clearly a generation who cares only about themselves and their money. I truly believe that if we can document this graft, there is enough good left in the souls of the American voters to end this unnecessary war, and get these bums out of office and behind prison bars. So far, we have lost 42,000 men in Vietnam. Time is of the essence."

"Now listen very carefully to what I am going to tell you. All of our lives depend on a perfect execution of the plan. Our plan of infiltration will be about the same as getting a job in a Michigan bar or a car dealership." Dave smiled. "You will need to go to the Marine Corps recruiting center after they announce the numbers for this year's draft. Your birthday will be the first to be drafted, and if necessary, I can have the University of Tennessee fail you in all your subjects so your student deferment will be canceled." Bubba looked up at Dave and said, "That won't be necessary." "Tell the recruiter you are going to be drafted, and that is why you choose to enlist. Everyone knows that the only way to survive Vietnam is if you are trained by the Marine Corps. Everybody else comes home in a body bag, due to a lack of proper training. After Boot Camp, you will be getting orders to go to a location where we are certain most of the armaments and products are being delivered, before they're destroyed by our own military. This camp is run by an insane Colonel named Rat, and his major, named Phil Laychio. Both of these men have active accounts in the Caymans that keep growing every month. This certainly isn't the normal profile for a Marine officer, but even the best of our military has those who are only in it for themselves. I will be transferred in as one of the Corps of Engineers as an equipment operator. There are two others working with us. All of us have photographic memories. We need to remember the dates and times, who was present, and what products from America were destroyed, how, and why. Let me repeat this. Locations are important. Dates are important, along with knowing who else witnessed the moment when the American products were destroyed. If we can catch Rat and Laychio, we can convict both Robert and Ted Kennedy. The war will end much sooner, and thousands of lives will be saved. We must never act as if we know each other in the camp. The other two operatives are assigned positions: one as a demolition expert; the other as a helicopter pilot. If anything weird happens to these two men, you and I need to go AWOL. That stands for absent without official leave. You will immediately be tagged as a deserter, and if caught, you will spend the rest of your life in prison. Get out of there and hide in South America until the war is over. Use your Cayman account for funds, but always have a different person make withdrawals from the account and bring the money to you. If that person is ever apprehended, leave the area immediately. Have your escape plan in place, and regularly practice portions of it to make sure everything will go well. We think the General and the Major are using some of the Lurps in the camp as a tool of fear to keep everyone in line. Get out of line, and one of the Lurps will slit your throat."

"What is a Lurp?" I asked.

"These are the green faces that operate only at night," said Dave. "Green faces? Who are the Green Faces?"

"Let me explain what is really going on at this FOB," said Dave. "What is an FOB?" I asked. "It stands for Forward Operating Base. Colonel Rat is one of the persons involved in forming a special-operations unit to fight warfare in an unconventional manner. He is right on target, as they have been very successful in Vietnam. Our problem is that American forces move forward in the same manner as we did in World War II. We attack with large columns of tanks and personnel carriers, with soldiers behind them. Much like the fighting in the Civil War where whichever side has the most men usually wins. But there is a problem with this. The Viet-Cong hear them coming, attack and kill a few troops, then pull back and disappear into the jungle, into holes in the ground, into tunnels in the jungles. It is estimated there are ten Viet-Cong to every American. Their leader is fighting a war of attrition. Kill an American to every Viet-Cong, and they will win. Kill two or three and they win faster. They don't ever try to destroy more than one or two of our tanks and personnel carriers. They kill the men inside by firing recoilless rifles into them, but seldom damage the vehicle. They want the noisy sons-of-bitches operable, so that they will have another opportunity to kill more men. As long as we use these noisemakers, they can always hear us coming."

"As it turned out, one of the platoons of Marines at this FOB was all from the South. They were used to dense forests, and they all had hunted while growing up in the mountains. These men formed the first platoon of "Green Faces." What they did was to smear their faces with green paint, and camo their clothes. They started patrolling into the jungle to find the Viet-Cong camps. They approached the entire thing using their stealth, as if they were at home poaching in the Great Smoky Mountain National Park for deer or bear. Slip hunting, as it was called back home. Stay downwind of the target; move so slow that no one notices you are there. Layer the attack so your opponent doesn't know where you are, or how many of you there are. Above all, adopt the "one shot, one kill" policy. When one single round goes off, you can't really locate where it came from. It is the rapid fire that tells your opponent where you are. Never leave a fallen soldier behind. With these men, "never" means "never", and they own the night.

"Their success was incredible. The Viet-Cong thought this was a different race of men. They had seen our white and black soldiers. But the Green Faces could not be killed. The Viet-Cong was so afraid of the Green Faces that when one was rumored to be in the area, they would pull back by at least a hundred-kilometer radius."

"As with all groups of men, they became jealous of each other's accomplishments. This happened with the Green Faces too. You see that some of the soldiers in the platoon were deer hunters, and some were bear hunters. The bear hunters always looked down on the deer hunters as a second-rate, lower-class hunter. And this is rightfully so. Back in the South, bear hunting is much different than deer hunting. Deer hunters hunt during the day. Bear hunters hunt at night. The bear hunters meet each other with their hounds at a predetermined destination, deep in the woods, a few hours after dark. The reason for this is so they can sit talking in the dark for a couple of hours, prior to the hunt. What happens while they sit there is that their eyes form visual purple, the substance in your eyes that allows you to see in the dark. The more visual purple you have, the less light you need to see. Light destroys visual purple. That is why you can't see in a room for a few seconds after the lights are turned off. Once they turned the hounds loose on a bear track, they would run behind the hounds in the dark. When they bayed or treed the bear, they would bring it down with one shot to the head, using only a .22 rifle."

"The park rangers who were trying to stop these poachers would come through the woods with flashlights. The hounds, because they are real shy, would only go to their owners, so the park ranger couldn't catch them. The bear hunters would be right amongst the rangers, but they would never turn on a light, and the rangers would run right past them all night. The stakes of this game were high. If you were caught poaching the park, you were sent to federal prison for long sentences. They would confiscate your truck, and while you were in prison, your wife would usually leave you for someone who could help her raise the children. Getting caught was not an option. It is arguable that it was totally irresponsible for the park superintendents to send rangers into the woods after dark to chase these guys. Soon, out of frustration, the methods for trying to catch poachers started to change. The rangers would start harassing the local hound owners on the public roads outside of the park. After the wives and children of some of the hunters were stopped, the park started having forest fires. Stop a truck and the park burns. Keep harassing us and we will burn the whole damn place to the ground. Finally, the business leaders of Gatlinburg stepped in and brokered some solution that also included the transfer of the park superintendent.

In Vietnam, the bear hunters decided they wanted to start hunting the Viet-Cong only at night, the same way they hunted bears back home. From their perspective, this would be some back-home fun. It would beat the hell out of sitting around camp the entire day, doing nothing. Entire platoons were formed. These men would stay in dark tents all day, and only come out at night. These were the Lurps. (It stands for "Long-Range Reconnaissance Patrol" – LRRP) They were the most feared fighters in Vietnam, by both sides. These bear hunters would also hunt the Russian boar in the Smoky Mountains in the same manner. The only difference was that instead of using hounds, they would use pit bulldogs; and instead of a .22 rifle, they would use Bowie knives. The pit bulldogs, when they were turned on a hog, would grab the boar in a death grip, usually by the nose or ear. One of the hunters would enter the foray and grab the boar by a rear leg so that it would lose its balance. The other hunter would stick the hog behind the front leg in the heart with the knife. Back home, the park rangers have no chance, nor quite frankly any desire, to try to catch these hunters. In Colonel Rat's base camp, every once in a while, someone would be found with his throat slit while they were sleeping in their tent or quarters. Some said it was the Viet-Cong, using some sort of psychological warfare. Others, who had completed their tour and were now stateside, would tell their congressman that this is how Major Laychio disciplines those he fears are onto his scheme, and who don't want to join him. Major Laychio's story is that these men were supposed to be guarding the camp's perimeter, and when they fell asleep, the Viet-Cong would come during the night and slit their throats. The fact is that we believe these are planned "hits" by the Colonel and/or the Major. Maybe someone was getting too close to their operation, or asked too many questions. It is worth noting that Colonel Rat's entire Lurp platoon has Cayman Island accounts, and every time someone shows up dead with a slit throat, there is a deposit into all their accounts. Remember, if you ever think they are on to you, get the hell out and hide in South America until the war is over. "Bubba, do you think you can handle this mission?" asked Dave.

Pitbull dogs and Bowie knives are how the Russian boars are hunted in the Smoky Mountains. This hog is being delivered a death blow by a hunter.

I arrived at Parris Island, North Carolina, and after suffering through Boot Camp, I was off to Vietnam. Once there, I arrived at Camp Glory, approximately fifteen miles inside the South Vietnam side of the DMZ. My first day was spent meeting my new platoon leader, a young second lieutenant fresh out of Officer Training School.

Chapter 5

I don't give a Damn,
Next stop is Vietnam!

...That night I dreamed of hog hunting in a large forest. I was following a game trail used by the hogs, and I came upon a cleared area that was growing beautiful grass. It was a holler, with one side cleared about halfway up the mountain. Large gray rocks protruded throughout the field, unwilling to yield their space to man's improvements and intrusions.

I sat in the game trail waiting to kill a hog. A group of twelve men arrived, and they started building a wall in the trail to hide behind when the hogs came. They were scared, and yet committed to the task...

It was the next week when I first saw Major Laychio. What a piece of work. Major Laychio was "meditating," kneeling as though at an altar and staring in the direction of the DMZ.

He was a very small man. While kneeling there, Major Phil Laychio was remembering how, in high school, some kid would always smack him on the back of his head while another one would knock the books out of his hand. This would start to put his mind in a dark area that caused him much pain. They always changed his name to sound like something queer or degrading, and they shouted it in unison as they ran by. Phillaychio! Phillaychio! Phillaychio! He knew that the meaning of this word was to suck a dick. It was not his fault that his name sounded like this word. No matter how many times he tattled to the teacher, no matter how many times the other children were punished, it always continued. Laychio knew that some day he would have a chance to be in charge of something – and when he was, he would get even. He hated tall children, and after he grew up, he hated tall men. After thinking of his miserable childhood, he would bring the misery to his young- adult years.

Dating was always different for him. Most women in his school preferred the tall men. He was limited to dating the short, fat women, or those who were mean, or the ones everyone had already used and rejected. What really bothered him was that the better he treated those women, the less likely he was to get more than a goodnight kiss. Dinner at a fine restaurant and a goodnight kiss. A movie and a nice ride through the evening – a goodnight kiss. His entire dating history could be recorded as spending money on a rejected female, a kiss goodnight, and then a personal session masturbating with a dirty picture of a woman with whom he would never get a date.

Laychio remembered that the most enjoyable moment he'd had in college was when he joined ROTC. He always wanted to be in charge of something – to be viewed with respect. This was his chance to be admired: to wear a uniform that demanded respect from everyone. The highlight of his college days was his third semester, when he was allowed to carry one of the flags and march in front of the drill team. Everyone had to be noticing him. He was concerned that he would not look tall enough, so he invested in some lifts to put into his boots to add a half-inch to his height. He would never forget how badly his feet hurt from that march, as the lifts had cut into the back of his heels. But it was worth it, and he noticed that some of the girls who were looking at him were not fat.

When he graduated, he had to make a decision. He had barely passed, with a baccalaureate degree in logistical engineering. There would not be much opportunity for such a half-assed guy, who had regularly cheated on his tests in his last two years in order to graduate. In the real world, it would be a matter of time before his superiors realized how incompetent he really was. He had an alternative. With all his ROTC credits, he could slide through the back door into the

Marine Corps Officer Training School without the required commission. Even if he didn't have to qualify like all the rest of the officers, he knew he could pretend he was as qualified as everyone else. One thing he had learned over the years was that everyone would like him if he acted positive, and agreed to do the jobs no one else wanted. He became popular by default: everyone had to like him. Who didn't like someone who was willing to do the shit jobs? Now he was in Vietnam, and it was time to get some ribbons for his chest. Yesterday he decided to create some action. The colonel would never know what had really happened, as he knew he would be the one to do the paperwork detailing the incident. After completing his meditation, he climbed into his Jeep and told the driver to go to the front lines. As his Jeep pulled up to the defensive position at the DMZ, he was immediately saluted by Second Lieutenant Murphy. Laychio loved when people saluted him. He knew they could not drop their salute until he raised his hand and returned the salute. This gave him a rush. Over the years he had perfected this delayed salute presentation, and it gave him great satisfaction.

Instead of immediately returning the salute so that his subordinate could drop his hand and assume an "at ease" position, Laychio would go into his dominance routine. He never did this when there might be a higher-ranking officer present, but he cherished those moments when only he, his driver, and a subordinate officer were there. His dominance routine would start by first approaching the subordinate, then moving within two feet of his face. He would then stare directly into his subordinate's eyes and hold the stare for at least five seconds. Then, slowly, he would lower his glare and continue to inspect the subordinate by slowly looking down his chest, his belt line, and then his boots. Once his eyes reached the boots, he would slowly walk around the subordinate, who was still holding his hand in the salute position, until he was once again staring directly into his face. After a pause of another few seconds, he would return the salute, thus ending his military greeting ritual. He noticed that during this greeting ritual, if the soldier was tall or handsome, he would often feel the blood rushing to his penis – and he would achieve a slight, unnoticeable erection. Controlling the moment truly excited him.

But Laychio had arrived at Second Lieutenant Murphy's platoon with a purpose. He was going to instruct the platoon to fire mortars across the DMZ, and initiate some contact with the enemy.

"Lieutenant Murphy: I instruct you to place a mortar barrage on that ridge, facing us at three o'clock, with the flat, cleared field in front of it."

"Major, where on the ridge do you want us to target our ordnance?"

"Lieutenant, bracket that cleared area in front of the ridge."

"Major, the cleared area is designated as a graveyard by our sector map. It is a court-martial offense to unnecessarily fire on a human graveyard."

"Lieutenant, do you know for a fact by your personal observation that anyone is buried at that location?"

"No, Sir."

"Proceed as ordered. Give me the coordinates that are on the map for the graveyard."

Lieutenant Murphy barked the proper sequence to bracket the target and then fired for effect, successfully hitting the very middle of the clearing. "What are the coordinates of your last round, Major?" "Southwest, ninety-seven meters by northeast, seventeen meters on quadrant four map 103.

"Major Laychio to air command. We have hostile fire from quadrant four maps 103 southwest, ninety-seven meters by northeast seventeen meters. Requesting air support in quadrant four map 103.

"This is air command. Please give us your clearance code." Laychio paused. He knew he would have to use his Colonel's security codes, as he was not authorized to call in an air strike. President Johnson had decided that only he could call in an air strike, unless an officer of the rank of Colonel or higher called one in to keep from being overrun. This was America's new "fight for a tie" policy. It is now reasonably obvious why we lost the war. But this was Laychio's chance to call in an air strike before the war ended. He would need to use the Colonel's clearance code, as his rank wouldn't allow for it. He could slip the paperwork by Colonel Rat by saying they were being overrun. He knew he could convince the Colonel that he was covering for him.

"Clearance code Alpha Four, Lima Six, Bravo Nine; fire for effect immediately."

The F-16s arrived almost a half-mile ahead of their sound. Coming in low at 850 miles per hour, they dropped their ordnance and broke out of formation, surging upward with afterburners blazing. The detonation was spectacular, and the ground beneath everyone's feet shook from the impact of the explosions. What happened next was an incredible display as bodies, caskets, bones, and debris were blown high from the graveyard into the air.

"Lieutenant Murphy." "Yes Sir, Major Laychio?" "We were lucky we were successful in destroying that position, considering all the enemy fire you were receiving. It was clear that your platoon was pinned down and about to be decimated. Wasn't it?"

Lieutenant Murphy looked at the Major in disbelief.

"I repeat, Lieutenant: We were very lucky we were able to take out that enemy position that had you pinned down and that was about to overrun our position, weren't we?"

Reluctantly, Lieutenant Murphy answered, "Yes sir, Major – thank you for saving me, and all my men's lives, with your brilliant attack of the enemy position. I am sure Colonel Rat will be very proud of your leadership, and will request that you receive proper recognition for your brilliant action and strategy under such extensive pressure."

"Continue, Lieutenant," Laychio ordered, as he entered his Jeep and proceeded to drive back to the base camp. The sarcasm in Lieutenant Murphy's voice really pissed him off, but he could deal with that later tonight.

Upon arriving at the base camp, he saw the Colonel standing in front of his quarters, unshaven and with hair uncombed. "Major, what the fuck is going on in the fourth quadrant?" "Sir, I arrived to find Lieutenant Murphy's platoon pinned down and about to be overrun. I observed the location of the enemy, calculated its location, and called in an air strike to defeat the threat. I am proud to say that Lieutenant Murphy and his platoon are without casualty. May I speak to you in private, Sir?" The two men went into the Colonel's quarters. "Colonel, I knew you were not feeling well this morning and were unavailable, so I bypassed the proper protocol for getting approval and used your clearance codes for the air strike. I felt that any delay would have caused Lieutenant Murphy's platoon to be overrun, and that we would be dealing with many causalities. Shall my report indicate that you were directly involved from the command center and aware of the situation, and that you ordered clearance for the air strike?" The Colonel looked at the floor and as he turned away from the Major he said, "Fill your report as stated, Major." He knew Laychio had made the whole thing up, but he also knew the war was soon to be over. How long would the American people buy into this stupid "fight for a tie" policy while their sons kept coming home in body bags? Sooner or later, everyone was going to figure out that the war was only being continued to keep the jobs that were making all the materials it takes to fight a war. The opportunity that he and Laychio had, to make the money they were making through their contacts in Washington, was too good to screw up over something as dumb as his Major wanting another ribbon for being in a battle that never existed. All they needed to do was to see that everything that was being sent to Vietnam was destroyed, so that more of it could be ordered. It was just that simple. Keep the union-controlled factories full of orders, and that would keep everyone happy and voting Democrat. It would all soon be over, and he would be able to retire to Florida and enjoy his retirement fishing with his friends. His short, "Napoleonic" Major had told everyone he was going to retire in the Smoky Mountains. It was doubtful he would ever see that small man freak show once this was over. Laychio left the Colonel's quarters and proceeded to the administration building. Laychio knew that if he took his time, and wrote the report carefully, he would get a chance at a medal, or at the very least a ribbon. After all, at great risk to himself, he had stormed into the fighting at the front lines, and in the heat of a furious battle, made life-saving decisions. Now all he needed to do was get the narrative right, and give the battle a really Vietnam-sounding name. He would have his glory moment from the incident, and he was sure the Colonel would sign the report to cover his own ass for being asleep in his tent with a hangover. This program of developing "issues" when the opportunity presented itself would almost guarantee him promotion at every opportunity. Unfortunately, Vietnam would end two years later, with him still a Major. He would find another opportunity to apply his skills of smoothing out situations and "issues" that seemed to always develop around him. After Vietnam, he was talking with some other officers at the Officer's Club in Wilmington. He learned there was going to be some opportunity in Washington for military personnel with people skills to act as lobbyists on behalf of the Marine Corps in Congress. Everyone was talking about what a brown-nose, shithead job that would be. Laychio couldn't wait to apply.

Laychio recognized the possibilities one could have by knowing all of the Congressmen on a personal basis. This was his chance to become a General if he really worked these Congressmen properly. The thought of stroking the best excited him. Were his people skills strong enough to bullshit the very best of the bullshit artists? He would have to be very careful, as about half of the Congressmen were honorable, and were really trying to do what they felt was best for the country. He knew that Washington was a lousy place to live. Several years later, he married a promiscuous tall woman from Memphis. He needed a wife to take to all the social gatherings in Washington. Most of his past relationships with women had involved photos in Hustler magazine. But after all, sex with the real thing was better than sex with a picture of one. Well, maybe that was an exaggeration, as his wife did not look anywhere as good as the women in the pictures – but she was tall. Maybe the other men would think he was really hung like a stud horse if they thought he could satisfy such a tall woman. In time he had a son, but his son would be a real disappointment. His son had his short stature, and his mother's frail bone structure. Laychio was embarrassed to introduce him, as he always felt his son reflected very poorly on the image he was trying to give everyone. After all, he wanted everyone to believe he was a manly man despite how short he was. The re-assignment to Washington as a lobbyist would allow him to develop friendships with every congressman. A lot of them would make appointments with him, and some would have little to do with him. Some would be quite impressed with his ability to take care of "issues" that kept popping up out of nowhere. With a little help from his new political friends, maybe he would be given regular promotions and retire as an officer of high rank. Maybe one day he would be a General. Maybe he could get two or even three stars, if he was really careful to always seem 100 percent on the correct side of the political moment. But before he could do anything like socializing with congressmen and Senators, he was going to have to close some affiliations from Vietnam. This was going to be a little tricky, as it would take a lot of scapegoats and carefully crafted storylines to get one Marine to turn on another Marine. The Lurps were going to have to get really busy before Vietnam ended, and then destroy themselves without any connection to anything associated with him.

Chapter 6

Whoopee, we are all going to die!

...I dreamed I was living in a house on a cleared hill, when a mother bear and two cubs came over the hill. I thought how pretty it was to see the three bears digging for food in the green grass.

A pack of coyotes descended upon the bears. The mother and cubs ran to the edge of the woods. The mother put the cubs up a tree, and then fought the coyotes at the base of the tree. One of the cubs became too scared, and climbed down the tree to be with its mother. The coyotes instantly killed the cub while the mother was distracted by the rest of the pack.

By this time I had grabbed my pump shotgun, loaded with five rounds of buckshot, and arrived at the tree. I began slaughtering the coyotes. I killed three with the first shots. The rest of the coyotes ran away, and the mother bear also ran away. The remaining cub climbed higher in the tree. In my mind's eye, I saw myself sitting on my porch after reloading my shotgun. Dark descended, and I saw myself drifting to sleep. I then saw the small cub

come down the tree and crawl into my lap. As I held the cub, it went to sleep lying on my chest...

Dave arrived a couple of weeks later at Camp Glory. This was the signal that everyone was in place. A few days later, I was ordered to go with him on a mission on the other side of the DMZ. Apparently, other than the fake attacks, Major Laychio was documenting that there was little to no activity in our area. Washington was perplexed. Was a new boundary by proxy between North and South Vietnam being accepted? This was similar to what had happened with the Korean War. There was a lot of talk in Washington about how we could leave Vietnam with honor. Or was it possible that North Vietnam was using our very publicly announced "fight for a tie" strategy as an opportunity to set up new supply routes, closer to the present DMZ? The plan designed by the Major was to advance into the DMZ boundary on the North Vietnam side of the line. An amazing number of personnel carriers were flown into Camp Glory by the large Huey helicopters. The next day, one fire team of three men was put into each personnel carrier. This was strange, as normally each personnel carrier held three fire teams. The personnel carriers were brand new, having just been manufactured by Chrysler Corporation. As the last of the men loaded, I saw how obvious it was why there were so many personnel carriers, but not enough men to fill them. The plan was to advance about a mile, then wait for orders as what to do next.

They crossed over the boundary that was considered the perimeter of Camp Glory. The column of new personnel carriers entered the dirt road that led into the jungle. Immediately, the Viet-Cong started pounding the personnel carriers. Everyone still alive bailed out, and began to run back to the base camp. Just as the last of the men were clearing the DMZ, the F-16 arrived. Hell fell from the sky and started obliterating everything, including all of the vacated personnel carriers. Where there was once an advancing column of personnel carriers, there were now smoldering trees, burning tires, and some lost souls. The official report stated that after hours of fighting we were overrun, and that the Colonel had to call in an air strike. The report also stated that we had killed hundreds of Viet-Cong, who had supposedly been trying to take ownership of the personnel carriers. Another fifty million dollars lost in personnel carriers, a few letters to sleepless parents at home, and another ribbon for the Colonel to wear – and what the hell, give the Major one too. New purchase orders were sent by the Department of Defense to Chrysler for some more personnel carriers. Pay the hard-working factory workers overtime. Give them whatever the unions asked for, because we needed these personnel carriers immediately if we were going to win the war.

Management at Chrysler announced overtime for the next three months. Overtime pay was approved through the union negotiations at twice the normal rate, for every hour over forty hours worked in a week, plus a week of paid vacation for every ten weeks worked. The marketing department at Chrysler "invested" in a Cayman Islands campaign to sell their new "K Cars" in South America. The CIA watched the Colonel's and Major's Cayman Islands accounts jump another $50,000 each in deposits – not much, though, compared to the millions transferred to executives and congressmen who voted for the appropriation to build the personnel carriers. Five thousand dollars was deposited to the account of each Lurp on active duty at Camp Glory. The factory workers in Detroit partied hard when they watched the news anchorman announce that work was guaranteed for at least another year at the Chrysler plant. Smoke another joint, and let's do some tequila shots. What a great economy President Johnson has given us! Vote Democrat! Vote union! Kick ass in Vietnam! Support your troops! Go America! Re-elect your Congressman! Don't worry now, times are good. In a few years and after over 58,000 men are killed, we can worry about the effects of the war and how to keep Chrysler out of bankruptcy from all these insane war contracts.

When I got back to my tent, it was too hot to breathe. I had just sprinted a mile back to camp, hoping not to be shot in the back by a Viet-Cong, and I fell on my bed. I was very motivated after seeing the man next to me get his head blown off from a round sent through the side of our supposedly bulletproof personnel carrier. I lay there, drifting along the edge of being in shock, half asleep and half awake at the same time, in a scrambled effort to try to reconcile what had just happened. I needed to remember times, locations, who was involved in giving what orders, and when they were given. Who was present? Who stayed behind with the Major as we pulled out of the camp? While neither asleep nor awake, I had an incredibly clear vision warning me to get ready for another violent confrontation. It was as if it was a dream, but I was awake. It was if it was a daydream, yet I seemed to be in control of the direction, or what was going to be the narrative, of the dream.

I sat up, and while staring at the entrance of the tent, I realized I could control when I received a dream. I could take myself to a mental state that was halfway between awake and asleep. I might not be able to control the message, but like answering a ringing phone, I could control when I received one. Most importantly, for the first time in my life, I could tell that these dreams were coming from a great force. Truly this was the power of the Holy Spirit, and I now understood why the Roman government of yesteryear so feared the Christians. The Christians could enter their dreams at will. By entering their dreams, they could see history's plans for them and prepare for their upcoming challenge. They might not be able to defeat the challenge, but they had the knowledge to know it was coming. Knowledge is a great power. With knowledge, one can formulate a plan. With a plan, one can take action. With action, one can create history.

Chapter 7

Keep calm, you are
smarter than they are

...I lie there dreaming as the strongest of the stars continue to shine, hesitant to pass the torch to the spirits of the morning.

Strips of clouds begin to show, waiting for the sun to caress their edges. Shards of light pass through their voids all the way down to Mother Earth. In one great moment, the clouds blush with color.

A thin line of yellow begins to show on the eastern horizon as the sky's blackness begins to change to a pale blue.

No longer willing to wait, the clouds burst pink, blue and red from their soft undersides, streaming the color to the waiting mountains below.

Thermal currents begin to flow around the trees, caressing the leaves and making them twitch and tingle as they dance in the warming air.

The climax of color and warmth is cheered by all the forest residents as Mother Earth births another day...

I went to the latrine to take a good shit. As I sat there, swatting the flies away from my mouth, Dave Sadowski kicked in the door. "They're onto us." "Our stateside support at the agency has sold us out. I'm going to create a diversion in front of the latrine, and when I do, kick out the back wall and get to the Huey that's getting ready for takeoff. It is full of dead bodies: get in one of the body bags. In Hanoi, use your Cayman Islands account for one large withdrawal, then go to South America. I have told Headquarters that you were killed in this morning's firefight, and your body is being sent to Germany to be processed. Take care and don't hesitate." With that, Dave exited the front of the latrine and slowly walked toward the Lurp tent. I watched through the cracks between the boards as I pulled up my pants. Two men were following Dave about 200 feet back, trying to act inconspicuous. As Dave got to the Lurp tent, he drew his Ka-bar knife and slit open a large hole to let in the bright sunlight. The Lurps, blinded by the light, started swearing and threatening that whoever had done that was going to pay. Dave tossed a grenade into the tent, pulled his .45 Colt, and started to fire on the two men following him.

Before he could get the second round off, they cut him down with automatic gunfire. The grenades went off. I reeled around and busted out the back of the latrine.

The Huey helicopter was behind the latrine, and men were loading the last of the body bags. I approached the helicopter, got on my knees, and started praying out loud over the death of an apparent friend while making the sign of the cross. The men paused a moment, then left me while they went to check out the explosion in camp. The minute they were out of sight, I entered the helicopter. I found a body bag that had only a few remains in it, crawled in, and zipped all but the last couple of inches shut. I could hardly get enough air through the opening, because they tossed the last body on top of me.

The chopper lifted off and headed for Hanoi, where the bodies would be stored overnight before being sent to Germany for processing.

The fumes from the exhaust were entering the cab of the chopper. Between the smell of the blood and the dead bodies, along with the fumes of the exhaust, I became sick. I could not prevent myself from gagging. I held my nose closed with my hand as I puked a puddle of vomit under my chin. I tried to envision myself happily swimming in the ocean, but it was not working.

Every time I choked and gagged, I would feel the head of one of the dead bodies pressing on my back, and the hand of another body, stiff with rigor mortis, pushing on my side. As the helicopter pitched and turned, the stack of bodies would shift and the pile would get tighter as they settled among themselves on the helicopter floor. The feeling of claustrophobia was overwhelming, and I knew that I was not able to stand the sensation any longer. It was sweltering hot. I needed air, and I needed to stop gagging. I reached up and zipped the body bag open, and popped my head out of the bag.

I found myself looking at the backs of the heads of the helicopter pilot and co-pilot. The fresh air in my face stopped me from puking. I kept holding my nose so I would not smell the stench. The back of my throat was burning from my vomit. I had an iron taste in my mouth from the blood of the dead soldier who had been tossed on top of me. I slowly pushed the soldier off me onto the back of the pile. When the helicopter started to descend, I lay back into the vomit, and zipped all but the last few inches of my body bag shut.

Once in Hanoi, all the body bags, including mine, were carefully placed on a large tile floor in a long row. When the job was done, the lights to the room were turned out, and all the personnel left. I unzipped myself from my bag and noticed I was on the floor of a large locker room. On the walls were showers. I quickly turned on the shower, rinsed off the best I could – uniform and all – and then stood there, dripping wet, looking out the crack in the door. The stench of death was still in my clothes and hair. I needed a plan, and I needed to act soon. There was a long, wide hall full of people. After a few minutes it would become almost empty, for up to twenty seconds at a time. Occasionally, groups of soldiers would come through the hall. Having dripped dry for about ten minutes, I waited until one of the groups passed through. When they were just about out of sight down the hall, another group of soldiers passed through. I fell in behind them, but slightly out of their sight so that I would look like I was the beginning of the next group. As I knew I was leaving a trail of wet spots on the floor, I took the first exit out of the building. Apparently, I must have exited from the rear of the hospital, as I walked immediately into the bustle of Hanoi. I walked into one of the many spas that were set up to attract the off-duty military for the prostitutes. I had to get the smell of death off of me. "Ten dollars American you have a shower and girl," the Mamasan barked. I handed her a ten-dollar bill, and went to the locker room. Dozens of G.I. uniforms were on hangers there while the soldiers were being entertained by the girls in the spa.

I took a good shower, even taking the time to get the blood out from under my nails and in my hair. When I'd finished, I picked a sergeant uniform that seemed to be my size. I stuffed my old uniform down the dry toilet so it would not be found. And I smirked as I wondered how the sergeant was going to get back on base without his uniform.

My first stop was the bank. I was to make one transfer – only one. I gave the officer my routing number and transferred $175,000 into a local Swiss bank. I then walked about two blocks to the branch of that Swiss bank. There I deposited $100,000 to "American Life Insurance Company," and I set up monthly automatic transfers, for my mother, in the amount of $1,000 per month. I withdrew $50,000 in cash and left the remaining $25,000 in the account, establishing protocols with the banker for future deposits and withdrawals.

In Hanoi I purchased some obvious tourist clothes. I also bought a camera, a camera bag, and a spare lens, along with my Humphrey Bogart hat, white shoes, and green khaki pants. I stood out like a sore thumb. Sometimes the most obvious is the least obvious.

From there I took a taxi over to the docks, where a second-rate cruise line was in port for the day. People would take the ship from Hawaii to Hanoi to buy all sorts of stuff at extremely low prices. I convinced the security guard I had left my wallet and papers on board, and he let me pass in order to get them. Once on the ship, I went straight to the bar. I figured I had about fifteen to thirty minutes before security might come looking for me. At the bar were a few average-looking women who had decided to drink the afternoon away instead of shopping in Hanoi. I noticed one who had the mark of a wedding band, but no ring, on her left hand. In talking to her it became clear she'd just been divorced. Twenty minutes later, Jane and I were in her suite. I estimated it would be at least three hours before the ship left port. Using every technique I could remember, I slowly, methodically, pleasured this lady Jane until Hanoi was only a twinkling skyline in the distance.

Even horny women want to eventually come up for air and food. I told her I'd been traveling with my girlfriend, only to come back to the cabin and find her with some foreign man. I couldn't go back to the cabin, as I was so angry I might hurt him – but instead, I had come to the bar, where I'd met her. I had her completely convinced that destiny had placed us together. Jane went to the ship's on-board store and purchased a couple of sets of clothes for me, and we ordered room service. For the next three days, we found out how many ways I could pleasure Jane.

I arrived in Hawaii, promised Jane I would call her, and got on the next flight to Colombia. Once in Colombia I went to Belize, where I spent the next four years living as a beach bum off my Swiss account. I missed my mother terribly. I didn't even know if she was alive, but I was scared to check, as it might blow my cover. While I was enjoying the sunrise one morning, I decided I wanted to go home to Tennessee.

Faking transcripts to appear as an extremely smart Belize exchange student, I applied to the University of Tennessee Law School under my nickname Bubba, a name that I'd received from a bartender back in Michigan. I re-named myself with a new last name, "Savage." That fall, "Bubba Savage," as a Belize exchange student, started law school at the University of Tennessee in Knoxville.

Real women hunt deer.

Chapter 8
Real Men (and some women) Hunt Deer

When I was admitted to the University Of Tennessee School Of Law, it was 1971, and I was on schedule to graduate in 1975. It was the fall of 1973 when I first met Tom. We were in this hole-in-the-wall, somewhat unheard-of bar called the Maltese Falcon. The bar was located in the ground floor of an apartment building called Shelbourne Towers. It was one of the most popular bars in the campus area, just a short walk from the Presidential Complex. This is where most of the coeds lived for their first and second years at U.T. It was a short and safe walk back to the dorm after a night of partying. It was also one of the bars that the student athletes could go to without being busted for violating curfew, as all the coaches patrolled the bars on "the strip" – a slang term for Cumberland Avenue. If you were a cute coed who wanted to meet one of the student athletes, this is where you went to party.

I had learned that men in law school also had the same star power as the jocks, if you could get a chance to work the fact that you were attending law school into the conversation. My favorite technique was to zero in on someone I knew from a previous evening who'd had a lot of "followers," and start a conversation with him as if the girls didn't matter and weren't even in the room. This always ended in an introduction, with the star athlete telling the girls I was his lawyer friend. That is all it took, as from then on I could pretty much have my pick. I had just entered the Maltese Falcon on a Thursday night when I first met Tom.

He was a large man, about six-foot-five, and somewhere between 225 and 235 pounds. He was in incredible shape, with every vein and muscle showing in his arms. And all over his arms were women. Every few minutes, another co-ed would drink herself brave and throw herself at his mercy. He was polite and warm to all of them: fat, thin, pretty, or ugly. He melted all of them with his warm eyes, wavy hair, big smile, and soft squeezes on their shoulders with his massive hands. I think this might have been his first trip to the Maltese Falcon, as I was there about four nights a week and I had never seen him before.

I introduced myself to Tom. After all, it seemed like a good segue to meet some of his pretty followers. I dropped the fact that I was in law school, but it did not seem to make a difference with the girls. They wanted Tom, and they couldn't care less if I was in law school. Somehow, the conversation changed to how bad the school food was. Tom remarked how much he would appreciate a good, home-cooked meal. I am actually quite a fine cook, so I started talking about cooking. After describing some really good food, and getting several "Oh, I would do anything to try some of those dishes" remarks from the girls, I thought the timing was right to invite Tom and two of the pretty, hungry-looking girls to my place, and I would prepare them any dish of their choice. Tom seemed intrigued, and he appeared to be going along with the newly developing plans. He could easily see what I was doing, but seemed uncertain about the plan. I may have stretched the truth a little by telling them I had graduated from culinary school, before deciding to become a lawyer. Thinking the deal was closed, I asked the girls if they had any wine preferences. I knew if I could get Tom and two of the girls back to my apartment, things would be going in the right direction and the night would almost definitely end in a score. But even the best of plans don't always work out. Apparently, Tom had a couple of male friends with him who were sitting at the next table. Until now, neither of them had been introduced or had been involved in the conversation. All they seemed to hear was the offer for a gourmet meal, and they immediately agreed to take me up on the offer. At the last minute, the two pretty girls came to their senses, or simply decided they no longer wanted to go eat with four men, and immediately left the bar to try their luck somewhere else. Now I was stuck with having to feed three hungry men a gourmet meal.

I was thinking about how I was going to ditch these guys, but I was actually hungry, and I figured we would return in a couple of hours and pick up the hunt where we'd left off. I would convince Tom to ditch his tagalong friends, so we could score some quality trim. We left Shelbourne Towers, and headed to the new Kroger in the Bearden district of Knoxville.

Kroger had just started a new concept in marketing. The store was open twenty-four hours a day, seven days a week. Normally, late in the evening was when the supermarket had the stock boys come in and replenish the shelves. Someone had decided to have one cashier and one checkout lane open during these times, and so was born the twenty-four-hour supermarket. It was a pretty smart idea by someone in operations who really understood the big picture. I hope they gave him a raise.

We arrived after what seemed to be hours. The store was only a couple of miles away, but we were really stoned because along the way we had smoked a joint. I will never forget how bright the place was when we came through the door. The lights were so bright I could hardly see. Tom, his friend Ron, and a guy I think was named Mike walked with me by the cashier, and for a moment we just stared into the endless rows of food.

We turned right, and the first row of food we came to was the produce.

Mike was so stoned he was walking with his hands out in front of him. He was really creeping me out, as he reminded me of one of those zombie characters from a second-rate movie I had just seen. The first thing that he came to was the lettuce display. There, in front of this completely stoned zombie eyes, were dozens of heads of lettuce wrapped in clear plastic. As if in slow motion, he reached down, picked up a head of lettuce, and took a bite out of it – plastic and all.

While he was chewing the lettuce and plastic, his head slowly turned, and he looked at me with a smile of satisfaction. I decided to move on and place as much distance between him and me as possible. At that point, I was worried he might envision me as a candy bar or something.

As I rounded the corner, I saw Ron by the dairy section. He had a can of pressurized whipped cream, and he was squirting all he could into his mouth. Eventually he started choking, and when he started to cough, the whipped cream blew out his nose. I really needed to get these guys out of here. Tom was walking along, eating a peach, when I shouted to him to get some Oreos, and that I would get a gallon of milk. Ron, Tom, and I were rounding the aisle when we noticed that two of the stock boys and the manager had surrounded Mike.

Mike was standing there with the same head of lettuce in his hands, still trying to chew the plastic. He was helpless. I shouted at him to bring the head of lettuce to the checkout counter where we were standing. He was frozen, and they did not appear as if they were going to let him come to the checkout lane. I told Ron to create a diversion to get the stock boys as far away from Mike as possible.

Ron was huge. He was about six-foot-two and 255 pounds. He was always lifting weights, and he was incredibly strong. Ron strolled slightly out of sight, picked up a cantaloupe, and threw it over six or seven rows of food. The cantaloupe crashed into a can display at the other end of the store. Ron casually stepped back into view, looked at all of us, and said: "What the hell was that?" The stock boy and the manager went running to the other end of the store to investigate. Seeing a reprieve, and knowing we only had a moment, we grabbed Mike and advanced to the checkout line.

Everything was going okay. The lady rang up the milk, the Oreos, and the mutilated head of lettuce. Then Tom placed a peach pit in front of the checkout lady. "How am I supposed to weigh that?" she asked. "Charge us double what you think is fair," I said. She choked up, started to laugh, picked up the peach pit, and threw it in the trash can under the counter. We paid her and left the store, just as the manager and the stock boys came back into view. As large as Tom and Ron were, they wisely decided not to follow us into the parking lot. When we got back to my apartment, we polished off the Oreos and milk. Tom no longer seemed stoned, but he was deep in thought. He seemed as if he had tuned out and gone to a different place. It was if he was displeased; bored, disgusted with himself, and nervous to get on with something more productive, all at the same time.

I asked Tom if he wanted another beer. He looked at me, a little confused, and then said, "Sure, that would be real nice." After a few minutes, I asked him what his major was. "Business law," he said. "There is no such major," I stated. He looked askance at me and said, "Yes there is – because that's what I am taking." I told him I was in law school, and there was no such major. This time he looked straight at me, put down his beer and said, "I think I am tired of hearing your shit." We stared at each other, and it became clear Tom was not going to back down. At this point I was trying to figure out how to calm him, but Tom seemed to be getting madder by the second. Remember, the first one who speaks or looks away loses. Ron got up and placed himself between us.

That night we got drunk and continued to smoke dope. In the wee hours of the morning, we made these great plans to go deer hunting the next day. I had access to this 8,000-acre hunting camp, owned by a man I had been doing some estate planning for in Georgia. We agreed to meet at the U.T. Safety and Security building at 9:00 am so Tom could check out his bow and arrows. Yes, U.T. will store your hunting gear, while you go to school there for free, at the campus police department. The South will rise again!

Tom had called a friend who also wanted to go. When I arrived at Safety and Security, there were Tom and his friend John, waiting to go to Georgia. We all loaded into my C-J5 Jeep.

Just before we reached Marietta, we turned east into the Piedmont section of Georgia. Before we left the hard surface road, we stopped at a two-pump gas station and we filled up the two five-gallon cans of gasoline from the rack on the back of the Jeep. We were going so deep into the woods that we would need to refill our tank to get out of this true wilderness. We turned off the highway onto a gravel logging road.

At first, every fifteen or twenty minutes, Tom would ask a question. Where were we going? Who owned the land? How did I know him? Then he started asking questions every five minutes. I kept dodging his questions because I really did not want to talk about Mr. Little's finances with someone I barely knew. I could tell Tom was getting really suspicious of me, and I was now regretting this whole trip. His next move caught me by surprise. After about an hour and a half on this gravel road, and after I dodged another one of his questions, he pulled out a .32 caliber pistol that was hidden in his belt and said, "Turn the vehicle around if you are not going to answer me." I stopped the vehicle and looked deep into his eyes. I knew he wasn't bluffing.

"Settle down, and I'll tell you the whole story," I said. Tom replied, "Just start explaining, and I will lower the gun when I feel comfortable. For all I know, you are some weird pervert." "Listen, Tom, you are twice my size and you could easily take me. Put the gun down!"

Tom didn't flinch. He just kept staring at me and said, "I was raised next to New York City, and I've seen small guys take big guys. Just start talking." At this point, I decided to tell him the entire truth. I was afraid that if he caught me in a lie, there was a good chance he would shoot me. "I am an attorney – well at least I go to law school, but I haven't passed the bar yet. I'll explain that to you once I get to know you better. I make a living moving money for rich people into tax shelters in the Cayman Islands. Large sums of money. For this service, I get 5 percent of everything I move into the Caymans.

"This is a lot more affordable for my clients than the 50 percent the federal government charges taxpayers in this tax bracket.

"Take the gentleman who is letting us hunt his land, for example. His name is Mr. Little: at least this is the name he goes by. He is a timber man; he buys large tracts of land, cuts the timber, and then moves on. He's really good at it, and over the years, he started keeping large tracts of land. Years passed, and the timber re-grew.

"Now, with no land costs, he was cutting timber and making a killing, until the IRS showed up and took most of it. So he started cutting timber, with cash money being a part of every deal. He used the cash to buy brand-new four-wheel drives. He built the huge hunting lodge that we are going to – and everything else imaginable, until he had everything he wanted – but he was still making a lot of cash.

"After a while you can't keep spending the money, as you will get above the IRS radar. Mr. Little was dangerously close. He couldn't buy any more stocks or land, and he ran out of relatives in which to place the ownership. He didn't need any more toys, and he couldn't put the money in the bank. That is where I come in. I launder money for rich people. I go to the Cayman Islands and open an account in a company name. I smuggle the money to the Caymans, and I place the funds into that account. The bank will then start investing it as my client instructs them. There are no taxes to pay to the IRS on any gains in this account. The account grows and grows; the Cayman government gets 1 percent of every transaction – both deposits and withdrawals. That 1 percent runs the entire government.

"The Cayman Islands people have no property taxes, no income taxes, and no government fees of any kind. All the schools are built by the government. All health care is free. There is one set of laws that no one ever breaks: the confidentiality laws. No banker will tell your business to anyone, ever. If he does, he will spend his life in prison, with no parole.

"Mr. Little's holdings have continued to grow. He is old, but his family will avoid the 50-percent death tax on all American estates. I will charge them another 5 percent to get money back to Georgia when they want it."

Tom kept the gun pointed at me, his face tense. Then he said, "We left the highway at mile marker 333 by turning right. We then turned left after crossing the creek. The next right was at a grove of cedars. The next turn was a left at a large white oak. You then crossed the creek twice more before turning right at the dead cypress stump. The next turn was a right at the bottom of a steep grade. I am now running out of memory and I want to know where we are going." I laughed, "I know where I'm going, the same way you know where you are. I too have an excellent memory. We will be there in one more left turn." Tom lowered his gun and looked ahead as if nothing had ever happened. It was then that we both knew we were going to be friends for life.

You see, real men don't spend all their time chasing women and getting laid. Real men do chase women, but they also hunt and fish. Hunting is like traveling to a foreign country. You don't speak the language and you don't know the customs. You have a short time to figure everything out and then blend into the surroundings. Only if you are successful in doing so do you get a shot.

The killing of the animal is anticlimactic. This is why many older hunters never load their guns, and just enjoy the moment of seeing the animal they are hunting.

Hunting camps are a reflection of the owner. As Tom was pondering what this deer camp was going to look like, he started to fall asleep, and began to dream about the perfect deer camp...

It is all about location, the rural area of any state. The dwindling financing of the road system, culminated by the final approach, the four-wheel-drive road. It is why a man owns an SUV, Jeep, or a four-wheel-drive truck. It is why you endure horrible gas mileage, bumpy rides, and the embarrassment of being unable to parallel park.

Proudly, you place your vehicle in neutral and reach out with authority to engage the four-wheel-drive into the low lock position. The vehicle seems to rise and bristle as the transmission locks all wheels

into power. How a person drives into the camp on the four-wheel-drive road is an important statement.

One's driving skills are challenged. Are you and your truck one? The thump of a rock hitting your skid plate causes looks of disapproval. What are you, a novice or something?

I hope he can shoot better than he can drive, thinks another. After all, in deer hunting, it is not about how well equipped you are, but how good you are with your equipment. Fashion statements and name brands are for snobby city folks.

The tires spin and dig until the rubber finds rock under the mud for traction. Creeks are forded and bogs are challenged and conquered. GMC rules! Finally you arrive at the cable: not a gate, never a gate. There is always a cable with a lock that appears to have been on steroids – thus enabling it to survive decades of logging roads. It's an American lock from American steel, Carnegie steel from the Pittsburgh Foundry: bulletproof, hacksaw proof, time proven.

The host of the camp exits the vehicle with a flashlight. The "Where's Waldo" of key searches begins. There is only one key for this lock; there has only ever been one key for this lock. It is always hidden within a twenty-five-foot radius of the cable. As it is always lost, it in fact can never be lost.

Up one tree and down another, all the hunters' flashlight beams crawl. Minutes pass. "Don't worry if I can't find it; the camp is just over the hill," an embarrassed host remarks. Soon the key is located, the cable is dropped, and the four wheel drive vehicle pulls forward. With a final turn in the road, the beams of the headlights shine down from the treetops as the hill is conquered. The camp is proudly exposed for all passengers to admire.

It is all about location. Most deer camps are built in hollers. The one in Tom's dream is built on a small knoll surrounded by tall trees. White five-gallon buckets are lined up under the edge of the roofline to collect rainwater. This must be an improved camp. You know, there must be an inside toilet, and this is the water to flush it.

A fire pit surrounded by large rocks is centered in front of the entrance porch. The uprights holding the shed roof over this porch are cedar logs cut from the surrounding forest. The branches have been trimmed two to four inches off the trunk, leaving a series of stubs or wooden pegs on the posts. Hanging from these stubs are coats, guns, and old deer skulls found by young hunters in the woods, along with rusty leg-hold traps placed there by the more senior members.

Coleman coolers line the wall side of the porch holding the camp's provisions; a time-honored decorating statement to complement the architecturally distinctive five-gallon toilet water collecting pails.

Surrounding all the structures is the camp's past history. An old school bus that must have been pulled up there by a dozer and used for shelter before the cabin was built. The first try, a three-sided structure where old roof tin was used for the walls, and a matching doghouse with page wire strung between the trees.

Every camp has a shooting stump. This stump is placed so that when you are on the front porch, you can do target practice. Usually, there's a two-by-twelve board in front of the stump for targets. There are cans and cartons with holes littering the surrounding ground.

The structure itself is an art-deco version of Appalachian leftovers. Peachtree casement windows, next to aluminum windows reclaimed from government-funded housing. Walls lined with tongue-and-groove pine meeting ceilings trimmed in mobile-home laminate. A loft with a leftover aluminum ladder for access, and of course, tanks of propane. Propane runs everything: the heat, the stove, the lights. Propane is the life blood of a hunting camp.

There's a butcher block table with cross legs. The seats of its chairs are split from years of use, exposing the yellow-stained foam rubber padding. A yellow-gold, now yellow-brown Broyhill couch awaits the weary traveler and soon-to-be hunter. The bathroom toilet is pretty much out in the open, and really a sub-room of the living room. If you are modest, your other choice is to go to the woods: a painful experience in the winter. This is not a co-ed environment. The first freeze broke the trap out of the bottom of the toilet. Protocol of the camp is to place the paper you wipe with in the container next to the toilet, so the paper doesn't clog the system during a flush.

Do your business – and follow your deposit with the water from one of the five-gallon pails from the porch – and your comfort is assured. True to East Tennessee, the rains come in time to refill the buckets. There is the muted pattering of the rain on the tin roof. The hunters have slept as deeply as one can sleep and still awaken afterward.

The host is always a great cook. Mom taught him well: deer stew, fried deer tenderloin, fried bluegill, and pork greens to keep it all moving through your intestines.

As always, there is some level of concern over the water supply for the toilet.

It is time to rise, about two hours before daybreak. Morning food is always going to be a three-skillet breakfast. Last night's potatoes browning in butter and garlic salt; steak carefully marinated in a blend of ginger-based seasoning, grilled, sliced thin, and fried in butter. A thick slab of bacon, artfully fried to golden perfection. The egg pan awaits the campers' requests: sunny side up, over medium, or scrambled. No Teflon here. Steel and cast iron are the tools of a Real Man's kitchen. Skillets that have been perfectly seasoned for many generations – Grandma's non-stick surface. The air fills with the aroma of coffee, steak, and home fries. The day has started at the camp. First light. City people don't understand the spiritual feeling of being awakened by first light in the deep woods. It is

God's work. A bird braves a very short chirp; it fears a late-flying owl, but nature demands that it announce the beginning of the morning. It is too wet to hunt today, but we have enjoyed an incredible breakfast. Coffee percolates on an old fifties-era stove fired by propane. No need to light the Coleman lantern: it is past first light.

Tom continues to dream of himself standing on the front porch at first light, watching the trees swaying in the rain. The wind is blowing mist in his face. He is being healed, anointed by Mother Nature. Every nerve in his body is awake. His sight is crisp, his senses clear, he feels the cold in every finger and toe. The host will bring him a cup of coffee as they stand on the porch. They will talk about yesteryear, high school, the draft, and raising kids. They are friends; it is the essence of deer-hunting camp.

Tom's mind clears as he awakens from the sound of the straining motor. The RPMs of the engine seem very high, and occasionally the sensation of a slipping tire creates a shuddering chug throughout the vehicle. Tom, pondering what this deer camp would look like, was trying to clear his head after having been asleep.

I pulled the final hill a little fast, so that when the headlights dropped from the sky, everyone could see what was in front of them like a large flash picture. "Holy Shit!" said Tom. "Where the hell are we?" "This," I said, "in front of us, is Mr. Little's hunting camp."

It was huge: the large stone structure built to look like a European mansion. All of the exterior walls were stone, and it covered over twenty thousand square feet. I could tell that Tom could not believe his eyes; he just got out of the Jeep and stared. Armed with a flashlight, I disappeared around the back of the building. I fired up the twelve-cylinder Caterpillar diesel generator, counted to thirty, and threw the large switch. The diesel growled as its governors dumped fuel to the injectors, and the entire hunting lodge lit up in the dark. Only in America do they build hunting camps like this. Completely self-sufficient – and off the grid and tax rolls. This was one asset that the IRS would never find. I came back to see Tom and John just standing in front of the lodge, frozen like deer in headlights.

"Come on in," I said, as I walked through the unlocked front door. "When everyone in the county respects you, you don't have to lock your doors." Tom and John followed, speechless. The first room we entered was a large banquet hall. The walls were covered in framed hunting pictures, and above them were trophy deer, bear, and boar mounts. Even if the people in the pictures weren't important celebrities, they were on the wall of honor, and they were Mr. Little's friends.

He honored them by making them permanent fixtures in a place that meant more to him than most things in his life. The large-planked loblolly pine floor was pegged, and random width. The beams that held the roof system were virgin pine logs, at least three feet in diameter. All the walls in between the massive superstructure were stucco or round river stone. The table in the middle of the room had chairs for forty guests. This was no mere hunting camp. This was a gentleman's retreat. Tom commented on how much labor and how many employees it must have taken to build the structure. I remarked how much employment there is when the IRS doesn't take everyone's money.

We unloaded our gear, marveled at the rest of the building, and decided to take the canvas top off the Jeep so we could look for deer trails crossing the four-wheel-drive logging roads. We turned our flashlights on and got into my CJ5 Jeep. I was in the back seat, Tom in the passenger seat, and John was driving. We crept along a deeply rutted logging trail while Tom leaned slightly out of the Jeep with the flashlight, looking for obvious deer crossings. This way we would know where to hunt, early in the morning.

You know how you can take a spoon and place it over the edge of a table, hit the side that is hanging over, and the spoon flips up instantly? It happened that fast. They were cutting pulp wood in the area. A log eight feet in length and about ten inches in diameter was lying over the edge of the tire rut in the road. As the Jeep crossed over the end of the log, it flipped up so fast that no one had any time to react. The log hit Tom squarely in the face, then fell on John's head, knocking him out. The Jeep crashed into the thicket on the uphill side of the road.

I fumbled around for my flashlight in the floorboard. I lifted the log off John. He held his head, but he appeared to be okay as he had the use of his arms. Tom wasn't so fortunate. He was having trouble breathing through his mouth, as he no longer had a nose. It was smashed, and the part of his face between his cheekbones was completely flat. The blood going down his throat was choking him and getting into his lungs. He kept coughing up lots of blood, and he was only semi-conscious and drifting into shock.

I grabbed the back of his coat and dragged him out of the Jeep. Once I had him lying on his side and spitting out the blood, he started breathing regularly. John backed the Jeep out of the ditch. No damage. He positioned the Jeep so that the headlights were on Tom.

After about twenty minutes, Tom stood up and asked me how his face looked. I told him that it was crushed, but I could fix it. I told him that if he would lie on the Jeep hood I could straighten his nose. When he asked if I was a doctor, I told him no, but that I had seen it done on Channel Two. He paused a minute and looked around, as if weighing other options, then said to go ahead.

I got two small sticks, cleaned them up, and blunted the ends with my pocket knife. Slowly I worked the sticks into his nose, pushing it up with my thumbs. I had never seen it done on Channel Two, but I had helped a doctor in Vietnam perform the exact same procedure. At about two inches in I stopped, as going any further could put the sticks into Tom's brain. Once I removed the sticks, his nose was back to a proper height between his cheekbones. He actually was able to breathe a bit through one of his nostrils again. We decided to return to the hunting palace. We helped Tom to a chair at the large dining room table. I got some beef jerky, chips, and onion dip from our grocery stash and placed it within reach of everyone. I offered Tom some water, but when he drank it he got sick and started bleeding again. Eventually we were able to get a couple of glasses of water into him.

Tom was looking kind of rough, covered in blood, leaves and pine bark. He also looked a little pale, and I was trying to decide if we should take him to a medical facility in Marietta. I was worried about the Jeep ride in the dark, and the possibility of getting lost on the way. In the dark, none of the trails look the same. This could cause us to get into a much worse situation than we already had, and for now at least, he appeared stable. I wanted to observe him for a while – as I felt he probably had a concussion – so I asked John and Tom if they wanted to play poker. Tom just wanted to go to bed, but I knew not to let him fall asleep if, in fact, he did have a concussion. I knew we had to observe Tom for several hours, and risk the drive back in the dark, if his condition worsened in the least little bit.

We all sat down at the table with a bottle of Jack. I took a hit on one of John's joints and we started playing poker. I have no idea where John was getting his weed, but it was either the best that Mexico had to offer or it was laced with something. I only took one hit in an effort to settle down a little, yet I was amazingly stoned. I let Tom drink a limited amount of Jack Daniel's, as he was in a lot of pain. After a while, all good judgment was completely gone. We got so messed up that our poker game was reduced to dealing each of us one card, everyone betting, and then each of us showing his card.

The high card would win. About every five hands we got into an argument whether aces were high or low. At about the time we were so fried that we couldn't remember which cards were higher than the other ones, there was a big disturbance outside. We just kept looking at each other for leadership, but everyone just sat there not knowing what to do. It started to sink in that a huge pack of four-wheel-drive vehicles had come roaring into the camp. I kept hearing truck doors open and close, then voices, and then a group of over twenty men wearing pistols, dressed in orange or camo pattern clothes, came into the great hall. The leader assessed the situation and shouted, "Who are you, and what are you doing here?"

It must have been quite the sight. Three of us drunk, two totally stoned, and the marijuana smoke still in the air. Tom still had leaves and caked blood all over his head and face. I was so stoned I couldn't speak. Finally, I was able to say the word, "Little."

The leader immediately smiled and said, "You must be his lawyer," while he shook his head in disbelief. "He said you might come down. Well, I guess the proper thing to say is 'Welcome to Georgia!'" He then asked, while pointing to Tom, "What happened to him, and does he need medical help?" Tom just stared at him. I tried to tell them that I didn't know where the closest doctor lived, but some of the men laughed while the others kept asking what I had just said. A middle-aged man stepped forward and started evaluating Tom. He had one of the other men help him move Tom to a different chair, a recliner of sorts. After about ten minutes he said that Tom would be able to make it till tomorrow – but no more booze, and get that marijuana out of this house. Mr. Little disdains drug use. And you are disrespecting him by bringing it into his camp. Give all your illegal drugs to that man there, and he will dispose of them. As the man stepped forward, and John handed his bag of weed to him, I noticed a State Trooper emblem on the man's jacket. The trooper took the weed to the bathroom and flushed it. "Keep this man here, and I will check on him every hour tonight. Tomorrow, take him to a hospital." "Okay, then we will be in this end of the camp, and you stay in your end, and we will all hunt."

We went to bed. In the morning, we got up about a couple of hours after the rest of the hunters, and they were all in the woods. None of us could eat breakfast, and I asked Tom if he was ready to go home. He said he still wanted to give it a try, so we loaded up the Jeep and drove to the first deer crossing. When Tom tried climbing the tree with his tree stand, he started bleeding again. He looked at me and I could tell that he'd had enough for one trip. We all decided it was time to go back to Tennessee. We arrived close to dark, and we were tired. I kept admiring what a professional job I had done on Tom's nose, but I decided not to bring it up, as his mood was not so good. After I dropped them off, I went home and headed straight to bed. I fell into a dream of vivid clarity.

...There were a large and a small dog growling at something on the other side of the screened porch. On the ledge, on the other side of the screen, was perched a large, fat, red fox. Neither the dogs nor the fox wanted to move. They seemed to just want to observe each other. All at once two coyotes appeared, and tried to catch the fox. The red fox already had its escape route planned, and it disappeared into the forest unharmed. Immediately, the two coyotes tore through the screen and grabbed the smaller dog. The larger dog attempted to fight off the coyotes, but she was too old to inflict any real damage. I entered the porch with my pistol and immediately started firing at the coyotes. I kept firing, but they were moving so fast I kept missing. The coyotes, in an effort to escape, dropped the small dog and dashed out onto the lawn in front of the house. I had fired all the bullets in the pistol, and the coyotes seemed to realize I was no longer a

threat. They stopped their retreat, and again began to advance on the little dog that was obviously hurt, and almost lifeless. I ran to my gun cabinet, grabbed the twelve-gauge pump shotgun, and went back to the porch. One of the coyotes was leaving the porch with the small dog in its mouth, while the other one was fighting the large older dog. This time I carefully aimed and took out the rear hindquarters of the coyote that was carrying off the smaller dog. Now completely paralyzed in its hindquarters, it dropped the smaller dog. Hearing the roar of the shotgun, the second coyote attempted to flee, but I killed it with my second shot. I then shot the first coyote, killing it instantly. I placed my shotgun on the ground, and ran over to see the condition of the little dog. It was dead. I picked it up and held it in my arms. As I started back to the porch again, I heard the growl of the larger dog that was lying in the screen porch, too hurt to get up to help me. As I looked in the direction of the porch, I now saw a large cougar between me and my shotgun. The cougar stared at me in a crouched position, with only the tip of its tail slowly moving back and forth. I very slowly placed the little dog onto the ground, eased my pocket knife out, and opened the blade. I locked my eyes onto those of the cougar and advanced toward it...

Stream fishing on Norton Creek,
Gatlinburg, TN, in the late 1970s.
Natty Crotchkell on left and Bubba Savage on right.

Chapter 9

"Real Men (and some women) Fish For Trout"

It was the spring of the year when I got Tom's phone call. I had spent the winter in South America, working and chasing women. I had just returned to East Tennessee and I was surprised to hear his voice. "Want to go trout fishing?" he said. "Do you have a place in mind?" I asked. "Yes, my grandfather owns some mountain land in Gatlinburg. He has his own stream." I asked if I could bring an old friend from law school named Natty Crotchkell. We all met for breakfast and headed to Tom's grandfather's place. Tom called it Norton Creek.

We exited on a road between Pigeon Forge and Gatlinburg and passed a few homes by a beautiful, spring-fed mountain creek. We headed up the mountain and passed through the first gate at the entrance of Tom's grandfather's property. There, beside the gate, was one of the caretaker's homes. Tom waved at the man, who stood there scowling in a very unwelcoming manner. As we continued up the mountain, we crossed the creek several more times. The road was one lane, but paved and well maintained. The bridges were all concrete and seemingly over-engineered. We had traveled a couple of miles when I asked Tom, "Is this a driveway or something?" "Yes," he replied, "it's my grandfather's." We passed another home on the left, where we were stopped by a man whom Tom called Uncle Doug. I don't know what the past history was between Tom and this man, but one day I was going to find out why Tom disliked him. I have always been a good judge of character, and I hated this son of a bitch the first time I met him.

He was approximately six-foot-two, with the slender build of a man who had never done anything physical in his whole life. He was extremely handsome, and had polished nails and pretty hands. Obviously he had never worked, and he was enjoying a life of extreme leisure.

Tom made our introductions, and his Uncle Doug started quizzing us about who we were and what we did. Our friend Natty was an attorney in Knoxville, and I said I worked for him as a paralegal. He kept coming back to me, obviously, not buying my story. He was incredibly intelligent and perceptive, yet overbearing and cocky. He had been well educated, but had spent too many years in isolation, up on this mountain. As Tom's uncle talked, I went into a daydream and saw Uncle Doug's future.

...Tom's uncle was sitting in front of his computer screen, staring at the picture of himself and waiting for an opportunity. He shifted his weight in the chair, as his remaining leg was sweating and pulling on his underwear. The prosthetic leg was slick and never sweated.

Doug thought the image of himself on the computer screen looked good. Yes, the picture was taken years ago. The computer gods had made him the Almighty in the world of Cowbell Golf. As he sat there staring at his own image, his mind drifted into a deep sleep. His dreams used to be good memories, but now they were just depressing. Realizing and finally accepting that he was a failure made him nervous and uneasy. He had nothing important to worry about. He had been reduced to a life of insignificant, mindless staring at a computer, hoping to receive an email response to his website.

In his younger years he would have been out hunting, fishing or playing golf. When he had extra time, he might have gone to see his father and have a talk about some conservative political topic.

His first wife was from Spain. Poloma was an excellent wife, a fine mother, and a great housekeeper. He knew that living in East Tennessee was hard for her, as she was a foreigner, and considered a second-rate person by most locals. She had a strong accent, and she barely spoke English well enough for the locals to understand what she said. As far as the locals were concerned, she might as well have been black. She gave him three children Cantina, Richard and Kirt. She did all the cooking, even making her own bread from her own yeast, baked fresh for each meal. The clothes were always clean, the house spotless, and the children well loved.

In hindsight, he treated Poloma like a slave you could have sex with, and who would bear your children.

He never spent any time with Poloma. She was there for his beckoning. Life was good. His dad gave him a house along Norton Creek – one of the best, if not *the* best, trout streams in the United States. Norton Creek, named after Sam Norton, ran in front of his house and was teeming with trout. One day his slave/wife Poloma went to the doctor. She had cancer – and she was going to die.

He still had three children to raise. There was housework, and there were domestic duties. Home-cooked meals and fresh-baked bread. Sex whenever

he wanted sex. How was he going to replace her? Doug knew he needed to keep Poloma alive.

There was no hope through any of the standard treatments. Some of the treatments outside of the American Medical Association guidelines were really weird. One doctor was using low doses of electricity on his patients. Another doctor was trying to heal tumors with magnets. One resort in Florida was offering baths in alligator dung to fight off cancers and assure a long life, but there was one treatment in Mexico that looked promising. They called it Laetrile.

I snapped out of my daydream and walked away from the group. I had been awake, yet dreaming. I could, for the first time, not believe how clear and exact it was. I was able to control when I turned it on and off. I felt the presence of some force or spirit controlling my body, yet I had no fear. I knew I had just dreamed "Uncle Doug's" future. For the first time, I now fully understood there is another force among us that can be accessed at will.

We soon left Uncle Doug, and drove another half mile, then we pulled over by the creek. It was incredible – the stream flowed as if its only purpose was to raise trout, and to please those who were fortunate enough to fish there. Tom established the rules: we would each take a turn fishing a pool, and then continue up the stream. Watch for snakes, yield to bears, and stay together. He rigged our fly rods appropriately, and then led us into the stream.

I felt as though I had entered a rainforest. The canopy of trees blocked out all direct sunlight, placing us into a semi-dark, damp environment. Cool mist hung between the creek and the protective overhang of trees. The rocks were covered with moss on all sides, and on almost every rock, at least one salamander of a different color was perched on top.

Tom started with his teaching moment as he faced Natty and me. "Place your fly on your first cast at the bottom of the pool. This will catch the small sentry trout that warn the larger ones of our approach. Pull him into the pool under the one you're fishing, before he can spook the fish at the head of the pool."

Tom demonstrated by floating a Royal Coachman fly onto the surface at the lower end of the pool. Immediately, a small trout struck the fly. Tom strong-armed the fish out of the water, and released it into the pool beneath the one we were fishing. "Now fish the upper part of the pool," he said. "The biggest fish will be lying where the whitewater becomes dark blue. Watch this!"

Tom took a little more line out of his reel, and placed the fly directly where the white and blue water met. Smack! The large rainbow trout slurped down the dry fly. Tom played it for about thirty seconds to a minute, then placed the fourteen-inch fish into his creel. "Your turn," he said, with a mischievous smile.

I was so upstaged it wasn't funny. Here I had taken Tom on a deer hunt that got his face smashed and almost killed him. Now I was standing in possibly the finest trout stream in the country – being schooled by Tom on how to fish. I wasn't even close to Tom's league when it came to trout fishing. Tom would gracefully move throughout the stream in a manner that would not spook the fish, while I kept slipping and falling into the creek. Natty seemed to be doing really well, and he was catching fish like Tom. He had these special shoes that kept him from slipping on the moss-covered rocks. I noticed that Tom was wearing a pair of tennis shoes that had a piece of carpet glued onto their soles. It was keeping him from slipping on the moss-covered rocks. I was wearing a regular pair of tennis shoes, and I was falling with almost every step. Every time I would wipe out, both Tom and Natty would make a remark on how spastic I was. It was really getting to me, and I started wondering if Tom was getting even with me for getting him hurt on our deer hunt. It was like the "death by a thousand cuts." If I took a step, I would slip and scratch my calf. If I took another step, I would slip and hurt my ankle. If I tried to walk on the big stones, I would completely wipe out and then get more insults from Tom and Natty. I don't know why I even had a fishing pole with me, as I could never stand up long enough to cast. I finally got out of the stream and walked along the bank, watching them catch fish in every pool. As we worked our way up the stream, I learned the whole story of how Tom had been graced with the opportunity to be fishing this paradise. As a boy, Tom had spent his summers growing up with his grandfather, who was an avid sportsman and very wealthy man. Tom's grandfather owned 3,600 acres next to Gatlinburg, a popular tourist town adjoining the Great Smoky Mountains Park. Running through the middle of this property was a watershed called Norton Creek. During the summer when Tom stayed with his grandfather, they would trout fish almost every day. When he was older, Tom was allowed to join the caretaker and his sons, when they ran bears with their hounds in the evenings.

We fished about a mile of creek, with Tom patiently coaching us (or should I say Natty, as I was no longer in the stream) the best he could. We were now upstream about a mile, so I left the stream to retrieve my Chevy Blazer and drive it to where Tom and Natty were still fishing. They had caught quite a lot of fish, and we had come to a group of large, flat boulders that made a great place to rest. Tom cleaned the fish and started unpacking the duffel bag he'd placed in the vehicle. He made a small fire from twigs and branches he'd gathered along the bank. Out of the duffel bag came potatoes, onions and a stick of butter, which Tom proceeded to use to grill everything together in an iron skillet over the fire. He placed a foil-wrapped loaf of biscuit bread he had made that morning next to the fire. He then pulled out two plastic bags. One had raw eggs, removed from their shell, with a little milk added. In the other was a mixture of flour, cornmeal, and some type of seasoning.

He browned the potatoes and onions. Then he placed a trout in the bag of eggs, and rolled it around until it was completely coated. He then placed the trout into the bag of flour. Then he dropped the trout into the cast-iron skillet. Tom repeated the process, fried all the trout golden brown, then pulled out one more bag, full of lemon halves, and exclaimed, "Let's eat!"

His meal was as understated as his remark: "My grandfather owns his own trout stream." I have eaten almost every type of fish, prepared almost every way imaginable, but I have never had such a delicious meal as this. The bread was soft and moist, with a faint sweet taste. The potatoes and onions were the perfect complement to the trout, so fresh and firm with that delicate crust. The trout flaked off the skeleton, one boneless piece to each side. I ate until I could hold no more.

"Where did you learn to cook like this?" Natty asked. "Bessie," Tom answered. "Who is Bessie?" I asked. "She is my grandfather's cook. She is the sweetest black lady, and she lives with my grandfather at the big house. She is in charge of all his meals. My most favorite recipe of hers is when she cooks bear meat that has been marinated in fresh buttermilk," said Tom.

Tom wasn't telling me everything. He was enjoying his coy attitude and my overzealous curiosity. Natty chimed in, "The only thing your story lacks for the perfect world is a beautiful woman." Tom laughed, "Let me tell you my best-kept secret. This trout stream has delivered me more beautiful women than any bar in Knoxville."

This caught my attention. "How could that possibly be true?"

Tom leaned back, and in a bragging kind of way, he started his story. "To get really good action on a regular basis, you have to have a master plan. My plan starts like this. First I drive to Gatlinburg on Friday afternoon and catch a happy hour at a local bar. I pick out my target. I always look for the women who look like tourists. These women are away from their hometown, and thus their hometown relationships. They want a little excitement and action, but I never pick up married women – never. You have to have standards.

"I will have one drink with the one I pick, along with the usual small talk. Eventually she will ask why I'm here. I'll let her know I've come to the mountains to trout fish. I don't tell her that it is my grandfather's stream. I only tell her that I am here to fish. At this point I let her know that fishing starts early, and that I have to go. As an aside, I ask if she would like to join me fishing tomorrow.

"They never see it coming. Can you imagine what she was thinking? Being asked to participate in the sacred male rite of trout fishing? He is leaving me at the bar, without even trying to make a move on me? The perfect man!

"They always say yes. I tell them to bring a bathing suit, as we will be wading in the stream. I say, "Don't worry, I have all the fishing gear and an extra fly rod." I ask them what motel they are staying at, and I tell them I will meet them in the front lobby around 8:00 am.

"I leave and go around the block, and I repeat the process at a different bar. This is in case, for some reason, the first one doesn't show up, I will have backup."

"Have you ever had both women fail to show?" asked Natty. "Never," said Tom. "Sometimes one won't show, but never both."

I couldn't stand it. What a great idea. Mr. Wholesome invites the lady trout fishing, then seals the deal with a takeaway close by leaving her sitting in the bar as he leaves. It was brilliant. "Well, tell us the rest. Where and when do you fuck them?" I asked.

"After picking up my date, we go to breakfast, and then to the creek. Now, remember these girls have arrived with their bathing suits. The same bathing suit they planned to wear walking around a swimming pool – but we are climbing up a trout stream over slippery rocks. You can imagine what that's like, can't you, Bubba?" Tom and Natty started laughing their ass off at me, then Tom continued: "I excuse myself, so they can change into their bathing suit behind the truck door.

The only way a woman can navigate these streams is half bent over or on all fours. Either way, her back is arched, and her ass is in the air almost the entire day. I follow behind, giving instructions, while she tries to fish. You can see every detail of a woman from this vantage point. The cold mist makes her nipples hard all day. Of course she needs me to hold her steady, as she doesn't have the proper foot gear to keep from slipping." "Why didn't you offer to hold Bubba steady this morning?" laughed Natty. "I started to help him just before he left the creek, because he was being such a pussy over falling all the time," said Tom. With that, Tom and Natty could not stop laughing at me. Not being able to stand it anymore, I said, "Just get on with the story, asshole!"

Tom chuckled a little more, then continued. "After I have entertained myself for a couple of hours with the view, I make a point of holding her close and helping her catch a few fish. After all, I want her to feel in control and comfortable. I steady her during her cast by firmly holding her hips. Sometimes she turns around and just attacks me right there, and sometimes not.

Once we have caught fish, the only thing left to do is to go back to my place and cook them. I am a damn good cook, and that always turns women on. Half the time the women attack me while I am preparing dinner. Those that don't are always quick to offer to do the dishes. While they are doing the dishes, I come up behind them, lift their hair up, and start kissing their neck.

I wait for at least two signals before I make any further moves." "Signals? What do you mean?" I asked.

"Women will tell you when to make the next move by giving you a signal.

When I am kissing her neck, if she moves her head to the side to give me more access, that is a signal. If she arches her back and slightly hikes her ass up, that is a signal. If her shoulders drop as in submission, that is a signal. If she starts moving one leg toward the other, that is a signal. If she rises up slightly on her toes, then leans her ass against me, that is a signal. When I get two signals, I make my next move.

As their hands are covered in soap, they can only stand there and let me proceed. Off come their pants.

"I take a towel, reach out for their hands, and slowly and deliberately dry each finger. I usually do them on the kitchen floor – some make it to the bedroom."

I was impressed. "What is your success ratio?" I asked. "Actually, it's 100 percent," Tom answered. I marveled at the perfect plan, and decided I would try it next weekend. Natty said he wanted to fish some more. We told him we would wait for him upstream, where he would come to a dam.

Tom took me up to the road about a quarter of a mile. We came upon a small gorge, where each side rose almost straight up for 100 feet. There in the gorge was a dam. This dam was a miniature replica of the dams that the TVA built throughout the South. It had its own generating turbine. This power was used to power "the big house," and I was about to see how it worked. We went to the upstream side of the dam, where there was a concrete pool with a swim house. We walked out on the dam by a manual gate valve that operated the spillway. There we waited for Natty to approach us, as he fished upstream toward the dam.

Natty got amazingly close to the dam before he realized it was in front of him. When he first looked up at us, he was only fifty to seventy-five feet from the base of the dam, and fully surrounded by the sheer walls of the gorge. Tom was lying there, relaxing by the pool. I decided I would have a little fun, and started cranking open the emergency spillway. I only wanted to scare Natty, but way more water came out than I expected. Hearing the noise, Tom jumped up, and started cranking the spillway valve shut.

Natty had nowhere to go. He made a feeble effort to try to ascend one side of the gorge, but the rising water from the open floodgate immediately took his footing. He then went head over heels downstream in the current.

Tom finished lowering the floodgate and bellowed, "What the fuck were you thinking? "Do you want me to give you a turn, too?"

I stared in amazement. Not only had he completely upstaged my deer hunt from last fall, but I actually thought he was going to toss me off the dam. I tried to explain to him that I was only joking around, but he was pissed, and walking fast to get to the Blazer so we could drive down and check on Natty. We drove downstream and collected Natty, who was really mad and wanted to go home. He wasn't hurt; he was just pissed off. Soon he got over it, after Tom found his fishing pole. Unfortunately, most of Natty's hoity-toity gear had been lost from his toilet bowl flushing experience. We felt bad about that, but after a few minutes he forgave us.

It was almost the end of the day, so Tom drove us up to his grandfather's "summer home." It was amazing. "Pops," as Tom called him, was a very wealthy man. Not only did he own 3,600 acres and five miles of his own perfect trout stream; he also owned one very nice home.

Built in a ranch style, the home displayed workmanship lost years ago. The stonework had been done by the same stonemasons who'd laid all the rock bridges and tunnels in the Great Smoky Mountains National Park. The lawns were bentgrass, mowed daily, and Pops had a nine-hole executive golf course laid out around his home. The place looked like a miniature version of the Biltmore Estate, complete with gardens and nursery homes. It had mountain views from every direction. A short walk off the east side of the home, and you could enjoy a round of trap and skeet. Go south, and you could pick a fine horse from the stable and go for a trail ride. It was a sportsman's paradise – a real man lived there.

Just as we were a few feet from the front door, a man opened it from the other side. "Welcome, Master Tom. Your grandfather awaits you and your friends in the living room," said the butler. Tom introduced us to "Pops." His steel blue eyes looked right through me, and read my soul.

"It is nice to make your acquaintance, Mr. Savage, and likewise yours, Mr. Crotchkell." I knew immediately this man and I would spend hours together in the future. I could tell right off that he desperately wanted to talk to me. I wondered if Tom had told him about what I did with other wealthy men's money. I also knew things were getting desperate in the Cayman Islands. The feds were becoming successful in getting bankers to divulge information – by offering American citizenship, along with just about as much money as they asked for – as part of the deal. I needed to move my clients' money fast, and it dawned on me that this man, "Pops," might also have need of my services. After a couple of hours of talking, and everyone thanking "Pops" for letting us come up and fish his stream, we began to leave. Just as I was about to walk through the door, "Pops," while shaking my hand, invited me to join him for lunch. We made an appointment to meet in two days. On the way down the mountain I asked Tom why his grandfather would ask me to lunch. Tom answered, "He must like you." "I forgot to ask him where we were going to meet," I said, as I cussed under my breath. Tom laughed as he shook his head, and said, "At his house, you dumbass!" He continued, "Wear a coat and tie, and don't start eating until Grace has been said over the food – or it will be a very short lunch."

Chapter 10

If You Don't Have Looks, Money Will Do

...I dreamed I lay in an orchard, looking at a small bud of an apple tree. It was just starting to bloom, fragrant and beautiful. A fly landed on the blossom to lay its eggs. The larvae that grew from the eggs would soon enter the flesh of the future apple, tainting the first bite. So sad was it that such a beautiful fruit could be damaged by such a small worm...

I had a plane hangared at a small private airport, close to the U.T. Knoxville campus. Actually, I had several planes tucked here and there in several private airports in case I needed to leave the country in a hurry for any reason. This allowed Tom and me to travel to many places within a large radius of Knoxville, Tennessee, at a moment's notice. Want some fresh seafood? In two and a half hours, we would be eating oysters in Charleston. Want to go pheasant hunting in South Dakota? Six hours and 1,800 miles later, we would land in Lake Andes, South Dakota. East Tennessee winters depressing you? Hours later we would be drinking beer in the Bahamas.

One plane was only five minutes from the U.T. campus. Guess what was at the U.T. campus? Women. Lots of women. What is even cooler about the women at U.T. is that you can tell if they are new to the campus, or if they have been at school for a few years. The topography of the campus is somewhat hilly, and everything is spread out so that all the students have to walk between one and two miles a day. This creates a type of anatomy – known locally as the U.T. calf – on all the girls. After a few years of attending U.T., all the girls have strong, pronounced calf muscles. Don't get me wrong: they look great because by the time they have developed the U.T. calf, they have also developed very firm asses from all this regular walking. But this is an important feature to look for when trying to pick up women. Women with this feature who are in bars to meet a man have either just broken up with someone, or they are getting a little desperate to find someone who will spend time with them after they graduate. Both of these are fine targets of opportunity if you want some sex.

By 1976, Tom had dropped out of U.T. and opened Knoxville's first discotheque. It was called Bogies Club, and it was located on Cumberland Avenue across from a fashion shop called "Mary Gills" that was owned by a blind queer. Never has there been a bar, or other local place, as slathered with women as Bogies Club was in 1976.

Tom, along with a few other handsome men, would go out and personally market to the females of U.T. between class changes. They would give free drink tokens to any attractive lady, and her friends.

Likewise, Tom purchased a 1955 Cadillac, put a speaker on the hood, and started cruising Fraternity Row. Pulled behind the Caddy was an open trailer with a couch. Lying on, sitting on, and draped across this couch were women Tom had personally recruited for the job, dressed in hot pants and t-shirts tied below their breasts. These women would couch-dance, and gyrate to the music being played over the speaker.

"Bogies Club, Let the Good Times Roll" was painted on the sides of the Caddy. The ladies would entice the men out of the frat houses as the Caddy toured Fraternity Row, and toss them tokens for fifty-cent beers.

This sexual "Good Humor Man" marketing ploy was beyond successful. Students would wait up to two hours to get into the club. Operating at full capacity of six hundred people, the club rocked all night long.

A local disc jockey by the name of Dick Winstead spun the records. Light machines, strobes, fog and Bose speakers pounded the crowd every night. There were four liquor bartenders, and six beer bartenders, who stayed busy pouring drinks. At the end of the night, around 3:00 am, a "chosen few" would be allowed to continue the party at Tom's place only a few miles away. I was always there.

After about a year, Tom sold Bogies Club. The new owner completely remodeled it to look like the bridge of the Starship Enterprise. "Trekkies," as they were called, gathered at the bar. Most were in the school of engineering, arriving with their miniature slide rules and pocket protectors, and they would take turns sitting in Captain Kirk's chair. Within a couple of months, the bar closed. The building was later occupied by an "O'Charley's" restaurant. But not all was lost when Bogies Club closed.

Tom and I had discovered a particular demographic of women who were a whole lot easier to get to know. These were the ones who had completed school and were not yet married. They fell into groups. The first group was ladies who were climbing the professional ladder, and were trying to break through the proverbial corporate "glass ceiling." They were usually not very good looking, and they needed regular sex. This group was usually overlooked because of the second group.

The second group consisted of women who were beautiful, had nice bodies, and had taken jobs at law firms and doctor's offices as receptionists. They were holding out for marriage with someone who could support them in a rich lifestyle. This group also needed regular sex.

Remember that I had a plane? The Friday night drill became one where Tom and I would go to the Copper Cellar on Cumberland Avenue, where these women went for a drink to unwind after a long week of work. I do have one very unique skill. I had perfected this skill through careful research, and a dedicated effort to become a ninja in this newly emerging sport. I could meander, or drift up and down the bar, and scent which women were on their period. There were many factors involved in this new sport. The direction of the heat and air utilities was very important. How much makeup, and how it was applied, spoke volumes. The clothes selection, the color of those clothes, and how they were worn, was always a factor. But the truth is that I have a very refined sense of smell, and I can pick up the very noticeable scent of a hormone that women secrete when they are on their period. Tom would sit there drinking his screwdriver, while I would signal him which ones were good targets. Tom would determine when two women who were sitting beside each other, and apparently knew each other, were secreting the proper pheromones according to my scent check. When I returned, we would agree on which pair of women we would pursue.

It was too easy. I would wear a sport coat, looking as if I had just left work. After all, dressed like this, I must be a rich lawyer or doctor. Tom would wear nice slacks and an Oxford shirt. His large arms were noticeably bulging under the shirt. Because he chooses to keep them covered, it seemed as if they weren't the most impressive part of his anatomy. With such a nice feature not being openly displayed, women would immediately become intrigued as to what other goodies might be available in this package.

Within an hour or two, the girls would be asked to join us for dinner. At this age, women don't mind eating in front of men. Younger women always are too embarrassed to eat a full meal in front of their dates, as they're probably worried the guy will think they will get fat. A confident woman will take this opportunity to eat a full meal that someone else is paying for, then work off the extra calories later by having unbridled, aggressive sex.

After a look at the menu, I would pause, reach out, and gently take everyone else's menu from them and say, "I'd really like a quality meal – let's fly to Charleston and get some fresh seafood." Thinking they had hit pay dirt, the women would look at each other and smile. Tom and I would stand up to go, and the ladies would follow. A few hours later, after travel and a meal in Charleston, these ladies would be working hard to get rid of those extra calories.

The lesson here is quite simple. Dress and act the part. As an example: If you want a woman who doesn't care about anything beyond the size of your arms, then wear a tight t-shirt and don't have a very high expectation. Drink beer instead of a mixed drink if you want an inexperienced young lady or a redneck leftover. Be loud, and every woman in the bar will notice you, and any decent-looking woman will think you lack confidence. Go to a football game without your shirt, paint your body, and the women who notice you will think you have a small dick. Or, dress comfortably and relaxed, act as though you are in total control of your surroundings, speak in quiet, soft tones, and women will see a mature male who is quite confident that he can control the moment. These are the men whom women of all ages want.

One night, Tom and I were returning from a long weekend of nonsense. We had been doing this for a year or so, and I had now become tired of the routine. It was time for both of us to grow up and start acting more responsible. It just wasn't fun anymore.

In hindsight, I now am ashamed of my past behavior. But experiencing all of these moments does give me the ability to reflect, and to realize that all of this is part of a rite of passage. It starts with the young, and it never ends until a person can truly define how and where they are comfortable in certain situations. You know you are reaching maturity when you start caring about how you are being perceived by your associates. We celebrate certain thresholds: learning to swim alone, manhood, driver's license, womanhood, religious revelation, community stature, political power, wealth, and death. It is the rites of passage that we don't celebrate which may have the greatest impact in the formation – or the lack of the formation – of our personality. It is often these curious voids that were never addressed or experienced, but are still the part of our being that cause us our greatest grief, and often our worst behavior.

When it is all reviewed and weighed, there are only two types of people: those with honor and those without. Honor is a statement of our conviction to our values. Honor, or lack of honor, is the defining difference in how all of us are perceived. Honor doesn't sit on a shelf as a goal to achieve – but, ironically, it is something that can be gained and developed from all the rite-of-passage lessons in our lives. Unfortunately, some people – despite being given the opportunity to live all their fantasies and experience many rite-of-passage moments – never become honorable.

A good day of pheasant hunting in South Dakota.

Chapter 11
Real Men (and some women)
Hunt Pheasants

...I dreamed I was at least twenty feet under the water, yet there was no pressure on my chest or ears. I was suspended as though lying on my back: looking up through the clear water, seeing the silhouette of the aluminum johnboat floating on the surface. I looked for fishing line, yet I could see none. It was just there on the surface waiting. I swam underwater until I came upon a group of swimmers.

They were all swimming around a large Godfrey Hurricane deck boat, enjoying the warm water of Tellico Lake. Soon a boat with two game wardens came upon us. They began to swim with us. I was surrounded by people in the boat I knew, or used to know, but I really didn't know why they were there. Some were children, some were adults. Some were relatives. The game wardens were friendly, but they inspected the situation as they swam with me. The wardens told the captain to turn on the boat lights, as it was getting to be dusk. He complied. As the wardens began to leave, one got on the boat and

attempted to do a fancy dive off the side. His leg caught on the railing attached to the boat's gunnels, and it broke as he plunged into the water. I retrieved him from the water and carried him to their truck, which was parked on the shore. Two other game wardens entered the truck. One was driving, and one was in the middle to his right. The man with the broken leg was next to the passenger door. He was in pain; he was in anguish; he was sad. They drove off, hardly recognizing my presence...

The summer evenings were no longer humid, and the katydids' constant chorus was no longer lulling me to sleep. Replacing those humid nights were cool mornings and clear, crisp air. Soon Mother Nature turned the seasonal dial to fall – and it was now time to go pheasant hunting. Pheasant hunting isn't something you can do in your backyard in Tennessee. Apparently we lack something in our soil that these birds need, in order to reproduce and populate within our state. Years ago, a few semi-retired men from Maryville set out to find places to hunt and fish in the western part of our country. After a couple of seasons of traveling and hunting virtually every species of game, they returned to tell their friends where to go if you wanted to hunt various species common to the West. One of those was pheasants – and the place to go hunt them was Lake Andes, South Dakota.

Lake Andes was once a very popular spot, in the middle of an endless expanse of grain production. This natural inland lake, which was surrounded with beautiful lake homes and small strip motels, offered fishing, water-skiing, boating, swimming. Life was good, and this small tourism industry supplied additional economy for the surrounding farm community.

At one end of the lake stood a huge wooden event structure. It was called the Moonlight Ballroom. This was an impressive structure, two stories high. In this event hall was a nice restaurant, a beautiful Western-style bar, and a large ballroom for dancing and socializing. For over eighty years, virtually every farmer within a 100-mile radius would bring his family out on Saturday night to eat and dance to the oompah-pah music that was the local favorite. Sons and daughters would meet sons and daughters of other farmers, and at some point in the future, they would be married at their local church with the reception held at the Moonlight Ballroom.

Off to one of the small strip motels on the lake the nice couple would go, and a new generation of farmers would soon begin. Life was simple in South Dakota. Life was pleasant and innocent, with strong family values. The local people raised a lot of corn, milk, beef – and children.

Then it all changed. A cult-like group of an outside religious denomination purchased thousands of acres of the farmland, and decided to aggressively irrigate their crops. This was upstream of Lake Andes, and all of the water-retention ponds they had built to irrigate the farms upstream of the lake held back so much water that Lake Andes dried up – and was no more. Lawsuits were filed, but the religious cult had good lawyers who kept filing motions, successfully putting the trial off for years. Before the local residents around the lake could get through the legal process, most had moved, or they'd gone broke paying lawyers to proceed with the lawsuit. Justice delayed is without a doubt justice denied. Only the Moonlight Ballroom, an adjoining twelve-unit motel, and a few retirees who couldn't afford to move, remained. On Saturday nights the youth would still come to the Moonlight Ballroom, but that too had changed. Pool tables now were the draw, and disco had replaced the oompah-pah bands. The motel now might rent a room for an hour or two if some girl had had too much to drink, or if some young couple felt horny and thought no one would notice if they left the bar. The fine family fabric of South Dakota was rapidly becoming quite frayed.

In South Dakota, when the third Saturday of October rolls around and for the next ten days, an incredible phenomenon happens. The population of the state of South Dakota triples. People from all over the country come to hunt pheasants. With this surge of so many diverse groups of people, intriguing things happen. Farmers meet people from all over the country. Some establish long friendships. Many residents welcome these hunters and allow them to hunt their farms for free. Over time, solid friendships are formed. It is typical for these farmers to visit these Tennessee hunters in the hunters' home towns during the summer, once school is out, when the alfalfa is green and the corn is planted.

All the farmers looked forward to meeting people from East Tennessee, and the closer to Gatlinburg, the better. The local farmers were glad to take a mountain boy up on the invitation to come stay with them if they ever came to Tennessee. In turn, they gladly extended hunting privileges to these Tennessee people. The fact is that the pheasants were a pain in the ass that ate the farmers' grain, and cut into their profits. They hoped that everyone would kill a bunch of them, and they put the hunters in the best locations to assure a successful hunt.

Years went by, maybe even a decade after we first met, when I was asked by Harold Tipton if I wanted to go to South Dakota and hunt pheasants. I accepted, and I asked Harold if Tom could come along. Harold agreed, and was delighted, as long as Tom would drive with him in his station wagon with all the hunting gear. I was having no part of driving 1,800 miles in a car. That was why I owned a plane.

So began a series of years when Tom, Harold, and I, along with a few others from the Knoxville area, went to South Dakota and hunted pheasants. Soon our mutual trout-fishing friend Natty, and Tom's father, were regulars as well. We soon discovered that Tom was a natural salesman – and given ten minutes, he could talk any farmer into granting permission for us to hunt. Friendships developed, and often everyone got together outside of hunting season in East Tennessee. When we were in South Dakota, we stayed at the last remaining motel, next to the Moonlight Ballroom. Every year, at the end of the hunting season, our group would pre-pay for the next year's ten-day motel stay, to assure our accommodations for the next year.

One year, our gang arrived to find a new owner at the motel we'd been staying in. The new owner had no knowledge of any prepayment, and all of his rooms had been rented to other hunters. A couple of things are certain in South Dakota: Winter will arrive one day, and if you haven't already arranged your accommodations before pheasant-hunting season, you are not going to find anywhere to stay.

We started to turn around and go home to Tennessee. But I looked over, and saw the same "For Sale" sign, on the same house across from the motel, that I had been seeing for years. I walked across from the motel to the house and knocked at the door. Eventually an old lady answered.

...She had been asleep, dreaming of a crow in a deep green forest.

The crow tilted and slightly lowered its head in an effort to see every detail in the forest. Something was wrong and out of place; it just had not yet determined what.

It called to the other members of the gang in code: for concern, not alarm. It could have left, yet it was drawn by curiosity.

The woman heard a large flock of geese flying over, honking loudly. She noticed that the crow never looked up, or was even distracted in the least. It just kept looking for what was wrong in the forest. It knew there was something there in the shadows, yet it was not scared, only curious...

I asked if she would consider renting us a few rooms. "No," was her answer. She wanted to sell. The home was stone and stucco, all hardwood floors, and beautifully decorated with old oak furniture. It was fairly large, clearly over 4,500 square feet. There was an old, decayed wooden walkway that went to the dock where the lake once had been. Now, it just seemed to disappear into a thicket of weeds and shrub growth; a walkway into yesteryear or a date with a journey into oblivion was all that remained. The entire home was decorated with trophies of every imaginable animal. Obviously, her deceased husband had been a successful hunter.

The lady explained that her husband had died eight years ago, and that she wanted to move to Florida with her sister, where it was warm, and where she could be with her remaining family. They had all moved to Florida years ago when the lake went dry. She had no children, and no car – and she had a deed to her property already prepared. We thanked her for showing us the house, but she was quite certain she would not rent it to us. On the way out the door, Tom asked her, "How much are you selling the place for?" The old lady replied, "Ten thousand dollars cash." I stopped, amazed at the low price, and started asking several legal questions, for which the lady had clear, concrete answers. I asked her when we could take occupancy. She said, "The minute you give me the money," as she pointed to four suitcases in the hallway. "I have been packed and ready to leave for eight years." I asked her, "Is there a place we can get some beds? Is there anyone in the area that can sell us some furniture? Will anyone deliver this late in the day today?" She seemed puzzled. "Why do you need furniture? There are six furnished bedrooms, and the price includes all the furniture."

We went into an immediate huddle, then we all scraped together the money and paid her. Twenty minutes later, one of her friends picked her up and took her to the Greyhound bus station, thirty minutes away, in Mitchell. That evening, she boarded a bus to Florida. And we moved into our new home.

The next couple of years were glorious. What great hunts we had. There were four of us in the deal: Natty, Tom, Tom's dad Dick, and me. I would see that the property taxes were paid. Tom would oversee repairs. Natty, our attorney friend, would send $100 each year to the new owner of the motel to keep the grass mowed and keep an eye on the place. Every year, we would arrive a day or two before pheasant season. Tom would go out and re-establish our relationships with the farmers, and we always killed our limit in pheasants.

Then it happened. All of a sudden, everyone wanted to bring a friend hunting. Natty brought another attorney named "Rick," and some guy named "Snake," who owned a sports store in Knoxville. I got drunk in Miami one weekend and invited everyone. In turn, my old friend Harold, who had introduced us to South Dakota in the first place, invited a couple named Dean and Jo to do all the cooking. Additionally, there was a middle-aged couple from Miami who were actually gourmet cooks, who took command of the kitchen. I never really knew who invited them. Dean and Jo brought their Weimaraner dog. I invited an old high school friend named Smutter, who Tom promptly renamed "Midget" due to his short stature. Smutter brought his son Curtis. Smutter also invited a couple from Miami who turned out to be a "professional hit man and woman team," something I didn't know at the time. In addition to that, I invited a few other people who lived in Miami. One of my friends, while waiting in the Miami airport bar, picked up a beautiful stripper named Mary. There were several others: some nice, some not. Tom and his dad, along with Natty and Rick, were seemingly out of place with this fast-paced crowd. Everyone settled into the house in South Dakota. I lay down to take a short nap, tired from our long travel.

The first order of business by the Miami group was to convert their cocaine into a liquid solution that they placed in Afrin nose-spray bottles. This was so that they could do a "hit" anytime, in front of the locals, without drawing suspicion. All the non-locals got allergies from the dust in the fields while hunting pheasants, so nose spray was fairly common. Sometimes the most obvious is the least obvious.

The next order of business with the Miami crowd was to have various types of sex with the stripper Mary. She didn't ever do drugs or alcohol. She just really liked having sex, and she was constantly initiating and coaxing the different men into doing her. The girl obviously had psychological problems, and she was a complete nymphomaniac. Tom, his Dad, Dean and Jo, Ron, and Rick abstained; while everyone else agreed to fulfill her requests. The camp was in chaos, and the only thing that seemed to keep everything from getting completely crazy was the fact that Smutter, or "Midget" as Tom called him, had brought his eleven-year-old son Curtis. When Curtis was around, Smutter tried to act "normal." Curtis enjoyed catching the non-poisonous garden snakes that were everywhere in the surrounding yard. By dinner, he had filled a large cardboard box with at least fifty of them.

Finally, those who were not doing coke ate the dinner that the gourmet chef had cooked. Eventually the cokeheads got really drunk, and they passed out on the large living room floor. The last logs were placed on the fire – and the first day was over. The night became long.

Tom, who was sleeping on the living room couch, was the first to awaken to the low growls of the Weimaraner dog. The embers, smoldering in the fireplace, dimly lit the room with a soft red glow. Bodies were everywhere, asleep on the floor. It looked like hell might look, with a bunch of corpses. Tom saw movement on the face of one of the Miami hunters. What was that? A mouse? A roach? His forehead seemed to be melting. As Tom's eyes focused, he noticed more movement everywhere, on everyone on the floor. There were snakes crawling over everybody. He rose up to make sure he was awake, and wasn't in hell, and he took a closer look. The garden snakes that Curtis had placed in the box were loose – and they were crawling over the sleeping hunters. On any other day this might have seemed very unnatural. Tom calmed the dog, closed his eyes, and went back to sleep.

The first day of hunting was not going smoothly. Some of the Miami crowd started their day with screwdrivers to get their hangovers under control. Some started doing coke. The gourmet chef was all in a twist because someone had left one of his gourmet cheeses out of the refrigerator. Tom, Natty, Tom's dad Dick, Dean, and Jo were ready to hunt or go back to Tennessee. I convinced them to stay. I was almost ready to hunt, but the stripper Mary was looking for someone's dick to suck, and this distracted me for a few minutes. I was a little concerned that this crowd might be a little overwhelming for even the friendliest of the South Dakota farmers.

As people started congregating at the vehicles, getting ready to go, Tom pulled me aside and convinced me we needed to go to the public hunting area. He was not willing to burn any of the bridges we had established with the local farmers over the years. I agreed, and within an hour we had loaded everyone into the various vehicles.

The rental vehicles in South Dakota, which we'd obtained from a local junkyard, are worth a mention. They would rent you a clunker for ten dollars a day. The problem was that these vehicles were all rusted out from the salt that was used in the winter to keep the roads open. In total, we had five vehicles. Harold's station wagon was full of beer, alcohol, and the chef's Galloping Gourmet road show. There were four clunkers that the Miami hunters had rented that Tom immediately named "Clone Mobiles." I wasn't sure if he arrived at that name by the similarities of the vehicles, or those who were driving them. Two of the four had no floorboards under the driver's and passenger's seats. The driver had to keep his feet on the pedals to keep from dragging his feet on the pavement or gravel. The passenger had to keep his feet on the dash. As the day went on, and the Miami people got drunk or high, they started driving these "clone mobiles" through the cornfields. The people in the back seat who were resting their feet on the back of the seat in front of them were shooting out the windows at the flushing pheasants. The more they drank, and the more coke they did, the faster they drove. One guy shot through the roof of the car while trying to reload. Tom watched in amazement as one guy missed a bird, then took his shotgun, and threw it out the window. The car never slowed down, but continued to speed into another cornfield. Tom and his Dad, Natty, Rick, Snake, Dean and Jo went back to the house.

That evening, the gourmet chef cooked some elaborate dish using only the pheasant tenders. He had it all garnished up when he served the only hungry people in the crowd, who were incidentally not from Miami. The entire Miami crowd was too coked up to eat, and Mary was over at the twelve-unit motel next door screwing all the hunters from Georgia.

After dinner, several of us went over to the Moonlight Ballroom pool hall. There were about eighty to 100 local people in there, between the ages of eighteen and thirty. I wanted to shoot some pool, so I asked Tom if he would be my partner. We put our quarter on the table to show our intention to play the winner. As the game ended, some really huge, dumb-looking son of a local farmer made some remark about my suede leather sport coat. Normally I would not give a shit what anyone says about how I dress, but I had been drinking. This huge dumbass, who could be a twin to Lenny in the book "Of Mice and Men," was insulting my totally cool suede leather sport coat. I thought an equal insult was in order, but instead of picking on his hog washer wardrobe, I decided to target his obviously low I.Q.

They broke the rack and made one ball. The next shot, they missed. Tom started to shoot when I stopped him. I wanted to shoot before the guy in the hog washers. I carefully studied the table, and made a shot that placed the cue ball in a location that left the dumbass who'd insulted me absolutely no shot.

He looked at me kind of funny, and as predicted, made no shot. Tom was next and made one ball, then missed the next shot. The big farmer guy's partner made one ball. With my turn, I again shot the cue ball into a location that left the dumbass absolutely no shot.

This time it finally sank into him that I wasn't trying to make a shot, but was just making sure he never had a shot. His face got real red, as I just stared at him with a kind of "fuck you" look on my face. "You had better stop that shit," he said. I continued to stare at him with that obnoxious smirk that always pisses everyone off.

Tom was quietly observing the moment, but I could tell he was getting very concerned. His eyes alertly dashed from one person to the other, carefully assessing who was going to get involved in the imminent confrontation. Tom slowly slid his right foot back and widened his stance; I could tell he was getting ready to throw a punch.

My low-IQ farmer opponent proceeded to try to sink a ball, but missed. As he rose from the table, he looked at the "fuck you" expression on my face and could no longer contain his anger. He made one move toward me, raising his pool cue, and Tom dropped him in his tracks. One over-the-shoulder right hook to the jaw, just below the temple, had done the trick. Tom shouted, "Anyone else?" There were no takers.

The Miami gang was in full swing. They had been going back and forth to the Moonlight Ballroom. Now completely coked out of their minds, and fully drunk, they were seeing how many times they could pimp Mary for blowjobs. They were so high they were offering $10 to any guy who would let her suck him off. They would then bet thousands of dollars on how fast she could make that guy ejaculate. Back and forth they would go, to get new recruits from the bar.

I decided things were out of hand, and I put a stop to their new-found fun. It was almost 2:00 am. Tom was looking at me with great disappointment over the fact that our hunting camp had gotten so out of hand. Tom's father, Natty, Snake, and Rick were ready to go back to Tennessee the next day. After some brief argument with the Miami crowd, everyone decided to stay in the house and stop partying.

I found a vacant bedroom and fell asleep, dreaming of being at a building show in Las Vegas.

...Set me free why don't you babe, you just keep me hanging on. The nostalgic music blares, carefully selected for its subliminal message. The music is

highlighted by lights modulating to the beat. My eyes are ablaze, and I feel excitement. The strobe lights make me feel young; even the guys older than me feel younger. The twenty-year-old girls somehow seem close to my age. They are all rocking to the music. What is that scent? The pheromones are thick in the air.

I look up from the blackjack table; a young, attractive lady whose mini-skirt doesn't quite cover all of her incredibly firm butt cheeks asks me if I would like a drink. A ginger ale would be nice. She forces a smile, trying to hide the disappointment. She was hoping I would order a double Jack on the rocks. After all, the drink is free, and her tip would bigger. I double my blackjack bet in an effort to regain my pride.

Las Vegas, Sin City, what goes on here stays here. This new marketing slogan seems to have abandoned the family market.

You can literally experience the world's finest vacation destinations while walking a four-mile strip. Last night I enjoyed New York City, and then watched the gondolas go down the waterways of Venice, Italy. The Eiffel Tower was pretty, but you can let the French keep Paris, along with their shitty, turncoat, backstabbing, codeless, careless government. I admit the whores hanging out in front of the Eiffel Tower were very pretty. I guess the French parents train their daughters early, sort of a national pride thing. We all know one's heritage is very important.

Egypt was impressive. The women in Caesar's Palace would have made Cleopatra proud.

The builders' show I was attending in my dream was designed for a Las Vegas setting. Kohler had an entire chorus line of hot women, dancing to project the company's slogan: "The Bold New Look of Kohler." Their competition, whose name I can't remember, had raised the bar by having a beautiful nude woman bathing under their "Rainforest" shower head. I am certain they turned up the cold water every time it hit her nipples.

A hot-tub manufacturer from the Southern "Bible Belt" had a fat, middle aged man in a worn-out polyester sport coat, with black horn-rimmed glasses, trying to convince people his hot tubs were best by telling everyone he owned one – a visual in my mind's eye that was downright scary.

Most of the attention went to the California brand that had the Hooters girls in string bikinis, suggesting you would have more fun in theirs.

The salespeople from the Bible Belt seemed disadvantaged: some people get it – some never do. It is the salespeople of Las Vegas who are ultimately successful in generating positive numbers, strong revenue streams, and loyal customers. The best techniques of a salesperson can be summed up in one word: female...

I awoke to someone moving in the room. Midget discovered he had left his coat, along with most of the supply of cocaine in its lining, at the bar. He woke me up and asked me to go with him to get his coat, but I stayed in bed. Everyone kept shouting for him to turn off the light and go back to bed, as the bar had been closed for hours.

I dozed back to sleep, but after about an hour I was awakened by the sounds of many people shouting. As I opened my eyes, there was a dull orange glow dancing over the room's windows. I sat up, looked outside, and to my amazement I saw the entire Moonlight Ballroom engulfed in flames. Standing between the house and the burning building was Midget, yelling in a sheepish voice, "Fire!"

The problem was that there was really no one there to hear Midget. There were no phones to call anyone. We all came out of the house, along with the people in the motel. We all watched as the Moonlight Ballroom proceeded to burn to the ground. About two hours after the fire started, some of the volunteer firemen arrived. By then the fire was almost out, and it had completely eaten the structure.

Sad would be the only way to describe the procession that we witnessed the next day. Cars from over 200 miles away slowly drove past the smoldering rubble. Old couples, often over eighty years of age, would get out of their car and stare at the ashes. Holding each other's hands, while trying to find some past memories in the ashes, they would eventually leave.

Tom was pissed off. He knew that Midget probably had something to do with the fire. He came into the living room and proclaimed, "The next person who does any drugs on this hunt is going to get his ass kicked." One of the Miami boys started to protest, when Tom started advancing on him. I stepped in between them and said, "No more drugs on this hunt." Within an hour, everyone from Miami was ready to go home. After some calmer talk, we all decided to try one more time to go hunting. The weather was starting to deteriorate. A large snowstorm was coming out of the west, and it was due the next day.

We arrived at one of the public hunting fields, formed a large, lazy "U," and proceeded to start walking the field. This is how you hunt pheasants when you have enough hunters. The plan is to drive the birds that are in the field towards the hunters waiting at the other end. Often the birds will try to run around you, and the hunter next to you will get a shot. As you get to the end of the field, the pheasants figure out they are surrounded, and they start flushing in all different directions. We sent Mary, the gourmet chef, and his wife, around to the other end, to act as blockers. They took the Pontiac station wagon, which had all our food, beverages and ammo. As we proceeded across the field, birds started to flush, but they were flying very low due to the strong west wind.

About halfway across the field, Ron's friend "Snake" pulled up on a low-flying bird and cut loose, with Tom in the line of fire. Tom must have seen it coming, as he turned just in time to catch a load of shot in his back and on the back of his head. He was knocked off his feet, but he got right back up, holding his head. None of the pellets had penetrated his scalp through his aviator's hat. His coat had stopped the others. Apologies were made, and accepted.

Everyone got back in formation, and we continued toward the end of the field. About the time we were 200 yards from the Pontiac station wagon, Mary started shooting one of the shotguns that had remained in the car. She kept reloading, laughing hysterically, and shooting up in the air. The gourmet chef and his wife just kept walking further away from the vehicle, trying to get as much distance between them and Mary. Once the group got within 100 yards, everyone stopped walking. Here we were, out in the middle of nowhere, with a crazy woman firing a shotgun from our only means of transportation. Furthermore, she was pointing the shotguns in our direction, and you could hear the shot rain down around us.

I decided I'd had enough of Mary's existence. There was no farmhouse within ten miles of us, and she was a deranged nymphomaniac who by now had probably contracted every fatal disease on the planet. The rest of the group backed further into the field, forming smaller groups of two and three persons. I took off my hunting vest and started searching deep in the pockets for some buckshot. I located four shells, and as I was putting my vest back on, Tom and his father arrived.

I looked at them and said, "I am going to shoot her." Tom's dad spoke: "No, you aren't, not until I first try to talk the gun from her." Tom objected to both of our plans, saying he could walk to the cars at the other road and drive until he found a farmer and get help from the police. I said, "Tell the farmer to bring a shovel, because we will need one by the time you get back."

The argument between the three of us was escalating when Tom's father Dick finally seemed to get truly mad, and his entire personality became that of someone we had never met. Dick was a retired Colonel who had fought in Okinawa and Korea as a scout sniper and forward artillery observer. "Bubba, no Marine worth a shit is going to let you shoot that woman. Before I thought she was just another slut from your generation who was enjoying her bad behavior. Now it is obvious she is nuts and needs help. From this point on there will be no more exploiting of this woman, as she is obviously crazy. I didn't fight in World War II to protect the innocent to watch someone shoot a crazy woman in a South Dakota cornfield." She was no different in his mind at that time than those Okinawa women who were jumping off the cliffs with their babies. Dick's eyes started to water as he had re-entered a very dark place in his past. "She needs help!" he shouted. Dick's grip tightened on his shotgun, and I saw him slip his safety off. He wasn't kidding, and there wasn't to be any further negotiation on this issue.

"What do you propose, then?" I asked Dick. "You and Tom get fifty yards to my left and right. Advance with me until you are within sixty yards of Mary. Then stop and keep a bead on her head. Load your guns with buckshot. I will continue to advance without my shotgun. If I drop to the ground, that will be the signal to shoot her. If I am standing, don't fire. I am going to try to talk the shotgun out of her hands.

Tom immediately started to protest, but seeing the look on his dad's face, Tom bowed to his authority when Dick told him to shut up and do as he was told. His father, who was always so kind and soft spoken, was now a different man. His eyes were piercing, his authority unquestionable, and his decision was not to be challenged by a subordinate. He was now the same Marine who decades ago had fought as a scout sniper in Okinawa and Korea, and expected those around him to follow his exact orders.

Travis handed Tom two of the rounds of buckshot and watched Tom chamber the rounds. At sixty yards away, we stopped and aimed at Mary's head. Dick moved toward her, and when he was within ten yards, Mary lowered the shotgun, put it on the car hood, and started crying. Dick emptied the shotgun and gave us some Marine signal that obviously meant for us to advance. I was really mad, but that quickly changed to relief, and then pity, as I saw Dick hugging Mary while she cried uncontrollably. I grew up a lot in that moment. To most of the camp, Mary appeared to be a woman who, like almost everyone in that generation, liked to party and just had no inhibitions or morals. This was actually more the norm. But now, at this moment, a very different woman showed Dick that she represented the weak. The weak he had traveled all over the world to protect as a United States Marine. Once it was clear she wanted and needed help, being the Marine that he was, he would be there to help her. It was also very clear to everyone, by the look in Dick's eyes, that there was to be no more exploiting this woman's weakness. Dick took Mary over to the side, and after talking to her for about fifteen minutes, it became clear that it would be best for her to go home to her parents. She was to stay away from the Miami people who brought her up here until we could figure out how to get her home. Several of us climbed into the Pontiac wagon to go get the cars from the other road, then Dick and I took Mary to the house. Once she was packed, we took her to the Greyhound bus station in Mitchell. We gave her money and some travel provisions, and waited until we saw her leave on the bus headed to Florida.

It was spitting snow by 4:00 pm, and everyone in the Tennessee group wanted to go home. By the time we got back to the house at Lake Andes, we discovered the Miami crowd had already left. It had become clear out in the field, and when we first returned to the house, that it wasn't over yet between Dick and the men who had exploited Mary. Tom had tried to calm him down, but he was unsuccessful. He knew his father suffered mentally from his war experiences. Almost weekly while growing up, Tom and his brother and sister would awaken to their mother trying to get Dick out of a nightmare in the middle of the night. But this was much different, as everyone was awake – and Tom had never seen this part of his father's personality. Dick had clearly returned to a time special in Okinawa and military history, and Tom could not get through to him. In Dick's mind, the enemy was from Miami. It was clear there was going to be a winner and a loser when he got back to the house, and he confronted the Miami crowd. I have always wondered if the Miami group left so suddenly out of concern that there was going to clearly be a penance delivered by Dick to those men from Miami when he returned to the house. They took two of the three planes at the gravel strip next to our house. A note in the cabin said to leave all their gear, they would get it next year. They hadn't cleaned or straightened anything up in the house. All their hunting gear, guns, clothes and everything they had brought with them was scattered about the house.

I talked the couple that had driven the car up from Tennessee into agreeing to stay here until the storm passed, and bring everyone's gear home. That way we could leave, if the only weight in the plane was the six of us. If we left immediately I was certain we could outrun the storm. Twenty minutes later, all six of us were in the twin engine Cessna, headed southeast.

The storm proved to be much closer than I thought. In fact I had no more than taken off and was setting my headings, when it was on top of us. There was no Doppler radar back then, or at least I didn't own one. I climbed up to 10,000 feet to try to get over the moisture. No luck. I told everyone to watch each other. If someone blacked out, let me know. The wings had started icing. I kept climbing to try to clear the moisture in the clouds.

Tom said he felt sick. Natty, sitting next to him, kept saying, "No, you are not sick." Natty was very nervous. He noticed that Tom's lips were blue, and he also felt very dizzy. About the time I took another hard look at Tom, I saw him vomit on Natty's lap. Once Tom got sick, everyone started getting sick.

I kept climbing to try to get above the moisture and out of the snow clouds. We were in a complete whiteout condition, and we were unable to pick up any of the navigation beacons. We were now at 18,000 feet in a non-pressurized plane without oxygen, and we had icicles about one to two inches on our wings. The plane was starting to lose the curvature in the wings and was having a hard time flying. I took an aggressive descent, and throttled back and feathered the prop to act as a brake as the plane started radically exceeding its maximum safe speed.

We were going to crash. I couldn't see anything due to the whiteout conditions created by the snow. The only hope we had was to find a flat area and try to land, before we lost all the lift in our wings due to the icing. I told everyone to tighten their seatbelts, and proceeded to call in a series of "Maydays." In all the confusion, the whiteout conditions, the ice, the vomit, being dizzy myself from the altitude, and about a dozen other horrible issues, I had lost track of our location and was unable to help those responding to my Maydays. There was zero visibility due to the snow. I couldn't raise any signal from any of the beacons on the chart I was using.

Everyone was very quiet as we descended into the abyss. I just kept watching the altimeter, and hoped the plane would hold together. We were now down to 3,000 feet. There was so much ice that the plane would only respond to the flaps and rudders if I kept the speed above 340 knots. Normal flying speed for this aircraft was 150 knots, and landing speed was sixty to eighty knots. This was going to be one tough landing in some farmer's field. I was just hoping we wouldn't catch any telephone lines on the way in. We would never know, as it was still a total whiteout. The first time we would know we were on the ground would be when we felt the plane hit a hard surface. I couldn't even see the prop clearly, the snow was so thick.

Then it happened. At about eleven hundred feet of elevation, I saw a break in the clouds. A small crease in the blanket of white exposed a small section of a road or runway beneath us. I descended at about ten degrees, turning as tightly as possible, and dropped the plane onto what turned out to be the auxiliary strip next to the main runway of a local airport.

Our speed was too great for the tires to keep up with the plane. One immediately burst on impact. I hit full left rudder to keep the plane from completely spinning around and flipping over. We slid approximately 800 yards at a forty-five-degree angle on the runway, and finally came to a stop. I tried to act like I was in control, but my adrenaline was pumping so high my legs were shaking uncontrollably. I tried to taxi around to the terminal, but with the ice on the runway, my shaking legs, and a flat tire, I parked off the runway next to some planes in the area used for long-term plane storage.

We all slid out of the plane and helped each other to the terminal. The traffic controller and the people in the airport were really nice to me, considering everything. I think they felt sorry for us and were amazed we were alive. The airport we had landed in was about eighty miles from where I thought I was. Actually, it was in the next state. They didn't even report the incident, as no one had heard my "Mayday" call for help from this far away. The truth is that I had used bogus call letters, as my plane was registered in the Cayman Islands as a tourist sightseeing plane. I guess somewhere in the West, they are looking for a crashed plane and six souls.

Natty, Tom and his Dad, Snake, and Rick decided to charter a plane to get them to Tennessee. A day later I hired the same guy to take me, and I told them I would come back in the spring to get my plane after the snow melted. I never returned to get that plane, as I really didn't want anyone to know I'd had anything to do with it.

Many years went by before anyone decided they wanted to go back to South Dakota to hunt pheasants. Finally, Tom started to resurrect the idea. For over a decade I had been sending the property taxes for the house to "Judy Solic," the tax assessor. For over a decade she had been cashing the checks. As Tom looked into hooking the power back up, he discovered she had not been re-elected as the assessor, and had been pocketing the money. Our home had been sold for back taxes to a local man for fifty dollars. The two-year redemption statute had run out, and we had lost our hunting camp in South Dakota. But I now had bigger problems. Most of the money in the Cayman Islands I had moved to Greece, as there was a way to quietly store money there in some privately managed banks. Apparently, a lot of people had moved money to Greece, and now the American Treasury agents were enjoying playing tourist and observing who was coming from and who was going to Greece. It would only be a matter of time before someone connected the dots.

Pheasant hunting in the hill country of Montana.

Chapter 12
My Sister Sissy

...I dreamed I walked across a gravel driveway, feeling the small stones crunch and give way under my feet. It was an old driveway, and the gravel was almost absorbed by the soil and plant life.

Across the river I saw a great mountain of limestone, crawling with equipment. Drills were penetrating the hard stone, and dynamite was blasting large slabs of stone from the mountainside. These slabs were broken into boulders that were crushed into gravel. The small fragments of their lesser self were hauled away to be spread over Mother Earth. There they lay, absorbed by the soil and ash of yesteryear. To what end was their purpose? I tossed and turned, trying to wake myself and get out of this dream, as I felt I had entered a dark space in time.

To make sense of my story I guess I need to come clean on how I'd made so much money. Yes, I had a few clients like Mr. Little, whose Cayman Island accounts I had managed, but I had one really large account. I had gotten this account through a family member.

She was my older sister. I called her "Sissy." She was a beautiful woman with long, thick auburn hair and bright Nazarene blue eyes. When she was sixteen years old she could no longer stand the fighting between my mother and father. My father's general disrespect toward women was not something Sissy was willing to tolerate. She moved to Miami and lived with our aunt and uncle. A week after Sissy graduated from high school, our aunt and uncle were killed in a car crash. As they had no children of their own, they left their modest block home in the Cuban district of Miami to Sissy. Although she had a place to live, Sissy fell into the routine of working hard and just getting by financially on a week-to-week basis.

Now twenty-two years old, she was waiting tables in the Coconut Grove district, outside of The Vizcaya Mansion. It was there where she met Julio. He was of South American descent, on vacation in Miami. Although street-wary and independent, Sissy fell head over heels for Julio, and they were married somewhere in South America. Sissy had three children by Julio. Her husband was kind and respectful, and he worshipped the ground she walked on. I had not kept up with Sissy prior to attending U.T., as we lived so far from each other. I kind of felt she had abandoned me the last years we lived in Tennessee, when she left to live with our aunt and uncle. It was only years later that I found out our mother had made her move for her own safety, because of the way my dad looked at her when he was drunk. My mother never told my father the truth of were Sissy was, and left him to believe she had run off with a motorcycle gang.

After escaping from Vietnam and hiding in South America, then attending U.T. law school for four years, I went to Miami and did a title search on the house that had belonged to my aunt and uncle. Just before I left for college, my mother had told me the whole story about her decision to send Sissy to Miami, and I was curious if my aunt and uncle and Sissy were still at that address. It had been over six years since I had made any attempt to contact Sissy. I wanted to keep her out of the loop, in case there were any wackos looking for me after my Vietnam experience. After finishing at U.T. law school and failing the law boards twice, I was somewhat lost as to what I would do for a career. I had now been back in Tennessee for years without anything resurfacing from my past. I felt it would be okay to make contact with my sister, aunt and uncle. It was there in the Miami courthouse that I saw the court probate papers giving the house to my sister. It was also where I found that she had transferred the house to the local Catholic Church. This piqued my curiosity, and I drove to the address. I was met at the door by a nun, who told me that the house was a safe house for young women who needed a place to live. The nun told me she could not let me enter the house, but if I wanted to make a donation, there was a box to my left and I could leave money to help them with their mission. I reached into my pocket, removed a twenty from my wallet, and placed it into the box. As I was walking away, the nun said "Cleveland, Tennessee," and just stared at me. I froze a moment, turned around, and asked the nun why she had just said that. She then asked, "What was tattooed on your father's right hand?" I answered, "Love." The nun then said, "Where was the Bible kept in your house?" I answered, "It was on the table in front of our couch until the night my father was so drunk he burned it in the wood stove thinking it was firewood." "What is your birth name?" she continued. "Grey Louise Carlton," I answered. The nun walked up to me and stared deep into my eyes. I could feel the kindness in her heart. She took my hand and kissed it, while slipping a piece of paper into my palm. She then stepped even closer and whispered into my right ear, "Sissy looks forward to seeing you." With that, she turned around and walked into the house, closing the door behind her. The directions were to a location in

Belize, in Central America. The location of their home was quite spectacular, yet very hard to get to. It had taken me several hours of driving on a really crappy dirt road to come to a high mountain pass, with sheer rock walls extending up hundreds of feet on each side of the road, and a valley below. On a high knoll in the valley was their house. It was quite large, and it actually looked a lot like the Vizcaya mansion in Miami. There were many smaller homes that surrounded the main house, which appeared to house families, as children played in the yards. All of the smaller homes also had multiple guards with assault rifles patrolling the perimeter. The family compound appeared more secure than Fort Knox. There were no fewer than 150 military-style guards surrounding the home. There was no gate or checkpoint, and I nervously pulled up to the front door. All of the military men seemed to melt into the jungle, reminding me of the Lurps in Vietnam. Then, as if I was in a Norman Rockwell painting, my sister came running out of the front door, hugged me, and started crying with joy. Soon to follow were three beautiful children shouting "Uncle Grey," and they also hugged me with their mother. A handsome man approached and introduced himself as Julio, my sister's husband. I had been there a week, and at breakfast one morning, Julio asked me what my plans were for the future. Sissy got up and hurriedly left the room. I talked about having completed law school, corporate law and tax law, but couldn't seem to pass the bar exam. He then looked me straight in the eyes and said, "Bubba, if I were to tell you something, would you always keep it a secret?" I nervously paused, as I had not ever been called "Bubba" by people I didn't really know, and only used this nickname in certain circles. Noticing my discomfort, Julio explained, "Your sister has required me to give her a report on your safety for years." Julio stared at me and said, "Your C.I.A. has less intelligence than I do." This made me nervous. I was having a hard time processing all that was going on, so I tried to buy myself some time. I went into a long explanation about the laws of client-attorney privilege and all that, to assure him that everything discussed between us would stay private. He asked me if he could hire me as his counsel. I again explained I hadn't passed the bar yet; however, this did not seem to matter to him. I agreed to work as his counsel on technical matters of the law for what seemed to be a very generous annual fee.

At this point, he reached into a briefcase on the chair next to him and removed a picture of a huge table full of money. He placed this picture in front of me and asked," If someone were to ask you to invest this money, could you do it without anyone knowing the owner?" I said, "Yes, it can be done." Julio stared at me for over a minute. "Would you care where it came from?" Julio asked. "Yes, I would" I said. "If you have hurt women, children, or adolescent boys I don't want to know anything else about this money." Julio stared at me another long minute. "I help women, children, and their families financially. No one is hurt or forced to participate in any way," he said. I stared back and said, "Then I don't care where it came from." Julio handed me a picture of a man and said, "This is Roberto, and he will contact you."

Over the next six months, Roberto and I had finalized our plans to launder Julio's billions, and it was now time to start executing these plans. There were many steps, many layers to each step, default plans at every level, and such a plethora of ownership that no one person or small group of persons could possibly ever connect the different entities to each other. So bold were some of the plans that there was no way anyone would ever consider it possible it was a front for laundering money.

All of the "fronts" and plans would require the investment of capital. This money, literally huge rooms of it, would need to be funneled into the different countries where the investments would take place.

It was decided by Roberto that only he and I would be involved in, or would actually know anything directly about, the actual movement of the money. If there was ever a leak, we would both immediately know who the informant had been.

The first load of money we were going to move would be $500,000. This would be a trial run. I'd always enjoyed the sport of sailing. After purchasing a forty-two-foot sailboat I named "Prophecy," Roberto and I proceeded to rig the sailboat for regular runs between the Dominican Republic and America. Of course we would be stopped, and we would be boarded by the Coast Guard.

The drill was always the same. Pick up a couple of attractive American women from the resorts in Punta Cana, and ask them if they wanted to join you sailing home. Never put any money on the boat, only under the boat. Roberto and I had been watching the America's Cup race when the Australia team took the cup from the Long Island Yacht Club. They did it with a sailboat that had a new keel design. The Aussies didn't want the Americans seeing their design, so they came up with an ingenious manner of disguise. They painted the keel the same color blue as the water. Even during the race, the Americans could not quite determine what the keel looked like. All the sore losers were calling the

Australians cheaters, as they would not dry dock the boat and let the other racers see the keel design.

Roberto and I took a pontoon from an old boat, and retrofitted it to attach to the keel of "Prophecy." What was really unique was our ability to scuttle the entire pontoon addition with the push of a button, similar to that on a garage door opener. The pontoon fit onto the sailboat keel like a shoe fits on your foot. Any trouble, and it would slide off the keel to the bottom of the ocean.

It is always about having a plan. This plan was simple: if the Coast Guard pulled up to board the sailboat and were being too thorough in their search, I would scuttle the load. After all, it was just money, and we had large rooms full of it. The pod would hold approximately twenty million, and it was painted dark ocean blue. It would sink out of sight.

I would note the longitude and latitude on my GPS and retrieve the pontoon later if the water was not too deep. They could be staring at the bottom of the boat and not see the pod disappear. I kept the garage door opener in plain view, clipped to my belt like a pager. Sometimes the most obvious is the least obvious.

After a long year of picking up women and sailing back and forth from America to the Dominican Republic, it was time to go to the next chapter in the plan.

I was going to start a plan of selling fast-food franchises in a new startup called "Uncle Bessie's Chicken." I had completed the entire standard operating procedure manual, training video, and business plan for future franchise holders. Every detail necessary for a manager to run the restaurant was complete. Commercial land would be purchased, buildings built and staffed, food served, and taxes paid. These restaurants would show way more income than they were really making – income from all the cash being smuggled into America by Roberto and me.

After the initial loss of the startup investment, the cost to launder the extra contribution of illegal cash was under 2 percent. The profits would be invested into legitimate investments such as stocks or "T-bills." The IRS was always welcome to audit us, and when they did the audits, everything went very well. After all, the IRS was looking for the nonpayment of taxes, not the overpayment of taxes. We were buying huge amounts of food that never was delivered to the restaurants, so it would look like our food costs were about 25 percent. All the extra food we weren't really selling was given to various food charities. Furthermore, I required the corporation to be properly set up, filings to be kept current, and investments to be made with the profits.

Keeping under the radar was important; we didn't want to grow any of the brands of restaurants too big. So after a while we applied the same program to a catfish franchise, then a smoked fish franchise, then a deli franchise.

The fish franchise offered another opportunity. You see, we were selling "fresh fish," brought in by boat on ice, and then shipped the next day on ice to our upscale restaurants. This required a network of stops along the way to deliver the fish to wholesalers, who would then distribute the fish to local franchise restaurants.

Each distributor would have to off-load the truck – all the fish and the ice onto a sanitary floor, in a refrigerated room – and then repack the fish into smaller loads to be shipped to the restaurants with fresh ice. Of course, this left a large pile of old ice in the middle of the refrigerated room. This old ice was removed and deposited outside in a concrete bin to melt and drain off. Other than a slight smell of ammonia that everyone assumed was caused by the fish, no one seemed to care about this large pile of ice melting outside of each distributor's building.

In fact the ice was actually a frozen blend of water, ammonia, and dissolved cocaine. The drain in the bottom of the concrete area where the ice was melting went to an adjoining building where there was a laundromat. As the ice melted and the water flowed to the laundromat, it would be boiled off until only the cocaine was left. No one would think anything about the steam coming from a laundromat, or the large natural gas bill. All laundromats are constantly venting steam, and they use a lot of gas for their dryers. We paid taxes to the government for all the money we were making from this laundromat. We then invested all these "profits" into legitimate institutions.

The reason the ice had an ammonia smell was not from the fish, but was because we would add ammonia with the cocaine to the water before freezing it into ice. Why do that? Ammonia kills a dog's ability to smell. Completely shuts it off. No ability to smell the cocaine in the ice.

What is even more interesting is how I came up with this plan. I was talking to Tom about his bear dogs. He was explaining how they could smell a bear in the woods while riding on the hood of his truck as he slowly drove on the logging roads in the mountains. He was explaining that when a bear dog is running a track, it would be as if we were following a large orange line painted through the woods. I remarked how it must be hard for the dogs to get any sleep with a nose that strong. Tom replied, "That is why dogs curl up and put their nose by their tail. They really are placing their nose by their asshole. Dogs shit every day, and the shit on their asshole gives off a lot of ammonia. By putting their noses there it turns their noses off. It would be the same thing to us as turning off the bedroom light and going to sleep."

I pondered on Tom's remark that night. Yes, chance favors a prepared mind. I had by chance been given a fact from a bear hunter in Townsend, Tennessee, that would allow us to distribute untold tons of cocaine each week, right in front of the DEA. Sometimes the most obvious is the least obvious. We kept opening up fine fish restaurants and laundromats, all up and down the Eastern Seaboard. Management to run these facilities was always imported from Belize. Do a good job, and you could come back to your family a very rich man, and retire after just five years into a nice home in Julio's valley. Your children would be educated by the finest teachers, and your family protected by a trained military that was more formidable than the Belize government's military.

The initial restaurant-franchise business was becoming a real pain in the ass. Almost every employee and assistant manager would eventually start stealing, first food, and then money. We didn't really care about the food, as I was giving most of it away. All of the restaurants started out well, and some were actually really making money, but eventually the lack of a proper manager's oversight always caused the store to start looking like a dump. I decided to completely stop this initial money-laundering effort, and focus on an industry that would be a little cleaner and less involved with dishonest employees. We would keep the fish franchise open for obvious reasons. This was how we were able to import and distribute our product. We no longer needed the middleman who would fly down to Colombia with a bunch of cash, and purchase our cocaine. These guys were often caught, and they were a source of exposure for us. We were also able to keep the money in America, and not have to transport the cash back to the States from overseas.

My plan started with the construction of airstrips, with connecting driveways to the owners' houses. This would be for the enthusiasts who wanted to fly up to their homes.

The next part of my plan was to set up a drop system for all our records in Tennessee. We needed to start hauling our cash by small plane between the different locations in the United States to speed up the process of re-patrioting our money. We had so much American money in South America, we couldn't stop the rats from eating and nesting in the warehouses of cash. By importing and selling our product directly, and investing the cocaine revenues locally, we avoided having to return the money from South America to the United States. We would only use the South American money to pay for the fish we were shipping in the cocaine-laden ice. This really helped the fishing economy in South America, and allowed us to speed up the process of getting rid of all the money in the warehouses. There were rumors that America was about to start printing new paper money, and one day stop accepting the old money.

After purchasing some acreage off Best Road in Maryville, I hooked up with my friend, the semi-retired, almost bankrupt builder/developer named Harold Tipton. Harold knew how to do almost anything in the construction field. He just lacked self-discipline to complete any task, and the ability to understand the effects of cash flow and financing on a business plan.

I was always intrigued by those machines that banks use to transfer money from an outside location to the tellers inside. You know those little round containers you put your check in, that is then sucked up the tube and then deposited at the other end? How far could one of those really go?

I got one of the girls at his bank to give him one of the shuttles they would use to place your check in for a birthday present as a joke gift. Harold went to Stokes Electric and purchased a huge roll of inner duct tubing. We took it out to a farm Harold owned, and unrolled the entire 5,000 feet of inner duct.

I attached a five-horsepower Shop-Vac to one end of the inner duct, plugged it into the generator in the back of my Blazer, and fired up the generator. I then beeped my horn for ten seconds. Harold, at the other end of the inner duct, heard the horn. He placed the cylinder into the inner duct, and poof! The cylinder started racing through the inner duct in my direction.

About forty-five seconds later I heard a "thunk," and then the vacuum started straining. I turned the generator off, cut the duct tape loose that was holding the vacuum hose and the inner duct together, and stared at the cylinder. Forty-five seconds was the travel time. Amazing!

When we built the subdivision on Best Road, all the utilities were underground so as to not interfere with the takeoff and landing of the planes. Extra inner duct was installed underground to all the future home sites. The airstrip was to be concrete, and there would be no patching from future utility work. In the event we ever had a house under observation, we could start moving our records and bearer bonds to the other homes and avoid any problems with a search. Sometimes the least obvious is the most obvious.

The subdivision sold slowly, and a few homes were built. Roberto and I kept four lots. We were getting ready to build four houses; all four lots were connected with the inner duct. If a warrant to search was for one house, we could beat the rap in court as our bonds and banking records could always be at a different location in a matter of seconds. Later that same year, some asshole with a plane was caught flying a load of pot into the airstrip. Game over: move on to the next plan. I found myself getting a little stressed, and I decided to take some time off and visit Tom.

Tom as a young man filmed by another bear hunter as he emerged from the woods after a successful hunt high in the mountains.

Chapter 13

Real Men (And a Few Women) Hunt Bears

...It was a large river, and it was the color of blood. It smelled like blood. I could taste that iron taste you get in your mouth when you get a bloody nose.

At first I thought I saw rocks protruding above the river surface. Then I realized they were large turtles trying to get upstream in the blood. Dragonflies landed on the turtles and drank the blood.

One of the dragonflies landed on my arm. Its feet were wet with blood, and it got blood on my arm when it landed. I stared into its eyes, yet they were lifeless. It left and I couldn't seem to get the blood off my arm. I wanted to get away from this river of blood, but my feet were stuck in the mud and I couldn't move...

I was back in America, so I called Tom to see if he wanted to go chase a little pussy with me. He said he was going bear hunting. When I asked, "Why bear hunting instead of girls?" Tom looked at me and said, "You don't understand, and I can't do it justice trying to explain it: you just need to go with me." I kept trying to get him to explain himself.

"Bubba, people come to these mountains by the millions each year to film the scenery. They then go to their cabins and motels and go to sleep. There is something greater out there that is so much grander than anything these tourists have ever experienced."

"The bear hunters are a private cult of people who are more secret, have more stealth, and are more tight-lipped than the Mafia, the KKK, or any military group. In the mountains at night, something happens that bridges all economic and social structures. Something that is superior to all rules of authority. Men stand as men, and they completely own the night."

"The mountains breathe life, and these men feel every breath. And while the tourists and retirees sleep, these men bear hunt. During the day when the tourists and retirees try to mix with the locals and try to become locals, the bear hunters just humor these people and say nothing about their sport. There are no words to describe the feeling a man gets while bear hunting in the Smoky Mountains behind a pack of hounds at night."

I just stared at Tom in amazement! Bear hunting was grander than going to a cabin at night? With a woman? Greater than anything I have ever experienced? I had to find out for myself.

I always wondered how Tom got started in this weird sport. It is not like tennis or golf, where you can go take a lesson at the country club. Every year there were always great stories over what had happened during the last year of bear hunts. Although a very tight lipped cult of people, they would talk in front of me when Tom told them I could be trusted. I decided I had to find out for myself what Tom was talking about.

Tom was always fascinated with bear hunting, but to understand it, you would have to understand where it all began.

On Tom's ninth birthday, his family went down to visit his grandfather, "Pops," at his summer home. This 3,200-acre playground, called Norton Creek, put Tom in awe. Skeet shooting, horseback riding, snake hunting, swimming, trout fishing, golf, Jeep riding, helicopter rides, endless games of skittles and gin rummy after dinner with Pops, and stories of the bear hunters.

"They hunt at night behind hounds, with miner's lights called wheat lights," said Pops. "They run behind the hounds until they tree the bear. They use only .22 rifles." Tom's questions were endless. What about snakes? Do they ever get lost? Does the bear ever get them?

Pops, getting weary of the endless questions, looked up at his nine-year-old grandson and said, "Do you want to go?"

Tom's mother, Dusty, almost dropped her drink. Tom's dad looked at his father with a look of horror. Tom instantly replied, "Yes!"

The caretaker at Pop's estate was a man named Orville Ownby, a well-known bear hunter, who had two sons, Billy and Jean. And then there were the bear hounds. Dogs so different from any other dog Tom had ever seen. They seemed small, skinny, and shy. They did not seem proud or strong enough to fight a bear. The male dogs got along and didn't fight each other like the dogs in Tom's neighborhood. Tom had to stay in the Jeep, and no bear was killed that night. But the experience was all-powerful for a nine-year-old boy.

Tom was raised in the suburbs of Connecticut, just outside of New York City. In the suburban environment, "big game" was when the bird feeders in the formal manicured gardens were invaded by a gray squirrel or a crow. The prospect of entering the wild wilderness of the Great Smoky Mountains at night was scary and unimaginable for a young city boy. The idea that you would chase a predator large enough to eat you with these skinny shy dogs and a .22 rifle was beyond belief. Even though he spent the entire night observing this sport from the safety of the Jeep on a logging trail, Tom trembled with nervous excitement the entire time. It was the first time in Tom's life that he experienced the effects of huge amounts of adrenaline flowing through his body for long periods of time. That night his brain was reprogrammed, and he developed an obvious addiction to this level of excitement. For the next couple of decades, like a drug addiction, it caused Tom great problems before he learned how to control and channel this burning desire to re-experience this rush. Tom at that young age was experiencing the same addictive feelings as that of someone using heroin for the first time. To see other young boys only a few years older than Tom outside of their Jeeps, barefoot, running through the woods chasing the hounds with their fathers, was more exciting than any book Tom had ever read or heard of in school. It was as if he was witnessing a real-life example of what a story would be like if it was a cross between The Jungle Book and

Huckleberry Finn. He was seeing the events unfold first hand, and he couldn't wait to see more.

An old photo given to the author supposedly of
Wisconsin bear hunters taken in the late 1800s.

When Tom turned twelve, he was offered a summer job by Pops and his wife Peggy. Pops was in semi-retirement and would only be working until noon. Tom would work for Orville and help him keep the grounds, and then after lunch, he would hang out with Pops. It was a great summer, and it was also the summer of Tom's first real bear hunt.

One day, Orville's sons Billy and Jean took Tom down a ridge called Caney Fork Ridge. Tom was told he could bring the .22 rifle he got from his father last Christmas. He was told he was going to be allowed to shoot a bear.

So off into the mountains went Tom, with his .22 and these two sons of the caretaker. No parents. No backup. Just a mountain man's rite of passage to be experienced by a twelve-year-old boy.

The dogs struck and treed, about a mile into the hunt. It was not a large bear, probably only 120 pounds. Billy and Jean positioned Tom where he would have a clear shot at the bear's head.

Tom shouldered his rifle and tried to control his shaking. Breathe. Breathe like your father showed you. You knew how to do this. Your dad was a Marine sniper, and he taught you well. Deep breath. Slowly let it out. Feel the rhythm of your heart pounding in your ears. Breathe. One more breath. Time the pulse of your heart with the pressure of your trigger finger. Force your mind to check your heart, your trigger finger, and the focus of your eye on the target all at the same time, and when your lungs are half-full of air, the gun will go off.

The bear dropped from the tree, dead from a head shot. The dogs piled into the bear with an aggression Tom had never witnessed.

Billy and Jean retrieved the dogs and gutted the bear. They then took their hands, dripping in blood, and placed them on Tom's head, smearing the blood over his face. This ritual is time honored and true to mountain tradition, when a boy makes his first bear kill. Tom, now properly anointed and baptized in blood, was no longer just a twelve-year-old boy. He was now a young man who was a member of the bear-hunting tribe. He was confirmed, deep in the mountains. With his confirmation came the clear understanding that there are winners and losers. You must strike first, or risk death. You are either in control of the moment, or the moment will control you. This was not some frat house membership. This was real life. For when two opposing forces come together, someone always bleeds. Something is always sacrificed. For this knowledge, this bear's blood had to be shed, and from this knowledge Tom gained a great understanding of how life really works.

It was almost a decade before Tom got to go bear hunting again. He had gone to see a chiropractor named Doc Walker, who was an avid bear hunter. After Tom had made many trips to get his back adjusted, Doc

Walker finally asked him to go with them to the coast of North Carolina for a ten-day hunt. Tom asked me to go with him, and I decided the trip might be fun.

The hunting in North Carolina was much different from the mountain hunting.

We were on the coast, in particular a place called Luchous Island. Luchous Island was not really an island; it did connect to land at low tide. This weird island was about eight to ten thousand acres in size. Where it occasionally connected to the coastline, there is a large farming company called the Open Lands Corporation. This adjoining coastal land was owned by this company, which had purchased tens of thousands of acres. They then cleared all the land and cut roads, spaced one mile apart just like the farmland in the West. This ground was only a few feet above sea level. They dredged large canals by drag line along each roadbed, and all these canals emptied into the Puget Sound near Morehead City.

The company would not allow any hunting. Their main core groups of employees were local assholes, who would keep everyone off the property while they hunted it themselves. Land access to Luchous Island was through Open Lands, and unobtainable to anyone except these employees.

This really chapped the locals, who had grown up with these guys. Everyone had hunted this land for years as young boys, and now a few of them were selfishly keeping all the good hunting to themselves.

And good hunting it was. The Open Lands property was used to grow row crops like corn, soybeans, and peas; all of which were sent to Europe for consumption. At night, the animal population of deer, bears and turkey would move from the surrounding property into these fields, under cover of darkness, and gorge themselves.

Never in the continental United States has anyone seen such fat, huge, deer, bear, and turkeys. As a matter of fact, a bear hunter from Sevierville, Tennessee named Coy Parton, who had local connections, killed a world-record black bear in one of these fields. The black bear weighed 805 pounds, which is usually considered trophy size for an Alaskan Kodiak brown bear.

Doc Walker hunted for trophy bears. Not to be deterred, he hooked up with an old coon hunter named Tom Tosto. Tosto owned an old barge. With our method, we would place one of the four-wheel-drive pickups on the old barge, and Tosto would pull the barge about 3 miles across the water to Luchous Island with an old, worn-out shrimp trawler that looked like it might sink at any minute. Being the new guy in the group, Tom had to use his truck for this trip.

About halfway across the Sound, the chop on the water created by the wind began to come over the windward side of the barge, and the entire platform began to tilt. There were about twelve men and twenty dogs on the barge with the truck. Tosto signaled for everyone to move to the leeward side to level out the barge, and changed the angle of his approach to compensate for the strong outgoing tide.

We arrived at Luchous Island scared, wet, and ready to get off this deathtrap of an overloaded barge. Masterfully, Tosto navigated us into a small cove, where he used his shrimp boat as a tug and pushed the barge to a little, cutout place on the bank, about the height of the top of the barge. Once the barge was tied off to some large pine trees on the bank, Tom locked the truck into four-wheel drive and powered off the barge and into the wood line.

The island absorbed our intrusion without incident. Base camp was established and dogs tethered. We made our dinner by campfire light and retired to our tents.

This land was in exactly the same condition as it had been at the beginning of time. It was as close to uninhabitable as a desert, a mountaintop, or the Arctic Circle. The mosquitoes came upon you in huge swarms. Vines with one-and-a-half-inch thorns hung from every tree and tall bush. Like rose vines on steroids, they could cut you deep enough that you would need stitches. The ground was unstable, and quicksand a real hazard. Cottonmouth moccasin snakes were in every sluice, along with alligators larger than canoes. It was beyond me how a bear could even survive here, much less how we were going to go in there to get one. The jungles of Vietnam were more hospitable than this place. I can see why everyone just passed it by and settled the rest of the country. Even Tom seemed nervous and very concerned over the safety of his dogs. Retiring to my mosquito-proof tent, I lay down, closed my eyes, and got comfortable between two large roots that protruded under the bottom of my tent. The sound of the slight wave action, along with the constant whine of the mosquitoes outside my tent, was hypnotizing. I closed my eyes and instantly fell asleep.

I opened my eyes, awakening to the sound of an early-morning bird. I had slept so soundly I had not moved at all the entire night, and I was in the exact same position as when I went to sleep. That was a first.

Complete deep sleep. No tossing and turning. Waking up in exactly the same position. I may have discovered the best sleep therapy on Earth. A night's sleep between two pine tree roots, hiding from the mosquitoes, snakes, and alligators on Luchous Island. Who would have thought?

Old man Tom Tosto from
Luchous Island, North Carolina.

The next day, nothing went right with our hunting. We lost all our dogs, and in an attempt to find them, we too got lost. At about dark, we came out at what was once an old store along the water, whose previous customers would arrive by boat. You couldn't tell it was ever a store or anything else. It had long since been consumed by termites, and the only thing remaining of any traces of mankind were a few pieces of rusty tin from the long-ago roof. It was pitted, and it looked as if the termites had even given it a try. The old local man who had brought us over on the barge announced that we were going to have to camp here for the night, as our base camp was on the other side of the island and it would be too dangerous to attempt to cross the island at night. The plan sounded like the first smart thing anyone had suggested since I got here. Our self-appointed leader then told us we needed to go into the water to get some oysters for dinner. We all looked over the expanse of water, and then to each other. The inhabitants of this island were bad enough, and none of us wanted to go into the water and challenge the sharks.

The old man looked at all of us in disgust. One of the boys in our group mumbled something about not being able to swim, as he looked at his boots.

At this point the old guy proceeded to take off his pants, underwear, and socks. Off came his coat and shirt. Now naked and squirming in the sand, he awkwardly put his boots back on and trudged into the ocean.

It was only knee deep, yet it was about a hundred feet out to where the oysters were. Using a wooden shaft we had cut for him from a pine tree, he pried out chunks of oyster from the sand. Delivering these back to the wave of us, standing there dry at the beach, he made several trips until there was a pile of what looked like rocks on the beach.

It was November, and the old man was getting very cold and hypothermic. I remember having to help him out of the water as his legs started to fail from the cold. By now we did have a large fire blazing, and he stood there naked, next to the fire with us, until he was dry. Putting his socks and pants back on, he then placed his boots next to the fire to dry. I always wondered what someone would have thought if they came upon nine men and one old naked man standing next to a fire in the middle of nowhere. I mean, would you even stop to ask?

The fire started to get under control, and coal out. Our leader instructed us to place the old roof tin over the coals, and then place the chunks of oysters on the tin. After about thirty minutes, the oysters steamed open, perfectly cooked and ready to eat. The old guy still had one trick left. He pulled an old bottle out of his daypack. It was at one time one of those hot sauce bottles with the cap that only lets one or two drops out at a time. He had placed his own mixture of oil, garlic and black pepper in the bottle. Everyone would use their knife to retrieve a cooked oyster, and the bottle would circulate around the group. One drop per oyster, please! We sat around the fireplace like a bunch of little kids, eating oysters for the next few hours.

Oysters roasting over an open fire on Luchous Island.

I was really cold that night. We were instructed to cover ourselves with pine needles. No matter how many pine needles I put over me, I was still cold. If I moved at all to get comfortable, they would fall off. Whenever I placed them over my head, one would go into my nose. The next morning I got up hungry, sore and covered in seed ticks. By mid-morning we were back at base camp, and everyone except the old local guy spent the next hour removing ticks. Apparently there was another local trick he never shared with us, as he didn't have one tick on him. The one thing I really learned over the past twenty-four hours was that knowledge is power – the power to survive!

We still had not located our dogs. When we arrived the first day, we had placed Tosto's name and local phone number on all our dogs' collars. This way, if someone found one of our dogs we would likely get a call; usually locals would not steal another local's dog.

We decided, on the second evening, that someone had to go back to the mainland to check on and retrieve any lost and found dogs, then return the next morning. The only form of communication back then was the CB radio, and we were too far in the wilderness for anyone to hear our signal. Bud Wolfe volunteered, and appointed me to join him. We stayed in a cheap motel about half a mile inland. Never before have I appreciated a hot shower and a warm bed as much as that first night. We followed this routine until the end of the hunt. Every morning Bud and I would remark how jealous we were not to be able to stay on the island. Each day, with diminishing enthusiasm, everyone would thank us for our sacrifice. On the tenth day, we loaded the truck back onto the barge and were ferried over to the mainland. I looked at the faces of the hunters who had stayed on the island. It was a warm morning, and sweat was etching small lines through the caked dirt on their faces. Under the dirt was the evidence of mosquito bites, many scratched to the point of infection. If it is ever established in the future that acne is a plague instead of a condition, I am certain the plague started on Luchous Island. As we approached the mainland, I amused myself with the thought of how Tom would explain it to his insurance agent if he lost his truck in the ocean. I did decide this would be my last North Carolina coastal bear hunt.

Tom had become friends with a few men during this bear hunt. These men, Larry, Kenny, Dave and Rocky, hunted in Sevier and Cocke counties in Tennessee. He started making trips to Canada for a few years with them. Tom seemed to really like them. On one trip, they were picking up a man in Walland on their way to Canada. While they loaded up this man's gear, his twelve-year-old boy was crying to his mother. The boy's jaw was very swollen, and there was apparently a family argument underway before Tom, Kenny, Larry, and Dave's arrival. The issue was that the boy had an abscessed molar. The dentist had told the boy he could pull the tooth for thirty dollars, or do a root canal for $120 and save the tooth. The boy's father had told his wife and boy to go back and have the permanent molar pulled, as he was not willing to pay the $120 for the root canal.

When Tom found this out, he became really pissed off and offered to give the man $120 to fix his son's tooth. Tom knew the man had at least $500 on him to make the trip to Canada. This caused great tension within the hunting party. Mountain code requires that you let a man run his family as he sees fit, and Tom had just broken the code. At the same time, everyone knew Tom was right. You shouldn't be going hunting for two weeks if you can't afford to fix your children's teeth.

A 500+ pound bear that had killed a farmer's
Clydesdale horse in Canada.

When everyone was loaded into the truck and the truck was running, Tom said, "I need to piss," and stepped out. He went to the back of the truck as though he were going to piss, then stepped over to the boy, handed him $120 and said, "Your father said to go get your tooth fixed." Tom immediately got back into the truck and drove off.

The trip was twenty-two hours, straight through. The destination was Restoule, in Ontario, Canada, and the Ambassador Bridge in Detroit was half way. Before leaving Knox County in Tennessee, one of the boys innocently started quizzing Tom about his religion. They were comparing the Carter Town Pentecostal Church services to Trinity Episcopal Church, which Tom attended.

Tom explained how, as part of every service, he took communion. This was when you went to the altar, and the priest would give you a wafer representing the body of Christ, and then you would sip wine from the cup representing the blood of Christ at the Last Supper.

At that point, Kenny said, "You are going to hell."

Tom looked at him and said, "Why did you say that?" Kenny replied, "You can't go into a church and get drunk on the altar without going to hell. The Devil is running your church." It was at that point that Tom decided this would be his last trip to Canada. It was going to be a long drive to Restoul.

The next fall, Tom convinced me to go with him to find his own hunting grounds in Canada. What the heck. Let's try a Canada bear hunt!

The blend of personalities on the trip was unique. It was going to be entertaining at the least. Only three of the six of us knew anything about bear hunting.

Tom, of course, knew what he was doing. He hunted locally with a man named D.H. Webb, who knew what he was supposed to do. There was one older man named Bud Wolfe. I have never met a man strung so tight, and so excitable, in my entire life. Bud was about sixty-five to seventy years old, and lived off Boyd's Creek Road in Sevier County. He owned about 400 acres, and had a pet bear and a permit from the State of Tennessee to keep it. He also had pet deer, raccoons, and everything else you could imagine. The man had done virtually everything but have children. He had a collection of over 10,000 arrowheads and Indian artifacts, and regularly the Cherokee would come to his house to learn about their past culture. He was a self-taught expert in archaeology. Bud was an old farm boy who had made good in the heat and air business. He made his own knives, still trapped foxes, and truly believed he was still about twenty-five years old. Unfortunately, in the last few years, he had developed a heart condition and had to keep nitro pills with him for when it acted up or he got too excited. Bud was also the man who had spent three decades in an aggressive bear hound breeding program with Doc Walker. The two men had developed the finest bloodline of bear dogs around. Their signature dogs were the Black Plotts, Blue Ticks, and Red Ticks. Their hound bloodlines included a bit of Airedale and Doberman, and the dogs were extremely fast and aggressive. Doc and Bud only occasionally gave anyone a dog from this bloodline. Outside of Doc and Bud themselves, now thirty years later, the only people with the original bloodline were Mick Webb, the Kerr boys, Ray and Raymond Whitehead, and Tom. The Kings in Wears Valley may have the bloodline, but it was rumored they got it from one of their female dogs being accidentally bred by one of the Whitehead dogs during a bear hunt.

When Bud heard that Tom was going to find his own hunting grounds in Canada, he wanted to go. Bud had been the first one to take bear dogs to Canada. No one in Canada had ever heard of running bears with dogs. Canadians would come from miles to see this phenomenon. After a few years the local game warden would be waiting with a list of farms that were having bear trouble, and introduce the Tennessee hunters to the farmers. Bud had set the Ontario bear record at 740 pounds. He was also the man who took all the Tennessee boys on their first trip to Canada. Now older, and even shorter tempered, he was never invited to go back with them. He would ask if there was an open slot, but never got a call.

Bud sat across from Tom in Tom's kitchen while they drank coffee. "I hear you're thinking about opening up a new hunting territory in Canada?" Tom replied, "I plan to go just west of North Bay, about a hundred miles under the tundra line. Would you like to go?" Bud couldn't believe what he had just heard. He started shaking and stuttering, and finally had to take one of his nitro pills. Seeing his excitement and the obvious problem, Tom said, "Make sure you bring plenty of those. We're leaving from here on September 14th at 10:00 am, and that should put us in camp the next day by noon."

D.H. worked at the Levi's plant in Maryville. He lived on the same road as Tom in Townsend. Bud had introduced them. The first nine times they hunted together in Townsend, Tennessee, they treed nine bears. D.H. was on his third or fourth wife and had somewhat of a drinking problem. He was a very likeable person; he just got really drunk really easy.

Ash Moore was a heavy-equipment operator who ran a 'dozer that Tom and I co-owned. He had a best friend named Bob who was a stonemason. Both were at least six-foot-three or –four, and both were over 250 pounds. Both were raging alcoholics. They didn't fool around with beer; it was Jack Daniels by the shot; Black Label only; and a fifth a night each.

We left as planned, but about six to eight hours into the trip, it became obvious that Ash and Bob were not going to be able to drive their shift. This put a real strain on things, as a twenty-two hour drive needed all three drivers sober. With the trucks loaded with eight to ten hounds each and all our hunting gear, there was no way to stop.

At the next gas stop it became apparent that D.H. had also gotten drunk. That left three of us; me, Tom, and Bud; to drive the remaining twelve hours. We were only twenty minutes from the Ambassador Bridge, where we would leave the United States and cross into Canada. Tom took everyone's booze and split up Bob and Ash into different trucks. I had D.H. and Ash with me; Tom had Bob and Bud, both of whom would not shut up.

I pulled up to the Customs Agent. "Your nationality, please?" asked the Customs Agent. "United States," I replied. At this point, Ash bellowed out, "I'm from Tennessee." The Customs Agent looked at the man sitting to my right, "Do you have anything to declare?" she asked. "I declare I have been in this goddamn truck too long!" shouted Ash. Then he leaned over and looked at the lady and slurred, "Good Day, Eh? See, I can speak Canada!"

"What is your business in Canada, sir?" she spoke firmly. "We are going bear hunting." Where do you plan to stay?" she asked. "At Camp Horizon below the North Bay," I replied. Ash leaned forward and shouted another "Good Day, Eh?" "What is wrong with this man?" the Customs Agent asked. With the straightest of faces, I looked into her eyes and said in a quiet voice, "He is retarded; his father married his sister and all the kids are like this. That is his cousin next to him; he is retarded also, but they like camping. Don't worry, we never let them near any firearms."

The Customs Agent just stared at me; I stared back. Over ten seconds passed with our eyes locked. Finally, she broke. "You may proceed," she said, and then bent over where she could see Ash and said, with a smile, "Good Day, Eh?"

Tom was next. He could tell I was having a hard time, so he told both of his passengers to act asleep and told them to shut the fuck up. Bob leaned back, and I think he actually passed out. Bud leaned back, but kept opening one eye to see what was going on. Every time Tom would catch him, he would squeeze both eyes shut real hard and look absolutely insane. Tom finally told him he could be awake, but not to say anything.

Tom pulled up to the Customs booth, and there was the attractive lady. Actually, if it had been under different circumstances, he might have asked her out. "Your nationality?" "United States." "Do you have anything to declare?" "No." "Have you been to Canada before?" "Yes, as a child. My grandfather would take me fishing." She stared at his license and then asked, "Are you related to the people in the truck that was in front of you?" "Yes," he said. And in a moment of playful humor, Tom said, "Everyone from Tennessee is somehow related."

She looked at him somewhat concerned. "Are they related?" she asked, pointing to Bob and Bud.

Bud couldn't stand it anymore. He looked real crazy at her and shouted, "I'm not related to that stupid son of a bitch!" Tom just stared at the Customs Agent like nothing was wrong. "What is wrong with the other man? He doesn't look well." Bud again couldn't contain himself. "Because he is a dumb son of a bitch!" he shouted. The Customs Agent looked at Bud and asked him, in all seriousness, "Did his father marry his sister like the other man in the truck in front of you?" Bud replied, "I wouldn't doubt it: look at the dumb son of a bitch! All I know is I'm not related to him."

At this point, it was all Tom could do to keep a straight face. He then decided to go on the offense before it got any worse. "Do you ever travel to Tennessee?" Tom asked her, in a flirting voice. "Maybe we could get together for dinner some night?" She looked at him with fear and disgust, and replied, "You may pass now." We drove on into Canada.

The last few hours of the trip were a real grind. Finally we arrived at Camp Horizon. The camp was primarily a fishing camp, and no one had ever heard of bear hunting with hounds. Our cabin was nice, and like almost all cabins in Canada, it was right on the lake.

As we were unloading, we were visited by the regional warden for the Ministry of Natural Resources. He was a young man, he seemed to have many questions for us, and he was somewhat curious about bear hunting with hounds. He had heard about hunters south of us, but none were ever up this far north. Tom finally asked him if he would like to join us hunting. He quickly said yes, and we arranged to meet him at 5:00 am the next morning. He cautioned us not to go to the Field Hotel. This was the local tavern, and it was the only gas station within fifty miles. It also offered barracks-style housing for loggers from other areas. There were about thirty French-speaking loggers from Quebec staying there now. They would log all day, get drunk all evening, and sleep without bathing.

Two days earlier, there were four fishermen from the States who had stopped there to get gas. A fight broke out, leaving the fishermen severely beaten, and two men with broken legs. Those responsible quickly disappeared back to Quebec, and a new group, just as nasty and mean, replaced them.

The first morning out, it occurred to me why the warden was with us. The loggers were driving the same gravel roads we were. They would take their trucks, fully loaded with logs, and play chicken with us, forcing us off the road. The warden would call in the license tag and location. By afternoon of the first day, all that nonsense stopped.

At this point Tom wanted to leave. He was worried these loggers would hurt his dogs. The prospect of driving two hours to get gas was not very pleasant. We were out of gas now, and needed to fill up. The warden had already left. We decided to fill the tanks at the Field Hotel, and fuel to a dollar amount that did not need change. There was a small window where the owner sat to collect money. Our plan was that we would pay fast and leave.

A successful week long hunt of problem bears that the Canadian Ministry of Natural Resources asked us to eliminate.

It was as if they had been waiting for us all along. We had just started filling our tank, when about twenty or more of them came out of the tavern. One very small man, who apparently was the only one who spoke any English, came up to the truck. In broken English he said to me, "You had better get those tires smoking!" I saw Tom reach into the truck. I knew what he was doing.

What Tom didn't know was that I was quite fluent in French, as well as Spanish, German, and Vietnamese.

I looked at the little man. It was obvious he was sent out to start a fight, wherein the others would pile on in an effort to supposedly break up the fight and save their undersized friend. It was the perfect alibi.

I looked at the man and said in English, "These tires are burning?" He misunderstood me and responded, "Yes." I then said in French, so all his buddies could understand, "If my tires are on fire, I had better put out the fire." At which point I pulled out my dick, and started pissing on the tire. The entire group started laughing, and the little man got real red in the face. I shook off the last drops from the end of my dick in the direction of the man, who immediately took a step back, and zipped up my fly.

Again in French, I told the little man, "I am going to caution you: See that tall man there? He will shoot you if you start a fight with us." I am also going to warn you that the other hunters are worried about their dogs. If any of our dogs go missing, I am certain these hunters will return here in the night and set this place on fire while you are sleeping.

"We are going to stop here and get gas every day. We don't want problems or conflict. We come from a lawless area, the mountains of Tennessee. If you start something with us or our dogs, you will find out how we respond to assholes like you in Tennessee. Believe me: your foot-fighting pussies are not ready for the wrath of East Tennessee mountain revenge. With this, I walked over to the window, and paid for my gas. We all drove back to camp. Tom asked, "My French is a little rusty, what did you say?" "I told them you were going to fuck their women if they pissed you off." Tom just shook his head and said, "Not even with your dick would I have anything to do with their women."

We had gotten skunked the first day, but the next day we found a hot track. The footprint was that of a dollar bear. That is when you lay a dollar bill across the track and the front pad is larger than the bill. These bears are always over 500 pounds. We scouted the small ridgeline to our right, as that was the direction the bear was traveling. There were groves of chokecherries and many piles of bear crap. The dogs started barking, as they could "wind" or smell the bear. So Tom let "Prince," his strike dog, loose. Immediately he jumped the bear, and we started sending more hounds to him for support. We could tell that the entire pack was fighting the bear, and it was on the move. The ridge we were on was paralleling the logging road. There were a few thousand acres of woods to the left of the road. On the other side of these woods was a huge lake; you couldn't even see the far shoreline. The road ran to the lake, and as the dogs fought the bear, it was being squeezed between the lake on one side and the road on the other. The bear started trying to cross the road. We had CB radios in the trucks and portable units for those in the woods. I grabbed a portable unit and followed Tom into the woods.

Tom and I were behind the dogs, trying to close the gap. The fight was moving and about a quarter mile in front of us. We had called the two trucks on the CB radios but received no response. The truck that had Bob and D.H. was apparently headed down the logging road in the wrong direction, and was not even close to the fight. The other truck had Ash and Bud. They were paralleling the dog-and-bear fight in the truck. Every time the bear would start to cross the road, it would hear the truck running and turn back into the woods.

Tom and I finally came onto the road about 500 yards behind the truck; we kept calling on the CB but no answer. Finally Bud figured out the problem: the noise of the truck was scaring the bear back into the woods. He exited the truck with his rifle, took a nitroglycerin pill, and started running down the road to head off the chase. He told Ash to stay there, so as to not scare the bear again. This time, when the bear came to the road, he was going to be there and kill it.

Just as the bear was about to cross the road, right where Bud was waiting with a shouldered 30/06, Ash pulled up with the truck so he could get a shot at the bear too. This kept happening every few hundred feet. Bud kept telling Ash to stay put while he ran down the road, eating nitro pills. Ash kept advancing and scaring the bear.

The bear would drop back into the woods, fight the hounds, and advance another quarter mile and try to cross again. Tom and I were jogging, trying to catch the truck, but we couldn't get their attention. Tom was in a panic over Bud running in front of the truck with his heart condition.

Bud once again shouted to Ash to stay there, took another nitroglycerin pill and started running down the road to head off the bear. Ash took another large drink of Jack Daniel's. Again the bear came almost to the road, and again Bud was there ready and waiting. Again, seconds before Bud could shoot, Ash, now completely drunk, decided to pull up in the truck to see if he could also shoot the bear.

The bear heard the truck and retreated into the woods. Tom and I were now only a hundred yards or so behind the truck and closing fast. What happened next was unbelievable. Bud pulled up his 30/06 and started to shoot Ash. He then saw us, only fifty to eighty yards away and running toward him. I think he was worried about us being in his line of fire. He then threw down his rifle and proceeded to jerk Ash out of the truck. The fight was on: two old men going at it, bare fists and all. Just as Tom and I separated them, we all watched, as about forty yards in front of the truck the bear and the entire pack of dogs crossed the road into the endless boundary of forest to the right side of the road.

Bud just walked over, got his gun, unloaded it, and got into the truck. Ash got into the truck next to him, also without saying a word. Tom took a compass reading and got in to drive. I sat on the tailgate, and back to camp we went. According to the map, the next road for us to intercept the bear and dogs was over seventy miles away.

On the way to camp, we found Bob and D.H. drunk and stuck in the soft shoulder on the side of the road. They said someone had stopped to help them, but they couldn't understand him. He must have only spoken French. They said they offered him a drink from the Jack Daniel's bottle. They were mad, as the guy apparently drank more than they expected him to drink, all in a few large gulps. I got in and drove their truck after Tom pulled it out of the ditch.

About two miles down the road, we met the French guy who had gulped their Jack Daniel's. He was on the top of his truck, and the truck was half submerged in a swampy beaver pond next to the road. I spoke to him in French, and told him we would send help. He smiled and waved his hand in acknowledgment.

When we got gas, we told the owner where the guy was stuck. He sent about ten drunken loggers and a large logging truck to rescue him. Tom ordered everyone except me to stay in camp. The only way to get to where the dogs were headed was to drive into Quebec and backtrack. When pursued, bears almost always take a direct course. Tom had plotted where he felt the dogs would come out. The bear was so large he didn't feel it would tree. He also knew his dogs would not quit.

When you got as far into Canada as we were, there are no border guards or customs between Toronto and Quebec. All that is up there are logging roads without any signs. It was getting close to dark when we found the dogs at an outback fishing camp. There, next to one of the cabins, were all our dogs and a 500-plus-pound bear up a tree, with about twenty French Canadians taking pictures.

We walked up to the tree, fastened the dogs, and led them back to the truck. The bear came down and scattered the French Canadians taking pictures while we watered the dogs. We never said a word to them and just left.

It was dark when we got back to camp. The other truck was gone. We fed and watered the dogs, but still no truck. Suddenly, the manager of the camp came to our cabin, shouting that our friends were being beaten up at the Field Hotel.

Tom grabbed his 30/06 carbine, slammed a clip into the magazine, and grabbed a spare. I tried to calm him down but when we got there all he would say is "Fuck the French!" No sign of anyone outside. Tom crashed the front door with the 30/06 locked and loaded. Just as he entered the door, a very drunk manager and a few remaining loggers raised their shot glasses and cheered. There were Bud, Ash, and Bob standing; D.H. passed out hugging some French logger, and an entire bar of unconscious loggers on the tables and floor.

I translated for the manager: apparently Ash, Bud, Bob, and D.H. had arrived with a case of twelve fifths of Jack Daniels. They gave the bartender/manager $200 for his bar, and had him challenge every logger to do shots until the best man was the last one standing. The loggers, used to drinking weak Canadian beer, were not even in the same league as Ash and Bob. They made short work of the entire group.

After a couple of days of recouping for the dogs and men, we got on the track of another huge bear. This time I stayed on the local CB channel with the French loggers. They put us right in front of the bear. This bear was smart, and must have been harassed by wolves in the past. He knew how to fight the dogs. The bear would move from beaver pond to beaver pond, staying in about a foot of water. The dogs could not press him under these conditions.

We leap-frogged one beaver dam ahead, and spread out over the top of the dam waiting for the bear. As it approached us it must have smelled us, as it paused in an alder thicket at the base of the beaver dam. Bud, in his zone to kill one more bear, did something no one should ever do. He entered the thicket to confront the cornered bear, and was immediately charged by the huge bruin. He killed the charging bear less than ten feet in front of him, with one shot to the head.

There was celebration that night at the field hotel over old man Bud Wolf killing the bear. Once again, the Canada loggers lost the drinking competition to the Tennessee mountain men.

The next day, everyone was too hung over to hunt. It was Friday, and a Crew Cab truck full of Canadian loggers came to our camp. The short one who spoke a little English asked us if we would like to go to North Bay and drink and party with them. He made of point of telling us several times there would be women and dancing.

I looked at Tom, who was there shaking his head. Finally he said feed the dogs and we will go. Ash and D.H. sprang to their feet, but Bob tried to get up and fell over. Apparently he'd had a little too much of the "hair of the dog" that bit him last night. The Canadian loggers standing behind the little Frenchman couldn't stop laughing. They came over and lifted Bob up and loaded him into their truck.

After about an hour drive, we arrived at this large metal building on the outskirts of North Bay.

The place was packed with a bunch of scruffy men and middle-aged, unattractive women. Some feeding off the buffet, gorging on the pastries. Others were drinking while some were attempting to look sexually stimulating while dancing to some French-sounding disco music. Tom and I couldn't help but laugh. It was obvious that the Tennessee boys had been drinking Jack Daniel's with the French loggers all the way to North Bay.

Every one of them wanted a drink when they came through the door. If that didn't disadvantage and challenge them enough, now there were women to impress.

D.H. immediately went to the dance floor and started clogging to the disco. Clogging is an old dance style only found in the Smoky Mountains that is done to country Appalachian music. Although this wasn't country music, somehow he was making it work, and everyone started to surround him, clapping in unison to the beat of the music. Nobody in this part of the world had seen a man clog, and when others would try it, the entire crowd would break out in laughter until someone shoved the contestant off the dance floor.

Finally, a really worn-out greasy-headed woman with only one remaining front tooth took to the dance floor. After a couple of false starts, she broke into proper cadence, clogging along with D.H. The crowd erupted, and everyone standing on the dance floor attempted to clog. I stood there thinking that maybe if we could get this woman on the dance floor with President Reagan and President Gorbachev, the world would become a safer place.

D.H. came to the table with Mrs. Toothless and kept telling her she was as cute as a speckled pup. He then threw out his signature move, his tongue, which glistened slightly greenish brown from all the tobacco he chewed. She aggressively received his offer, almost sucking his tongue out of his mouth. In between French kisses, he kept telling her he wanted to get married and that his dick was getting hard. Of course she had no idea what he was saying. Tom got up from the table and told me to round everyone up, as he couldn't stand to watch D.H. and Toothless anymore. Tom went to the truck and waited, while I dragged the rest of the men to the vehicle.

But that was then, and this is now. Many years later I find myself on a small dirt road outside Townsend, Tennessee. This will be my last bear hunt. Tom and I are getting a little old, and this is a young man's sport. I had been working out really hard for the last two years, and I figured I might as well do something fun with my new, fit body. The truth was that we were starting to get too old to keep up with the hounds – or that the hounds were getting much faster.

It wasn't just my age that was worrying me. The tensions between the bear hunters and the game wardens in Tennessee had really ratcheted up over the summer. As we were walking down the road, I started remembering some of the main issues.

It started on the North side of Caney Creek. A local family had a hunting camp overlooking Wears Valley. It was a perfect jump-off place to enter the park. The location had been a secret for years, but now the state game wardens were teaming up with the Federal Park Rangers to stop poaching.

One evening, several truckloads of game wardens drove in to the backside of Norton Creek, and parked where the TVA power line descended off Eagle's Nest Point into Wears Valley. Their plan was to stay high on the mountain and try to hear where the hound dogs were coming from. This way, they could locate the camp.

The trucks were parked just short of the edge where the power line cleared the sharp cliff overlooking the entire valley.

Hours passed as the wardens quietly stood by their trucks. Suddenly there were five sets of flashlights paralleling the mountain, only a few hundred feet under the wardens. You could hear a dog bark occasionally as they headed to the gap next to the wardens in an attempt to enter the park.

The game warden quietly followed them by staying on the old logging trail above the poachers to block any escape into Norton Creek. The park rangers were spread out on the park line at the gap, waiting for the poachers to walk right in to their trap.

About a mile from their trucks, the game wardens noticed that all the poachers' lights went out at once. Everyone stood in silence, waiting for the poachers to move.

A few seconds later, the sound of truck windows breaking, and then the sound of trucks crashing over the cliff, broke the silence.

The game wardens ran back to find that their trucks were piled up, hundreds of feet below the cliff. It was then that it began to settle in that the five flashlights were only a decoy to get the game wardens away from the trucks. It took the wardens four hours to hike to where they could be picked up and taken home.

Now the Governor of Tennessee and the Park Superintendent were really pissed. Every game warden in the state was brought in to form a task force, along with the Federal Park Rangers, to stop the poaching.

The next incident was when a group off old Highway 73 went hog hunting on the back side of Mount LeConte. A man from one of the Webb families had some really great pit bulldogs, and a half-Airedale-half-hound as a strike dog. When the hunters came to a large laurel slick under the Alum Bluff trail, the entire forest exploded with the lights of dozens of rangers and game wardens.

Every poacher started running back down the mountain, with rangers and wardens following. The poachers had let go of the leashes holding the dogs when they started running. Two of the pit bulls immediately locked up in a fight. One of the pit bulls attacked a warden, and all the other wardens and rangers had to stop their pursuit to help him. The dog was immediately shot.

But the Webb boy was a Vietnam veteran. Instead of running down the mountain, he eased into the laurel thicket, and disappeared down one of the many tunnels made by the Russian boars. To fully understand how creepy this is, you must understand the properties of a laurel thicket.

This low-growing bush gets so thick it becomes completely impenetrable, and it grows so dense you can walk on it eight to ten feet off the ground. Only the Russian boar can push through the thicket, and in doing so, leaves small tunnels throughout the laurel slick. These laurel slicks are often several hundred acres in size.

When Webb was several hundred feet into the slick, he started taunting the wardens, just like the Vietcong would taunt him from the edge of the F.O.B.'s in Vietnam. On and on he would go, without pausing between sentences. It was obvious he was trying to get some of the wardens to come into the laurel and try to catch him. That in itself gave everyone pause.

Above the slick, one of the wardens could hear Webb taunting from within the laurel. He called over his radio to warn everyone not to pursue. This warden, a Vietnam veteran himself, had seen Lurps go out into the night to silence their Viet-cong tormentors. It sent chills down his spine to hear this dynamic happening again here in America. It was obvious the man in the laurel slick was a Lurp.

The head warden had all the rangers and wardens surround the slick. Webb just went on and on like a demonic whippoorwill, trying to lure in some prey. The

Vietnam warden pleaded with the head warden to pull all the wardens back and leave Webb there.

Suddenly, about an hour before daybreak, when the moon was set but before the next day's sunrise, Webb stopped suddenly in mid-sentence. Every warden and ranger's flashlight came on, as they nervously shined their flashlights into the laurel.

Webb peered through the laurel to see where all the wardens and rangers were. Quietly, he exited the slick in between two of the lights on the laurel's edge. Once back at his house, he showered and went to bed. All through the next day, SWAT teams combed the laurel slick, while military helicopters flew overhead. When the search team stopped to get gas for their trucks at the only filling station within miles, the local owner would turn off his pumps. Eventually, all the federal men left, and the mountains were once again quiet.

It was about a month later that Tom and a Webb from a different branch of the family tree did something really stupid.

They had a pet bear of about 200 pounds that they had been feeding at the end of Briar Branch Road in Townsend. They would take young dogs and turn them on this bear. The bear would run a few hundred yards, and then tree. The dogs would be encouraged by Tom and Webb to bark "Treed" at the base of the tree where the bear was.

After about fifteen or twenty minutes, Tom and Webb would put the hounds on a leash and take them back to the truck. After placing the dogs in the truck, they would re-enter the woods about 200 feet from the truck and wait for the bear. They had been feeding the bear for months, and now it was completely trained.

In a few minutes, the bear that was previously in the tree would come down the trail to where Tom and Webb were. The three of them would sit there while Tom and Webb fed the bear several dozen stale donuts that they got for free from the Walland IGA.

News of this got back to some of the hunters on the Chilhowee Mountain side of Happy Holler. Tom and Webb learned that these men were going to try to take the bear to their side of the mountain. A plan was made to move the bear over to Tom's house at the end of Carrs Creek, and continue feeding it there. At first, Tom and Webb tried to get the bear to follow them to the truck. After a few days they were successful. They then tried to get the bear to go into the rear of the truck, which had a camper shell over it. The bear would come to the truck but would not enter the truck bed. They tried everything from getting in the truck with the donuts to just putting the donuts in the truck bed. The bear would just go to the edge of the truck and then come back to Tom and Webb, start licking their fingers, and keep begging for more donuts.

The next day, Tom and Webb returned with a barrel trap in an effort to catch the bear without injuring it. There was just one problem: Webb had custody of his son, Stacy, and had brought him along to help. Sworn to secrecy, the boy joined Tom and Webb as they placed the barrel trap about a mile into the woods.

When walking back down the trail, Tom placed black sewing thread across the trail so he could see if anyone was on the mountain in between their visits.

The bear didn't enter the trap the first day. The second day, when Tom entered the woods, he found that the first sewing thread he'd placed across the trail was broken. He stopped and decided to get off to the side of the trail and advance very slowly.

The local Game Warden McMurray knew the area. He also had fresh intel that there was a bear trap on the mountain. His daughter had returned from school to tell him she overheard the boys at school talking about the bear trap. McMurray immediately reported the intel, and nine wardens were sent as a task force to catch the poachers. The wardens found the barrel trap, circled the area, and waited.

Tom was concerned about finding the broken thread. He could hear his pet bear banging on the inside of the barrel trap. He then decided to make slow, smaller circles until he could see the trap. As he came around a blooming rhododendron bush, he could see McMurray lying there, fast asleep. He panicked and started backing up without looking, and stepped on a stick that broke under his left foot.

McMurray opened his eyes to see Tom staring at him, ten feet away. McMurray said, "Tom, you are caught. If you run it will cost you another 500 dollars."

Tom just took a couple of steps forward, extended his hand, and helped McMurray to his feet.

McMurray pulled out his handcuffs. Tom looked at him and said, "You caught me fair and square. I will do what you say, but I am not letting you or anyone else put handcuffs on me."

McMurray stared at Tom. There, in front of him, was a man of six-foot-five, with arms larger than his neck. He knew he had no chance of putting handcuffs on Tom. He then said, "Let's go to the trap and get the other wardens."

Tom walked to the trap with McMurray following. The other wardens, now hearing two men talking, came running over to find Tom and McMurray joking over something they both had heard about the week before in Townsend. When asked why Tom wasn't in handcuffs, McMurray said, "He has agreed to do what I say, and he doesn't want any handcuffs on him." The other warden looked at Tom's size, and then said "Okay, let's go to the truck."

As they were descending down the trail, several other wardens joined them. They were listening to Tom tell the story of why he set the bear trap. By the time they got to the end of Briar Branch Road, the entire holler was full of green trucks with blue lights flashing.

As Tom and the group of wardens entered the road, a female warden stepped forward and started screaming at the wardens for not answering her on the radio. Apparently, she was in charge and could hear everyone talking as they descended the mountain. For some reason, none of the men would answer her. She asked why Tom wasn't cuffed. McMurray told her Tom was cooperating and didn't want to be cuffed. The two of them argued awhile when the female warden called

McMurray a pussy, in front of all the other wardens, for not cuffing Tom. McMurray, trying to save face, told her to cuff Tom herself. She approached Tom while holding her handcuffs in front of her, at which point Tom said to her, "I will do what you tell me, but if you try to put those on me I will shove them through your skull." She just stared at him, then turned to the other wardens and said, "Are you going to let him threaten me?" The entire group of men just stared back at her, not answering or cooperating.

The background story to this is that the female warden was an emergency quota hire to help get the State of Tennessee out of a lawsuit. She had been elevated to a senior position over all the men who had many more years of experience. Obviously, everyone was quite resentful.

She put her cuffs back and started ordering the other wardens to go get the bear and bring it back to her. Tom asked if they needed any help. McMurray said, "Sure, come on." At which point the female warden went nuts. She said Tom was her prisoner, and he had to stay there. McMurray looked at Tom and said, "I can be your witness that you were being tortured by staying with her." All the guys started laughing while Tom sat down on a stump at the end of the road.

After about twenty minutes, the men reached the bear in the barrel trap. They returned with the trapped bear to the logging road about an hour later. They started to let it out, while one of them was going to film it coming out of the trap as evidence.

The female warden started shouting at them to wait. She pulled her pistol out and said she was going to shoot the bear, as now it was a problem bear.

McMurray protested and accused her of wanting to kill the bear just so she could say she once killed a problem bear. Tom said, "If you want to go bear hunting, I can take you." Again all the men started laughing. The female warden, while standing in front of the trap, turned toward the men and started demanding they stop laughing, or she would write all of them up for discipline.

What happened next was never reported, as no one was certain what really happened. While the female warden was standing in front of the trap, either the bear got under the trap door or Tom had reached down and pulled the trap door slightly open, enough to give the bear the opportunity to escape. In a mad dash to get free and run into the woods, the bear came out of the trap at full speed and knocked the female warden over, as she was in his escape route. Tom was then cuffed. The female warden got up, crying and cussing, got in a truck, and drove off. The male wardens all agreed that the bear had slipped under the trap door on its own.

Of course, there were several other bear hunters in the woods watching the entire event unfold. By the time the summer breeze came off the mountains, everyone had heard in the wind what had happened in Briar Branch.

Tom got five years of probation as a first offender, plus a sizeable fine.

After that, Tom restricted his hunting to the area around his home at the end of Carrs Creek Road. He was too nervous to go to the big mountain, as he was afraid of what he might do if a warden tried to catch him. He wasn't doing five years, and he wasn't going to quit hunting.

Adjoining Tom's land, and about half a mile from his house, was an easement, purchased to build a future road known as the Foothills Parkway. This pork barrel of a worthless road project was started in 1948 as a scenic highway that started in nowhere and ended in nowhere. The truth is that it was being pushed very aggressively by certain Blount County power families, in an effort to give an alternate way around Townsend or District 15 as shown on the tax maps. Blount County did not want the negative image that Townsend had in the news. It would be funded for a few years, then mothballed for a few years. There was a four-wheel-drive road that went from Walland to Wears Valley. People would walk this road to get some exercise and get away from the crowds of tourists.

One day, a couple from Florida was walking the road from the Wears Valley side, when Prince, Tom's best strike dog, was wandering the roadway. They used a belt as a leash, and took Prince back to their RV site in Wears Valley. The next day they left to go back to Florida, and took Prince with them.

That evening, when Tom got home, there was a message on the recorder by his phone. A man delivering a package for Mize Lumber Company saw Tom's dog tied outside the trailer in Wears Valley. As this man was also a bear hunter, he knew something was wrong, with Prince being tied to a tree in the RV park. He didn't know if Tom was in the RV park with a friend, so he drove on and called after work and left a message. Bear hunters stick together.

Tom arrived about dark to find the RV gone and the fire coals still warm. They had just left. In the morning he went to the Sevier County courthouse, and looked on the tax map to see who owned the property. The tax card had a man's address and phone number.

Tom called the man and asked if he had just been in Tennessee at the site. The man asked why. Tom said that something personal and valuable was left there and he wanted to make sure he sent it to the proper person. Tom told the man it was a wallet, and if he could name the person on the driver's license he would send it to him.

The man immediately gave Tom the name and then the address of his son-in-law. Tom then asked for a phone number so he could call him and let them know he was sending the wallet.

Tom tried the number every few hours and never got an answer. On the third day a man answered the phone. Tom said, "I know you have my dog and you need to bring it back to me." The man laughed and said he had re-named the dog Bear, and he was going to keep it. Tom said, "I will come and get the dog." The man laughed and said, "My father-in-law, the one you talked to on the phone, is the Sheriff. We are going to keep the dog, and if you come down here, he will lock you up until you change your mind." With that said, the man hung up on Tom.

Immediately Tom called the lot owner, the sheriff, and tried to get him to do the right thing and have his daughter and son-in-law return his dog. The sheriff said his daughter had said that Tom wasn't feeding the dog enough, and they were not returning the dog. Then he hung up on Tom. Tom went to the Sevier County District Attorney, and asked for extradition papers for the man who stole his dog. The DA said he was not going to try dog cases, and refused to give Tom the papers.

I heard about all this, and went by to see Tom. He was distraught over losing his best dog, and was checking the RV site every day. When I asked him what was he going to do, he looked at me and said, "mountain justice."

I thought about it for a minute and I got very concerned for Tom's future. He was already on probation, and I knew, dog or not, someone was going to get hurt.

I looked at Tom and said, "Go to Delta Dash at McGhee Tyson Airport, the day after tomorrow, and Prince will be there for pickup in a dog travel case. He will be shipped under the name "Richard," no more, no less. They don't check your ID at Delta Dash if you know what it is and the main name on the container. He will be on the 6:45 flight arriving from Miami. Before that, go and spend all day with people you know.

I went home and called Roberto and made my request. I knew the dog would be there. It was ugly. The dog arrived as planned, but the bill at Delta Dash said the pet box contained a cat. That was one damn big cat! Anyone checking, trying to piece it together, would not know a dog had been sent.

The next day, District Attorney Al Smutzer called Tom and said, "You have warrants as high as your head on you in Florida. Whatever you did I don't know, but don't ever go to Florida. I am not going to serve these papers because you came to me first. I know you wouldn't do anything like what they claim, but whoever repossessed your dog went too far. No one got hurt. But don't ever go to Florida."

By the next morning, the wind had carried the news into the deepest hollers, and all the hounds men admired the outcome.

I was sitting in a bar in Knoxville, kind of proud of myself, enjoying a beer, when it happened. Although awake, I felt as if I was in a dream.

...And before me stood a large tree, its trunk almost reaching the heavens. The branches spoke of

the failures of man while dropping green leaves that drifted through the vast history of mankind. Some drifted together, then apart, yet part of the whole moment. All the leaves were of the same tree, yet each unique as to where they were positioned and where they remained. The large roots pulsed in a slow, deliberate pulsing movement, sucking up the juices of Mother Earth. The tree lorded over all beneath it, yet all lived off its opportunities.

Twelve young trees grew alongside this tree, waiting their turn to shelter humanity from the wrath above….

I sat there very depressed and started to tear up. I never cried; just teared. I had failed Tom, and put him at great risk, with the dog incident. He had no idea what I was going to do to get his dog back, but he trusted me not to do anything that would get him in trouble. I had not protected him, but tried to impress him. He looked up to me, yet I had envisioned myself as one of the leaves dropped to the forest floor.

Now, many years later on my last hunt, I find myself hunting bears with a bona fide, bear-poaching criminal. Tom and I entered the woods, leading the dogs down a small trail next to a trickling creek. We passed an abandoned cabin from yesteryear, completely engulfed with honeysuckle. The pungent aroma hung in the humid air. I could envision, years ago, a proud young couple completing this home, with the vines by the front porch, the flowers to enjoy. Now the vines had consumed and destroyed the cabin, growing free and undisciplined while fighting for the rays of light.

Tom's lead dog, Prince, struck a hot trail from a bear that had just watered moments prior to our arrival. Tom moved slightly up the ridge away from the creek, so that he could hear Prince more clearly. As the hound's voice changed, it was a signal to Tom.

Two hounds were released about one hundred feet apart, the ones with the best noses first, and finally the last two dogs, who were real bruisers named Wrinkles and Rowdy. These dogs looked incredibly powerful, being crosses between a Plott hound, redbone hounds, and a pit bulldog. When they arrived at the fight, something was going to get between their teeth.

We climbed higher up the mountain, and despite all my workouts over this last year, the increase in elevation strained my lungs. The chase of the hounds had a tempo similar to one of my favorite instrumentals, Megalomania, by the Alan Parsons Project band. About an hour and a half later, we were at the top of Rich Mountain, listening to the dogs in a furious fight on the back side of Cades Cove with a bayed bear. After a few moments, the dogs' barks changed to a rhythmic chop. The bear had treed. The dogs had won the fight.

It was late spring, and when we had started the chase, the air was thick and humid. Now, a couple of thousand feet higher on the mountain, the air was cool and dry. A summer breeze caused a slight chill on my back when it hit my sweat-soaked t-shirt. I actually felt cold, and wished I had a coat.

I looked out over several large valleys. The solace moon lit the valleys so brightly it looked like early morning. The high-elevation tree frogs were in chorus. The moonlight shone on thousands of white-spider eyes, hiding slightly under the leaves that carpeted the forest floor. In the distance, on every ridge, I could hear the mating calls of the whippoorwill, a night bird of the mountains. They would never stop singing, going on and on with fearsome determination to get the opportunity to mate. I finally understood why Tom loved to bear hunt. Never have I felt so in touch with my surroundings. Not only in touch, but in charge. I was the ultimate predator, the most feared animal in the mountains. I felt so strong, so large, so indestructible, so healthy, so young. I stood there in a moment of revelation, understanding the mountains as never before. And as the moon bathed my face in pale light, my senses were alive with the songs of the whippoorwills and the cries of the hounds.

My mind transcended into a dream. **...I had driven a Jeep into an open field that was dotted with trees. The grass was very high and thick, flourishing in a perfect environment. In the middle of the field was a large white bathtub filled with corn. There was a large mother bear and two cubs eating the corn. She noticed me and false-charged, stopping short of a full attack. My vantage point shifted to that of the hawk above, where I could see the entire field. From every wood line there were bears entering the field and heading in my direction. I immediately got into the Jeep and accelerated at full speed out of the field, narrowly escaping, between two bears...**

Tom had approached me and put his hand on my shoulder. I jumped with fear. "What the hell is wrong with you?" he asked. "I just had another freaky vision; I am very scared." "Would you feel better if I let you carry the gun?" he asked. I paused and thought a moment before answering. "No, I will be all right. Let's go get the bear."

Chapter 14

See the Keys on
Your Hands and Knees

...My eyes are burning from a day in the fields. I close them with the setting sun. The first sound of spring comes through my window. The tree frogs' choir ebbs and flows like the coming tide. I don't just hear them; I smell them, their musky, amphibious scent, so clean and earthy. My senses connect and I am hypnotized by their chanting. They are part of me and I of them. As they snuggle down in the ashes of yesteryear they promise a new beginning.

They spoke to me in tongues, and I clearly understood what they were saying...

What a great country America is for geographical diversity. You don't really have to travel that far to see huge changes in the terrain or weather.

Take the Smoky Mountains. You can be in Sevierville, Tennessee, and the temperature is 98 degrees. The same day, and without leaving Sevier County, you can drive to the mountains, hike up Mt. LeConte and enjoy 65-70 degree weather. Did you know that in over eighty years of record keeping it has never gotten warmer than 72 degrees on Mt. LeConte? Apparently, depending on the time of year, every thousand feet you go up in elevation you lose five to eight degrees Fahrenheit.

That is why I like the Florida Keys; well, in a reverse sort of way. No matter how cold it gets elsewhere, it is always warm in the Keys.

The Keys are sort of a string of islands that start off in Miami and continue south to within about ninety miles of Cuba. The one closest to Miami is Key Biscayne, and the one closest to Cuba is Key West. There is a road with a lot of bridges that connects all of these islands. Some are quite large; some are quite small.

The uniqueness is amazing. On the west side of each island is the entrance to the Gulf of Mexico. On the east side of the island, you are facing the mighty Atlantic Ocean.

Fishing is incredible, with opportunities for marsh or flats fishing to deep-sea fishing, all within a short boat ride.

In the winter it seems all the rich people from Canada and all the retired Americans who can afford it migrate down to the Keys. During vacation times, all the rich young females join their families at these vacation homes, and they are always looking for a fling with some tan, hard-bodied islander. It was around Christmas, and I decided it was time to take my friends Tom and Terry to visit my other friend Smutter, or Midget, as Tom called him.

Smutter owned a home on one of the Keys, about half the way down. It was one of the first Keys developed as a sleepy residential area, shortly after World War II. After screwing up our pheasant hunt years earlier by inviting the Miami crowd, Smutter was trying to make up for it with a good fishing trip.

The story behind the Keys and their development is almost as unique as the Keys themselves. Just after World War II, The Federal government sent thousands of unemployed soldiers who had returned stateside to the Keys, to build a road and bridges to connect all the Keys to mainland Florida. The automobile was now allowing Americans to travel greater distances to all the corners of the country. The Keys had no real need for a road, but there were no jobs for the returning soldiers.

Previously the Keys were accessible only by boat, and they had a very unique culture associated with them. This was the time of Ernest Hemingway, when

Humphrey Bogart and Lauren Bacall were famous. This was the time when great books like *The Old Man and the Sea* and *Islands in the Stream* were written. The Keys were the playground of the elite and famous, with some local populations of fishing residents.

During the construction phase of this road, a huge hurricane descended upon the Keys and drowned thousands of soldiers and construction workers. These poor men were unprotected, living in tents and shacks, when the ocean swallowed the areas where they lived. Everyone was outraged that these men were left so compromised, at the mercy of the surging seas. Ernest Hemingway even wrote a series of articles, openly accusing the Federal government of murdering these veterans who had so gallantly served their country in World War II. There were accusations that this was allowed to happen on purpose, in an attempt to lower the high percentage of unemployment that was destroying the morale of our country. It was true that men were sent to build a road that none of the residents wanted. It was also true that they were housed in low-lying areas that all the locals warned the government would flood during storms. Eventually the roadway was built.

Before there were any environmental laws, the government would dredge or dynamite canals into the

Keys to create dockable waters for boats. This way, a homeowner could step out of their home onto their boat and go fishing in the finest and most diverse fishing waters in the world. Smutter had purchased one of these lots, and built a nice house on the canal. There he had his fishing boat waiting, and we were going to escape the cold Tennessee winter to angle for fish and women in this tropical environment.

Some of the Keys are quite commercial, and known for wild partying. This was one of the small, quiet Keys that was primarily residential, with only one or two small bar/restaurants close to the main road.

We got in very late that evening and crashed early in hopes of getting an early start fishing the next morning. Smutter, our host, was a Delta 747 pilot who was starting a week of vacation.

Early the next morning, we went west in an effort to fish the Gulf side of the island. By 10:00 we were all drinking pretty heavily, and decided instead of fishing with a rod and reel, we would poach some lobsters for lunch.

We pulled the boat up in about ten to fifteen feet of water. To poach lobsters you need a mask and snorkel. You also have a small pole, maybe three to four feet long, with a reasonably large hook strapped to one end of the pole. You dive down to where these large coral formations, called "nigger heads," join the bottom, and look for the creases where the lobsters hide. You slide the pole, hook end first, into the creases, and try to snag whatever is in the hole. Sometimes things other than lobsters are in the hole. An occasional octopus or moray eel adds an unwelcome level of excitement. But when you come out with a fresh, juicy lobster, you eat well.

We grilled some of the tails on this odd-looking grill called a "green egg" that was popular with boat owners in the Keys. It is amazing how good fresh, grilled lobster tastes with just a little salt, pepper, and mayonnaise, wrapped in a slice of white bread.

After a few more hours of fishing, too much sun, and way too much beer, we headed home. A quick shower and some sunburn lotion, and we were on our way to one of the local restaurants in this ridiculously large Ford T-Bird convertible that Smutter kept at the house.

When we got to the restaurant, I felt as though I had stepped into a movie set from the years of black-and-white productions. This was one of the quintessential frozen-in-time veranda-type restaurants at the end of a gravel road.

A large screened-in area faced a huge gravel parking lot. Some people were eating on the screen porch. It adjoined a large dining area, and near the rear of the dining area was a bar that sat about thirty people. The bartender was young and incredibly hot. She had a rock-hard ass that was barely covered by hot pants, with legs that were firm, long, and tanned to perfection. Smutter just stared and drooled. I looked at him and said, "No chance."

We stayed for about an hour, waiting for a table to open up. Terry was way too drunk to eat. I was now questioning if I could eat. Tom was hungry as usual, and kept asking when our table would be available. Smutter just kept slamming shots and tipping the bar girl with $100 bills at every round. Sometimes he would tip her two to three hundred dollars for a single shot, while telling her how pretty she was going to look when they went skinny dipping later that evening. She would just smile, and stuff the hundreds between her tight hot pants and her incredible ass.

A four-top table opened up, and Tom told the maitre d' he wanted that table. When it was time for all of four of us to take a seat, Tom was the only one who wanted to eat. The maitre d' then said that Tom would have to wait for a two-top table to become available. Tom wasn't having any of it. He wanted to eat now. He told me to sit down at the four-top, and then walked over to a table of two Canadian girls who had just been seated at one of the two-tops. Within a minute they were joining us for dinner. The maitre d' started to protest, and I tried to politely explain that we were actually freeing up another table for him by all of us eating together. He kept protesting, as he was in charge of the seating and in a loud queer-sounding sort of voice where everyone could hear he protested that he did not like people changing his seating decisions. I pulled a hundred from my shirt pocket and held it up for him to take. He then shouted at me his seating skills were not for ransom. By then, Tom had had all he could take. He looked up, glared at the man, and then he politely said, "Sir, I am really hungry. We need a server taking our order within the next thirty seconds for me to remain calm. I am tired of your garish behavior. If I don't get really good service, with a fantastic meal, all delivered in a timely manner, I am going to leave this table, and on the way out I am going to totally maul your rude ass. The clock starts now." It became very quiet around our table for a few seconds, then the maitre d' snatched the hundred-dollar bill from my hand and signaled for a waiter. With that taken care of, Tom turned to the women from Canada and said, "So, what brings you to the Keys"?

They were kind of cute. I know I was now clearly drunk, but they were both rather pretty. One had her hair permed into a lot of small curls, and the other one had long, thick braids. They both had cameo features, and the long-haired one had cute freckles. Neither of them seemed embarrassed over our exchange with the maitre d'. In fact they seemed to be enjoying the action.

I started playing my rich American yachtsman act, but Tom wasn't following any of my leads. Normally, Tom was the ultimate wingman, but not tonight. I ordered a fancy, orange-glazed New England roast duck and a fine bottle of wine. Tom paid no attention to my "rich yachtsman, all the women love me" persona. He ordered a steak that must have weighed two pounds and a draft beer. What was really pissing me off was that he was getting all the attention. He wasn't even trying to do anything other than stuff his face with food, and they were all over him – both of them.

I talked at length about how I'd sailed my yacht in an exploration of all the uncharted islands in the Caribbean. I tried to eat my Duck a l'Orange in a sophisticated manner, but it tasted like shit. I think the maitre d' wanted to get even with us, and my meal was the target. Somewhere in between the next few drinks, I forgot I was checking out all the uncharted islands by boat, and started blabbering about how hard it was to land my plane on those small islands.

In mid-sentence I looked across the table at Tom, who was staring at me like I had grown another ear or something. The Canadian girls were also staring at me, when I finally realized I had switched my story from sailing a yacht to flying a plane to explore all these uncharted islands. I needed an immediate distraction, as there was not going to be any way to talk myself out of this mess of a story.

An old, gray German Shepherd dog was walking by the front porch, so I put two fingers together and let out a loud whistle. "Here Rattler, here," I shouted.

My whistle was all the old dog needed to violate the restaurant's "no pets" rule. Although I am sure that wasn't his name, he plowed by all the tables and came right to me. I dumped my entire plate of Duck a l'Orange, and all the other stupid shit they served with it, on the floor. The dog started wolfing it all down.

The maitre d' came over and attempted to get the dog's collar and remove the old boy from the restaurant. "Rattler" wasn't leaving his duck. The dog growled and snarled, and the maitre d' retreated two steps. A lady at the table next to us said, "His name isn't Rattler" in a snobby voice. Tom smirked, looked at the dog, then said to the lady, "Do you want to tell him that?"

There was a disturbance at the bar. Smutter, after having tipped the bar girl six or seven hundred dollars and possibly way more than that, assumed he had invested enough in her to get a "yes" to his invitation for her to come home with him. It was at this moment she explained she was living with her boyfriend up the road.

Smutter slammed down the last of his drink and proceeded to walk toward his huge T-Bird. I got up and followed him to see why he was so pissed off and wanted to leave. Behind both of us was the bartender, saying she needed him to pay for his drinks. Apparently she had not applied any of the tip money towards the tab.

That really set Smutter off as he was getting into the T-Bird. He tried to articulate that she needed to use some of the money he gave her for tips to settle the $86 tab. At that point he screamed at the girl, "Just stand there, so I can park this car up your hot ass."

Smutter fell into the driver's seat, and somehow, on the very first try, got the key in the ignition.

I jumped into the passenger seat just as the engine roared. Smutter slammed the car into one of the forward gears and floored it, right toward the restaurant, and the girl standing there holding his bar tab. I pulled the steering wheel all the way to the right. The car started doing a huge donut in the middle of the gravel lot. I was trying to get to the key, but Smutter was fighting me off, so I just held onto the wheel.

A huge dust cloud engulfed us, and as we went round and round, it also engulfed the restaurant. People started screaming and running for the back of the building to avoid the choking dust cloud.

Having now emptied the entire restaurant, Smutter let off the gas and said to me, "We'd better get the fuck out of here." I asked him, "If I let go of the wheel, will you drive straight home?" A large man from the restaurant was rapidly approaching the car. Smutter looked at him, and then he looked at me, and said, "Straight home, I promise." I let go of the steering wheel and we sped out of the parking lot.

We arrived at Smutter's house only to find Terry already there. Apparently when Tom and I sat down for dinner, he had walked back to the house. It then dawned on me that we had left Tom at the restaurant. I thought about it for a minute, and decided he would do better without us there trying to help.

When the great dust cloud engulfed the restaurant, Tom, the Canadian girls, and most of the patrons and staff exited out the rear of the building. Tom asked the Canadian girls to give him a ride.

When they arrived at the house, Tom took them to a table outside by the canal. We were all inside, and by now it was dark outside, and no one could see the girls.

Tom came in the house. "How did you get back?" I asked Tom. "Got a ride," he replied. I watched as he got a bag of stick pretzels and poured them into a bowl. He then took three beers out of the refrigerator and started outside. "Where are you going?" I asked. "I am going outside to sit by the canal," he said.

At first I thought he was pissed that we left him at the restaurant. I decided it would be best to let him cool off. Then I heard girls giggling and laughing. I peered out the window, cupping my hands to shield my eyes from the interior light. There sat Tom and the two Canadian girls by the canal, drinking beer and eating pretzels.

"What type of a wingman is that?" I thought.

I rubbed my fingers across my teeth and checked my breath. It could use some work but it would do. I couldn't remember if I was a pilot or a yachtsman, but I used my most confident strut as I approached the table. I decided to sit by the one with the small curls in her hair. I noticed I had forgotten my drink when I reached for it so I just grabbed her beer and hoped she wouldn't notice.

I thought I was using some pretty good pickup lines, although I can't remember what I said when the lady next to me looked and said, "Why don't you get into your boat-plane and sail-fly back to the house?"

Everyone at the table started laughing at me. I started to blush. I needed a distraction. For some unexplainable reason, I picked up the bowl of stick pretzels and dumped them over the lady's head. I stood up and listed hard left, but regained my balance. I couldn't believe how sad she looked, as she stared at me with her soft brown eyes and all those pretzels sticking out of her curly hair. I started to apologize, but then thought the best thing would be to act confident. I couldn't think of a thing to say and everyone was staring at me.

Trying to break the ice and change the topic, I then asked her if she would like to go swimming – and before she could answer, I reached down, unbuckled my belt, unzipped my fly, and standing there two feet in front of her, dropped my pants as if to go swimming in my underwear. It was then I remembered I was going commando – no underwear today. Everyone was so quiet. I could feel my penis getting smaller in the cold air. I walked over to the canal and jumped into the water.

The moment after I hit the water, I started thinking more clearly. I was in a shark-infested canal at night: not good. I was now too embarrassed to exit the water in front of the girls. I know my dick was now shrunk up to less than half its normal size, due to the cold water. I couldn't stand any more humiliation from the ladies or Tom, so I swam down the canal to Smutter's neighbor's dock. I got out and cut through the hedges so no one would see me going back to the house. When I got there, I put on a pair of underwear and started back toward the kitchen. Smutter was sitting there with a bottle of Scotch, doing half shots by himself. I sat down and started trying to catch up by doing full shots.

Terry was lying down outside, where the garden joined the concrete driveway. He tried to bury himself in sand so the mosquitoes would stop biting him as he tried to get some sleep.

Tom came in and looked at me, and shook his head. He had told the girls to leave. I looked away in shame. I know he was disturbed at me for dumping the pretzels on the girl's head. What the hell, I really don't know if he was mad at all, as by now I was so drunk I could hardly stand up. Then it happened.

As I walked by Smutter, he took a six-to-eight-inch fillet knife and tried to cut off my penis. He later said he was only trying to cut off my underwear, but I really think he was trying to stab me in the dick.

He was so drunk when he slashed at me with the fillet knife that he missed, and plunged it deep into his own thigh. Blood started squirting everywhere. I was really pissed, and picked up the knife and started at Smutter to stab him in the dick. Smutter started screaming like a girl, while holding both my wrists. As I was standing over him with the fillet knife, Terry came into the room, covered in sand and looking like an earth creature, and just froze in the doorway. Tom then entered the room.

I don't really know what happened next. I think Tom grabbed my wrist, the one with the knife in my hand, and broke it. I blacked out, and later came to with a broken wrist. Tom and Terry were binding Smutter's leg, and there was a tremendous amount of blood everywhere. I stood up, cradling my wrist. I really don't know why, but the next thing I started to do was pour Scotch over Smutter's leg. Smutter's eyes rolled back in his head, and then he passed out. Tom grabbed the bottle from me and punched me in the stomach. I fell back on the floor and started puking. Tom and Terry loaded Smutter into the Thunderbird and headed to the hospital.

They arrived back from the hospital just before daybreak. Smutter looked a little pale, but he started drinking a Bloody Mary the minute he arrived at the house. I needed medical help, as I could not grip with my hand, and my fingers were numb. My wrist and hand hurt so bad I kept getting sick from the pain, and of course the hangover. I drank a couple of Bloody Marys with Smutter.

Tom wanted to go back to Miami. I wanted to see a doctor. We all left in the Thunderbird by 10:00 am.

After getting a cast on my wrist, I crashed at my apartment, just outside of Coconut Grove.

Terry went to sleep on the couch. Tom crashed in the great room, and we left Smutter in the foyer. About 6:00 pm Tom was ready to go and meet this really hot Brazilian girl he had arranged a date with, the day before we left for the Keys. He said he needed a ride to a bar called Bachelors Three. Apparently they had dinner plans. I was feeling better, or at least the pain pills were working, so I cleaned up. At some point, Smutter woke up and changed his bloody clothes. He was all high on my painkillers and alcohol and was ready to go party. Although he really needed a bath and smelled pretty bad, I told him he could ride with me as I took Tom to a bar named Bachelors Three. Smutter got out and hobbled into the bar behind Tom. I think Tom was pissed over the Canadian girl incident and told us to keep the hell away from him. He met his date in the bar, and immediately escorted her away from us by taking her to the dining room.

As we were already in the bar, Smutter and I decided to have a drink before going home. Sitting at the bar were two huge linemen from the Miami Dolphins football team. Smutter, who was a diehard Miami fan, started talking to them. He smelled so bad they told him to get away from them. High on hydrocodone, and now with a few drinks under his belt, Smutter told them he was going to kick their asses. Of course Smutter had earned his nickname "Midget" because of his size. He was about five foot four and 130 pounds. It's not like he was in shape, either. He was actually this small, smelly man who was literally half the size of these linemen. They ignored him. I really needed to take a leak, so I went to the men's room. Upon returning a few minutes later I noticed that both linemen and Smutter were gone.

I asked the bartender where Smutter was. He just shrugged his shoulders. I went out front, no Smutter. I came back in, stared at the bartender, and said, "Tell me where he is, or I am going to kill you." He stared at me for about a second, then said, "Those two guys took him out back," signaling to the rear entrance.

There was no way I could come close to handling either, much less both, of those guys, so I pulled my 9mm Beretta from my hidden shoulder holster. I entered the parking lot from the rear bar door. There was no one there. I shouted for Smutter, and then heard a groan from the dumpster to my left. I looked over the side and there was Smutter. He was covered in food, and I thought he had been really worked over.

I helped him out of the dumpster and set him against the building. I ran back inside and got a damp towel from the bartender. Smutter kept telling me how he had done really well in the fight, and almost had both of them beat, until they got a lucky punch on him. It took about five minutes to clean all the food off him. It was then I realized he didn't have a mark on him anywhere. Apparently he followed them out, and one of them must have tossed him in the dumpster. What a wimp.

About that time, Tom came out and said he wanted to leave now. He was clearly shaken. We walked around the building halfway, carrying Smutter to the car.

"What happened to your hot date?" I asked. "We need to get out of here now," said Tom. "She said she wanted to take me back to her place for some sex." She then told me we would need to hurry before her boyfriend got back in town. She told me he was a Colombian cocaine dealer, and he would have my legs cut off if he saw me with her." We all got back in the Thunderbird and went back to my apartment and crashed. The next morning, Tom flew back to Tennessee with Terry. I took Smutter to the hospital, as he now had a serious infection in his leg. We had seen the Keys on our hands and knees. Once back in Miami, I met with Roberto for our weekly "board meeting." Things were not good. Years ago I had retrieved all the money I had been laundering for individuals other than Julio, and returned it to them. Apparently, in an effort to set up his own Cayman Islands account, a doctor had been charged with tax evasion. As part of a plea deal to stay out of prison, he had to tell the Feds everything he knew about anyone who was involved in the Cayman

Islands. One of my many aliases came up, but they were able to connect it to a video taken in the bank. I only spoke French when I worked or visited the Caymans. The problem was that the doctor told the Feds I communicated with him in English. Although not enough to put me on the radar, it did put me a little closer to getting there. Once on the Feds' radar, you are pretty much screwed. Julio, Roberto and I decided we would finish investing the last three billion dollars that wasn't already in the system, and then we all would stop, relocate, and retire. We decided that our last deal would be in a banking product that seemed so transparent that if reviewed, it would draw no further attention.

Chapter 15
Westover Park

...In my dream I saw a large oak that was without leaves. High up, mistletoe grew on the cold, gray branches. The mistletoe sucked nutrition from the bark of the tree, as it had no root system of its own. It produced a beautiful white berry from a seemingly nonexistent environment. This translucent berry shone in the dawn's light, ready for the beginning of its cycle. It had grown pure from its rootless beginning. No ties to the earth, yet glowing with opportunity...

After Tom returned to Tennessee from our trip to the Keys, he dove into his work, trying to keep everything going at his timeshare project called Westover Park. How this project became a timeshare project in the first place is a story unto itself. It was located on the outskirts of town, several miles from the closest tourist economy. The truth is that like almost every other timeshare project, it was a conversion of a failed real estate effort. Unfortunately, Tom's dad had been forced into early retirement by a proxy fight at the company. This was beyond difficult for his father, as Tom's grandfather had relocated the company to Sevier

County. This company, Cherokee Textile Mills, was the county's largest employer for over 35 years. The fact that the legacy had stopped with him was all too hard to stomach. Tom had come to the University of Tennessee to follow in his father's and grandfather's footsteps, and he was being groomed to step into the family business. Once it became apparent that there was no longer a business to step into, Tom started learning the construction trades. His father Dick, like many other people who had lost their permanent jobs late in their careers, became a real estate agent. Although Dick made few sales, he brought a touch of class to an industry that really needed some class. The lack of sales was not Dick's fault, as there was no business to be had, due to the terrible economy. President Jimmy Carter and the progressive Democrats had destroyed the nation's economy. They had passed legislation to allow softer requirements for savings-and-loan banks to lend money to people who couldn't afford the loans. These easy requirements allowed many loans to be made that shouldn't have been allowed. The borrowers were irresponsible, and often not even employed. It wasn't but a matter of a very short time before the defaults started. This killed the housing market, as it became flooded with foreclosures. When a bank foreclosed on a house, they would price the house about 10 percent under the market in an effort to make a quick sale and get the loss off their books. As all the banks started doing the same thing, soon everyone's house was worth much less than what they had paid for it. Owing more than the house was worth caused people who were employed and able to pay their mortgage to default and walk away from their mortgage. This vicious cycle continued until it caught up to the ones who had started the massive selloff in the first place. Banks failed, rates went up, inflation skyrocketed, and the economy collapsed. I think the Democrats and the progressives called their stupid legislation the Community Redevelopment Act. What a joke. With massive amounts of real estate inventory sitting idle, it fell on those creative businessmen in our country to solve the problem. This is how the timeshare industry started, and now these properties in the mountains and along the coastline were prime candidates for this new style of vacation ownership. What an idea! You can take my job, my house, my car, but for the love of Christ don't take my vacation. The one thing I deserve for putting up with this horrible economy is my vacation. Let me own a week of respect and relaxation, and somehow I will be able to suffer these dumbasses running our government into the ground. It all starts with a piece of mail offering you something free. Here you are feeling horrible about your financial life, and someone offers you the possibility of a loser like you owning a week in paradise, for less than you were going have to pay for some dumpy motel room. Yes you, the guy who will never be able to take your family anywhere decent to vacation, has somehow, through some unexplainable error, now qualified for an opportunity to be given the respect you have earned.

I was always intrigued by all the offers for free stuff I received from the timeshare industry. Someone was spending a lot of money. As far as I was concerned, if there was a place to spend a lot of money, then there may be a place to launder a lot of money. I was exhausted from spending months trying to help Julio with his big social experiment to try to help the poverty in his country. Julio and I were trying to establish a kind of "Farmer's Cooperative of South American Growers" to let the farmers enjoy some of the large profits from the product they grew and produced for export to the United States. This is more difficult than it sounds. We built small schools for all the Catholic churches to run in the villages. Next to these schools we built small medical clinics, complete with X-ray machines and pharmacies, to help with all but the most serious of medical needs. We staffed these clinics with some good doctors and arranged regular "outings" for these doctors in Belize or the Bahamas with the hottest women imaginable. The problem was the huge amount of money generated each year from our sales. If the farmers were to receive even a fraction of this money, it could ruin entire communities. A large bonus in any given year would allow all the men to quit farming, purchase a four-wheel-drive, and even a vacation home. They would start gambling, hiring whores, and staying drunk. Sometimes too much prosperity is more than a population of common workers can manage or endure. As bad as it sounds, not all of us should ever be allowed to become rich. Some people just can't handle the stress of wealth. Political parties, economic think tanks, people just trying to give each other a hand up, don't understand that it just isn't meant for everyone to have as much wealth as the next guy. We are all different, and it just doesn't work that way. After all, look at America, and at what the unions have done to destroy the productivity and the job security of our workforce. Start paying a person more than they are really worth, or lend them more money than they can pay back, and you run the risk of destroying that person financially and ruining all that they have that is good. When their job goes overseas and they lose their house from unemployment, how have you really helped them? This may be why over 85 percent of the people who win a large lottery in America are bankrupt within five years.

Back to the how Westover Park came into existence in the first place: Tom's grandfather, Pops, was a very wealthy man. After Pops died, Tom's parents were waiting for the probate time of one year to run out before they could receive this immense wealth. Wanting to be productive, and now in the real estate business, Dick borrowed money to build this upscale condominium development around the local Town and Country Club. They hired Tom, at $400 per week, to build the development, and after they recovered their initial investment, Tom would be given half the profits.

The Town and Country Club was the only watering hole in the Sevierville and Pigeon Forge area. In the state of Tennessee, to be a place that served alcohol in a dry county, you had to have at least a hundred dues-paying members for at least two years, and at least 60 percent of your sales had to be food.

Everyone who was in any way important: a judge, sheriff, lawyer, business owner, etc., was a member of this club. There was a poker night every Tuesday. During the day, the club hosted women's luncheons and weddings. There was a pool, and a couple of tennis courts. One of the judges used the club for fundraisers to build and maintain the local children's home. There were casino nights, with blackjack and craps and a full-scale Las Vegas venue up in the loft on a "you must know someone to be invited to play" basis. On casino nights, Tom would deal blackjack, with 10 percent of all winning hands going into some fund-raising campaign. This was the social hub of Sevierville. If you didn't belong to the Town and Country Club, you just weren't very important. Likewise, members of small Southern country clubs will tend to stick together and look after each other. There may be some internal squabbling, but this is where all the deals were done. Owning the Town and Country Club would immediately elevate anyone to the top of a social ladder. It would definitely help Dick in his real estate career, and it would be a lot of fun.

It was decided that the best way to fund this project would be to form a partnership between Tom and his father. Tom's parents would sign a promissory note through an old friend from Park National Bank. This would fund the construction of the first building group. Dick would list all the property and establish himself as a real estate agent in the local market.

The entire project was for 106 units to be built in a series of phases and building configurations. The first building had six units. After it was sold, Tom would proceed to build the next phase.

While Tom was building the first six units, the economy continued to deteriorate. The first building was completed while the Town and Country Club was remodeled. The local members seemed supportive, and at the grand opening event, one condo was purchased. Several other people wanted to buy, but they needed to sell their homes first, and no one was buying homes. In fact, there were contracts for all the units, but they were all contingent on the person selling their homes first. The interest on the construction note kept clicking away at 16 percent. Soon it became obvious that no one in America was going to be able to purchase any condos, as no one could sell any of their homes.

This entire project was a perfect example of what happens to visionaries who try to create a market instead of competing in a market. There was no condo market in Sevier County, or anywhere in the entire country for that matter. There is a huge difference in the skill set of these two different types of real estate occupations. Westover Park was way ahead of any future condo market for this area. Thanks to President Carter, interest on a home loan had now escalated to 19.5 percent, and the entire nation's economy proceeded to shut down. The best idea that President Carter's entire staff, cabinet, and inner circle could come up with to stop the runaway inflation was to print and distribute a bunch of lapel buttons that said "W.I.N." This was supposed to stand for "Whip Inflation Now." No one really understood the very deep economic principles and theories that were going to come into play by wearing those lapel pins, except for Carter and his Progressive staff. President Carter's economic principles were like a limp dick in a whorehouse: useless, totally useless. If this weren't bad enough, in one final move of insanity, Carter decided to embargo all the grain the USA was selling to the Soviet Union. The Soviet Union still got all the grain for about the same amount they were going to pay to America. But when grain futures tanked over the news of President Carter's executive action, Brazil purchased the commodity at forty cents on the dollar, and then brokered it to the Soviets for a huge profit. The only problem with this was that every grain farmer in the Midwest who had borrowed any money to plant corn on the family farm went broke. Soon thereafter, 80 percent of all family farms were lost at the auction block.

This same year, President Carter decided to stop the milk subsidies – and 90 percent of Vermont dairies then went bankrupt. Finally, someone convinced President Carter to hire Paul Volcker as chairman of the Federal Reserve. Volcker stopped letting the Fed print money, choked down the money supply, and started getting inflation under control. This took a while, however, and by then every building contractor and carpenter in the country was out of work. No business plan of any type will work for commercial real estate when you have to use a 20-percent capitalization rate. Residential real estate did not fare much better. Home mortgages doubled, and everyone was out of work. In an effort to generate construction, a new style of energy-efficient house was created by Carter's staff. Soon the Carter-era homes started appearing. They were supposed to be energy-efficient homes, but the windows were so small that you couldn't get out of the house if there was a fire. Contractors desperate to build energy-efficient homes started trying everything imaginable to increase R-values. Foam insulation took the industry by storm, but it wasn't long before all the pregnant women who moved into foam-insulated houses started having miscarriages from the high levels of formaldehyde gas being emitted by the foam inside the walls. If things weren't bad enough with these firetrap, death-gas houses to start with; all you had to do was wait a few years, and the foam would break down and crumble inside the wall into a small pile of dust at the bottom of the wall cavity. Now you had no insulation in your walls, and your utility bill would increase 400 to 500 percent. President Carter's leadership was equally great in the arena of foreign affairs. Remember the Arabs, our "friends"? While Carter's financial insanity was taking place, the Arab world decided to stop all shipments of oil to the United States. Now everyone had to wait one to two hours to purchase two dollars' worth of gas on the way to their new "energy-efficient Carter home." With America's weaknesses clearly visible, the government of Iran decided to take 400 Americans hostage. America had not had such a weak, spineless leader ever – and now was the time to show the world the strength of the Arab nations. The citizens of America were disgusted with Carter's weak leadership, and elections were around the corner. Trying to demonstrate some level of leadership and backbone, President Carter sent about a dozen helicopters with Marines into a raging sandstorm, to execute a completely ridiculous rescue plan, in an effort to gain voter support prior to the election. America always votes with the President in wartime. The sandstorm downed the choppers, and the Marines' bodies were paraded through Tehran and torn apart by the raging crowds. The American media, which was solidly pro-Democrat, decided not to air the coverage. Even the "progressives" couldn't handle this. Slowly but surely, the facts came out. Our nation's population was disgusted. Carter's opponent in the upcoming election, Ronald Reagan, never said what he was going to do to free the hostages. His only reply to the question was a defiant "When I become President, Iran will sure as hell wish they didn't have any American hostages."

It became impossible to sell anything. We had an incompetent peanut farmer from Georgia, who never had any business experience, running our country into the ground, telling everyone to get a solar panel, windmill or woodstove for their house and everything was going to be all right. The Department of Energy was created. Solar panels were put on the White House. There was talk of installing wood-burning stoves on Capitol Hill. At this point, even the Democratic Party started wondering about how the White House would look, covered in ash and soot. There were further concerns and opinions formed over how to blend the stately look of the Government buildings with the quaint look of a windmill.

While all the leaders in Washington were chasing kilowatts and turning off all the eternal torches in the country, the business community, the capital investors, the manufacturers, and other industry were all either dying on the vine or moving to Mexico and China.

Carter lost the election, and Ronald Reagan became President. Literally the actual hour President Reagan was being sworn into office, two jets arriving from the Middle East requested permission to land at New

York's JFK airport. Permission was granted. Four hundred American hostages exited the aircraft. Smart move, Iran. You don't screw with a Republican President. Carter's last economic stimulus suggestion in office was something about using wood stoves to heat the White House, and hiring the poor, unemployed, economically enslaved welfare recipients in the Washington, D.C. area to cut the firewood. That would have been a proud moment. Talk about history repeating itself. Maybe Carter should have taken some of these economically enslaved welfare recipients back to Plains, Georgia, to pick peanuts on his family's plantation. Ah yes! Back to the good old days when things were much simpler and everyone seemed so happy.

Stuck with five completed, yet unsold units, Tom needed a new game plan. As there was no market to sell these condos, he was going to have to create a market. After much research, he stumbled into an idea that just might work. A new concept in vacationing was being tried very successfully in Gatlinburg, called "Time Sharing." After studying the business plan, Tom started selling his condominium units a week at a time. As with all problems, the best way to solve your problem is to break it into smaller, more manageable problems. Westover Park was off and running, with strong sales, and Tom soon was building the next phase of the development. Before I get into how Tom really became so successful in the timeshare conversion of this defunct condo project, I need to sidetrack a little bit. There was a tremendous amount of conflict between Tom's dad and his younger brother, Uncle Doug. When Tom's grandfather died, there was an issue over where all the family jewelry had gone. Pops had graced his late wife Peggy with lots of pretty jewelry over the years. When Peggy died, all her jewelry was placed in her room in the Norton Creek house, as Pops had instructed. We are not talking about a few nice brooches or necklaces. There was over fifty years' worth of Tiffany's finest original creations represented in the collection.

The jewelry came up missing. "Uncle Doug" said that the maid stole it, yet there was no proof, and she was willing to take a lie detector test. Everyone was very suspicious, as Uncle Doug, a lady named Elizabeth (Pops's new bride), and the maid were the only ones allowed in the room. A week later, Pops died. The estate went into probate, and many problems were surfacing. The jewelry was never mentioned in the will, and to mention it now would only cause greater tax consequences, even if the thief was never caught.

Years passed, when Tom heard through his country club contacts that someone was trying to raise $95,000 in one week, and was willing to collateralize the loan with over two million dollars in jewelry, a Mercedes sedan, and a D-4 dozer. The borrower was working through the trust department of Gatlinburg National Bank, and was not to be identified.

Tom knew it was the missing family jewelry. There were only three or four families in the area that could afford this type of jewelry. None of them were in financial trouble except "Uncle Doug." Tom contacted his attorney, John Bradfield, and lent the $95,000 anonymously, securing the loan with a trust agreement from the Gatlinburg Bank to hold the jewelry in their vault.

The loan agreement was for ninety days, with several special stipulations that had to be met in order to get the jewelry back. Tucked into the body of the document was the demand that "Uncle Doug" name Tom's attorney as co-insured on the Mercedes sedan within ten days. It was clearly stated that failure to produce this proof within ten days would void the ability to pay back the $95,000 to retrieve the collateral. Tom patiently waited as the entire ninety days passed. When the ninetieth day arrived, Tom instructed John Bradfield to leave his office at 5 pm sharp and go to

Knoxville to get drunk, party, but not let himself be found until at least after midnight. Tom told John not to tell anyone where he was going, or answer any calls.

About 11 pm that night, Tom was awakened by a phone call.

"Tom, this is John. They found me, and they want to give me $95,000 for a signed release of their collateral." Tom paused and said, "Give me your number, and I will call you back in a minute." John blurted out the phone number. Tom recognized it as a Gatlinburg exchange.

Tom sat there in bed for a minute. What the hell was going on? He recognized the phone number, but couldn't place it.

After a few minutes he got up and found the Sevier County phone book. He looked up the Gatlinburg Bank phone number and it was a match. Why was John Bradfield in Gatlinburg instead of Knoxville? What was he doing, and who was he doing it with? Why was the bank open at 11:30 pm? It slowly settled in on Tom that his attorney was screwing him over. He picked up the phone and called the bank.

A man answered. Tom said, "This is Tom, who is this?" The answer was "I am the President of this bank." Tom could hear the echo of being on a speaker phone. He then said, "So, Uncle Doug, do you have my money?" A voice in the room said, "Yes, and I want your attorney to sign this release." Tom then said, "Mr. Bank President, I will be there at 6:00 tomorrow evening, with a different attorney, to get my money. Have your trust department have all the paperwork ready. When I am paid, I will sign the release." "John Bradfield, you are fired, and I will see you in your office at 8 am tomorrow." The bank president then said, "The bank closes at 5 pm." Tom responded, "Yeah, I can see that. I will be there at 6 pm, and the paperwork had better be right." Tom hung up the phone and called me.

The next day, I called the bank president at 1 pm telling him I was Tom's attorney, and I gave him the name of a highly renowned law firm in Nashville. I gave him a fax number that had the Nashville 615 area code. I told him I needed to review the paperwork and would be there at 6 pm with Tom, to get his money and sign the release. Of course, the fax just went to the house of an old girlfriend, who didn't even know my real name.

We arrived at 6 pm sharp, and a doorman let us through the entrance. Up to a conference room we went, where Uncle Doug was sitting, along with the overweight bank president and another bank officer. The cashier's check for the loan repayment was on the table, along with a sizable lock box of jewelry and a release. I signed as trustee for Tom. I would not let Tom touch the paperwork. They tendered me the cashier's check.

At that point, I pulled out my 9mm Beretta from inside my coat and pointed it at the president's head. He froze. I said, "You know that if this check bounces, the next time I visit, you won't see me coming." The bank president slowly spoke, "It is a cashier's check. It won't bounce."

I reached over and slowly pulled the signed release back across the table and put it in my pocket. I then said, "Let me tell you something, asshole, you need to keep this jewelry in your possession. I am going to have Tom file an order in court, with you and his uncle, that the jewelry be properly split between his dad and his uncle. This was his grandfather's instructions that he personally told me at a lunch date I had with him years ago. He told me to see that this happened before I moved the money that Doug had attempted to steal out of his personal Cayman Islands account. Everyone in this room is going to agree to this order, so that the Judge will have no reason but to grant the order. Any disagreement by anyone over these terms, and I can take all of it now." No one spoke. "As trustee, I am releasing the car and dozer tonight."

"To be clear, if any part of this doesn't go just like I have instructed, either I or one of my surrogates will be visiting every one of you one more time, and then none of this 'owning' stuff will matter to anyone."

"There is one more thing," I said, as I stared at Uncle Doug.

"You will have your banker give the maid you blamed for stealing all this jewelry $20,000 cash. As your banker is here, he is going to lend it to you tonight." "This is your penance that you must pay to receive my forgiveness for your trespass on her character." I then looked at the banker and said. "Your penance is that you are going to directly disburse this money to the maid, and it is doubtful that Doug will ever pay you back. Are we clear?" Both Doug and the bank president nodded their heads "yes."

Tom and I got up and left the bank. Three months later, Tom's dad and my uncle split the family jewelry, and the maid who used to work for my grandfather was driving a new car.

A few months after that, John Bradfield, Tom's previous attorney who had tried to screw him in the deal, died in a DWI accident after leaving the Town and Country Club. There were rumors that Tom might be indicted. Of course, Tom had nothing to do with the accident. I am 100 percent certain of that, given that a man who was terminally ill with cancer crossed into John Bradfield's lane, and it was a head-on collision. It happened in the middle of the bridge crossing the French Broad River, where there was no way for John to get away from the oncoming car. At least the guy had life insurance for his family. He'd been able to purchase a policy from a company called American Life Insurance Company. Apparently, once he discovered he had cancer, he was applying everywhere, and because of his cancer, he was being denied. A man from American Life Insurance Company visited him to see if he had gotten himself right with God. This was not a churchgoing man, and after a few visits, the salesman said that he could get some really good coverage for his family. There was a catch; he could only help him if he was willing to help them with a particularly dishonest attorney who was out there harming families like his when there was no one there to protect them. If ever this man was going to give forward to help his family from financial ruin, and make it right for all those other victims of this attorney, this was his chance. John Bradfield got drunk, there was a head-on accident, and the man with terminal cancer looked on from Heaven as his family started getting really nice checks every month from the life insurance company. While all this was going on, Tom was very focused on building and selling his timeshare resort, known as Westover Park. Tom had made some really good decisions in resurrecting the facility.

First, he re-staffed the country club and started offering an excellent menu with excellent service. He then decorated one of the condominiums with the finest of appointments, including Henredon furniture, beautiful wallpaper, and posh, rich-colored carpet.

The next order of business was to hire a marketing company to sell the units. He paid the salesman a commission upon the closing of each sale. After a sale was made, he would send the promissory note created by the sale to receive funding from the end-loan mortgage company. Tom had an agreement with a bank in Pennsylvania to purchase all notes created from each sale. The funds from these notes were used to pay down the construction note, while funding the marketing expenses and the operations of the facility.

All timeshare resorts operate on a similar principle. Over 50 percent of the cost of a unit was used to market that unit through the development of tours, and the premiums used to entice those potential buyers. Ten percent was used to pay the salesperson and the sales manager. Approximately 15 percent was needed to pay the finance costs of the building, along with the daily administrative overhead. Twenty-five percent was used to build and furnish the unit. In other words, when you purchase a timeshare unit, 25 percent is for the unit and 75 percent is for the bullshit. As all the old sales managers say, "We sell the sizzle, not the steak."

Tom had about $80,000 invested in each unit. His average sales price per week was $7,000. This would need some explaining. Part of the sizzle of the sale was the exchange rights you received when you purchased your week of timeshare. You could place a request to give your week of use at your resort to another couple, if they in turn would let you use their week at their resort. There were two exchange affiliations available for a resort to join. One was RCI, or Resort Condominiums International, and the other was Vacations International.

Both services recognized that all resorts had "in season" and "out of season" time periods. At Vacations International, the "in season" time frame was "Gold" and the "out of season" time frame was "Silver." With RCI they had three time frames. The in-season time was "Red," the "swing season" between the seasons was "White," and the out-of-season timeframe was "Blue." How patriotic. Tom had affiliated Westover Park with RCI.

The in-season Red weeks were priced at $8500, the White weeks were priced at $4500, and the Blue off-season weeks were priced at $2500.

To fully understand a timeshare sale you have to start with the beginning of the process. A marketing company will drop tens of thousands of "You have won!" cards to zip codes that fit certain financial profiles. This profile will basically be middle-class to upper-middle-class America. The prize they have won will require them to register at the resort for a certain morning or afternoon appointment to claim their prize.

When they arrive, the resort will require them to fill out a questionnaire to validate them and ensure that the right person is claiming their prize. This questionnaire will have a series of questions that are pertinent to the resort and the salesperson. The main one is, "Are you presently employed?" If not, the person is immediately nixed or non-qualified. This person is completely un-financeable in the event of a sale. "Have you been bankrupt in the last seven years? Divorced? Do you own your house?" The questions go on to include personal information that will be used in the sales process.

Non-qualifiers are sent out the back door. They should have read the fine print in the "Free gift you have won" offer. The qualified person is then introduced to a salesperson. The entire process works only if the marketing company is sending qualified prospects to the resort. The marketing companies who mail out these free offers have a toll-free phone number that goes to a large phone room full of reservationists. All the reservationists are paid on commission for every "up," or potential sales lead, that they can generate for the company. Often these reservationists would coach the "up" as to how to answer the questions on the questionnaire at the resort, in order to clear the prospect through the resort's screening process. Reservationists are paid a commission on how many people they book, and only if they show for the tour. The marketing company and the resort have agreed on a pre-determined set of criteria. Must be 21 years old, married, no bankruptcy, own their home, a combined income of at least $60,000, and so on.

Every time a prospect (or "up") clears the questionnaire process, the resort owes the marketing company a pre-determined amount of money. The usual cost of an "up" in the '80s was between $80 and $100, depending on what criteria were used.

Things started out well, and then Tom started having problems. The sales force was not representing the timeshare opportunity honestly. The bank, or the purchaser of the notes created with each sale, was not funding every sale under the previously agreed criteria. They were funding only those who had excellent credit. Tom was ending up with a large inventory of notes that he was going to have to hold "in house," and service with his own staff. This created another problem – there was not enough cash flow to pay the marketing company their commission. Because all the resort cash flow was tied up in these promissory notes that the bank was not buying, the resort could not keep generating "ups" or prospective clients for a tour of the project. With each sale, Tom was increasing his net worth while depleting his cash flow. Sooner or later he was going to sell himself broke, or rich, however you wished to view the circumstance. At the same time this economic phenomenon was unveiling, Tom started seeing a large number of these notes go into default. One week he sent the end-loan purchaser over $100,000 in notes, only to receive $12,000 back. They had the right to substitute an old, non-performing note with a new, good one. He needed to change the way the timeshare business was modeled. He needed to stop going to the school of hard knocks, and come up with a plan that was sustainable.

Tom had identified most of the problems. First, the sales force needed to be fired. They were telling so many lies that people would get home, wake up to the reality that they were being hustled, and then never make a payment on their note. By agreement, this allowed the end-loan mortgagor to swap an old, non-performing note with a new note from a recent sale.

But there was also culpability with the end-loan mortgagor. The end-loan mortgagor was not servicing any of the mortgages or sending coupon books out in time. People were in default before they ever got their payment book.

While studying the project's mortgage portfolio, Tom noticed that if a buyer could be responsible enough to make two payments, that only 30 percent of these would fail to make the next payment. If the buyer was responsible enough to make five payments, only 15 percent would fail to make the sixth payment.

From this understanding, Tom renegotiated his contract with the end-loan purchaser. They would let Tom assign all "seasoned paper" mortgages, with a history of at least three timely payments, for 90 percent of their face value. They would let Tom continue to collect the payments, thus giving the resort the opportunity to keep people reminded of their obligation.

Tom would send the bank a complete portfolio reconciliation within five days of the end of each month, along with proof of the deposits from the buyers. The bank was then paid its installment payment, and Tom would assign all new promissory notes to the lender and pick up all defaults from those who did fail to make their payments. Under these new terms, the bank gave Tom two million dollars of commitment for mortgages. Tom and the bank called this new banking product for timeshare notes "hypothecation."

Tom developed the following sales program for the project director. With each sale, he would give the new owner three coupons. The first coupon the owner could send in place of their third payment, one in place of their sixth payment and one in place of their twelfth payment. This cured the resort's defaults. Tom then raised the cost of a week by 20 percent to offset the cost of the coupons.

Next, Tom re-arranged the salesman's commission structure to be one-third on the day of sale (after Tennessee's required ten-day rescission period), one-third after receiving the third payment coupon, and one-third after receiving the sixth payment coupon. Most of those who had been misrepresenting the resort quit, and Tom fired the balance. The honest salespersons who were trying to make a career out of their trade all stayed, and started doing quite well.

Tom then decided that instead of offering a certain promotion such as a trip to the Bahamas, as an incentive to take a tour of the project, he would offer the person taking the tour a $200 shopping spree. Everyone liked to shop, and he would make sure there was something on the shelf for everyone in the family. The resort stocked a large room with everything imaginable: from tools to TVs; from quilts to romantic perfumes to Christmas decorations; to stuffed animals so cute they almost would not let them out of China. Displaying the room was one of the prettiest women Tom knew, with her arms spread wide, her perfect smile, a modestly short skirt with one of her legs slightly turned toward the other. In large print across the bottom of this picture were the words "Come shop with me."

Another trick up Tom's sleeve was that everything was priced fairly, and no one ever felt ripped off or misled. There were a few "loss leaders" in each category that were priced at the resort's cost. Seeing such bargains almost everyone touring spent an additional twenty to fifty dollars. As the rest of the inventory was marked up to similar prices in the area, usually the prospect would spend an additional fifty to sixty dollars doing their shopping for an upcoming birthday or Christmas. Through this marketing program, the overall cost for an "up" was reduced to less than forty dollars, and the response to the resort's direct-mail program for lead generation rose from half a percent to over two percent.

The first few weeks were close, but then Westover Park received its first check from the end-loan mortgage company. Then the next month, they received the next check. Soon, as if there had never been any worries, the checks kept coming and the sales kept flowing.

Things were now going great. Some weeks Westover Park was selling over $200,000 and sometimes much more. Tom started another building, as he was almost out of timeshare weeks to sell. Tom had snatched success out of the jaws of failure, and he was now a millionaire at age twenty-nine.

After seeing Tom pull his resort out of the fire, I started studying this business plan very carefully. I saw a gold mine, and a great opportunity to launder the last three billion dollars of Julio's money. I would form a marketing company, agree on almost any reasonable set of criteria the resort wanted, and drop however much mail it took to get prospective purchasers to visit the resort. From the income I received for the prospects, I would pay taxes, and then shift this "clean" money into legitimate investments in real estate or stocks and bonds. After all, I didn't really care how much I had to spend to get the prospects, or "ups," for these resorts. When you have rooms full of billions of dollars in cash, it really doesn't matter what something costs.

The resorts loved my new company, named Zachary Marketing. Within a few months I was selling resorts in five states their "ups" for 20 percent less than what it would cost to generate the same prospect with their own internal marketing staff. Everyone fired their marketing manager, and sub-contracted all the marketing to Zachary Marketing on a per-up basis. The average resort toured twenty persons a day, six days a week. I started depositing an average of $12,000 per week for every resort participating with my marketing company. By year's end, I had over 400 resorts buying "ups," and now depositing over four million into Zachary Marketing, right in front of the IRS's nose. The cost of this effort was approximately 20 percent more than I was depositing. Again, the IRS was looking for people who were trying to evade taxes, not people who were trying their hardest to figure out a way to pay more taxes.

I swung by one afternoon to see if Tom had hired any new waitresses. I also wanted to try to sell Tom some "ups." For some reason, he would not buy any from me. One fringe benefit of providing "ups" to all these resorts was the huge number of waitresses and office help who were always available for dinner dates and sex. Tom had a new problem, and seemed pretty stressed. The end-loan mortgagor was failing on their new commitment letter to Tom. The bank agreed to hypothecate on the first million dollars, but now wanted to go back to the old arrangement of purchasing the mortgages. Because of this underlying problem of being unable to borrow on the sales, the resort was again having cash flow problems,and it was about to go under.

Every time a sale is made in a timeshare, the person usually only puts down about 10 percent of the purchase price. This is usually put on a credit card. The balance of the purchase is then financed at high rates, over five to seven years. The mortgages are then purchased from the resorts by loan brokers, who then sell the mortgages to banks. Everyone takes a huge cut. The original mortgage from the banker is often for prime rate plus 4 percent. Additionally, the loan broker would take a $250 application fee, plus an origination point. Then the bank gets a discount point, plus it only funds 90 percent of the face amount of the mortgage. They also make the resort agree that if anyone is late on a payment and the mortgage is in default, it will be replaced with a new mortgage of equal or greater value. The original mortgage is returned to the resort, and often by the time it is returned, the buyer is three months late on payments. It is now impossible for the resort to get the owner current.

Tom's problem wasn't really the bank that was purchasing the promissory notes. He could work through that with the bank with their hypothecation program. The problem was the understaffed middleman, or the end-loan broker who wasn't processing the paperwork in time. These middlemen subcontractors promised the banks everything, but failed to do much of anything they'd promised. Just like under the old arrangement by the time the owners received their payment books, they were already one, or even two payments late. The bank auditors would receive the first payment, start to apply the payment, and then notice that it was already time for the second or third payment. The owner would be notified of the default, and be given ten days to send one or two more payments to catch up on the defaulted note. Most would give up and call the resort, wanting their money back. Some would call the Better Business Bureau; some would call the Department of Commerce and Insurance with the State of Tennessee. Before long, the Tennessee Real Estate commission was under the gun to do something.

I understood the problem. Tom was being screwed by the end-loan mortgagors' failure to process the paperwork in a timely manner. What an opportunity! I decided it was time to expand Zachary Marketing into Zachary Marketing and Financing. Westover Park would be our first client.

I would provide the "ups" for the resorts, and agree to take the end-loan mortgages as payment. The only catch would be that the resort would make the loan complete the day of the sale, print the payment coupon book, and give this payment book to the new owner before the new owner left the resort. Zachary Marketing would front the resort three months of "ups." After the third month, the resort would assign all the mortgages that had made three timely payments to Zachary Marketing. Ones that were late could be kept "in house" and be worked internally by the resort to get their payments. This way, the resorts would not pay marketing money up front. The resorts would still be responsible for processing all payments. Zachary Marketing would receive a payment coupon with a check stapled to it, along with the Resort's journal entry. As long as the resort stayed reasonably close to sending good promissory notes and timely payments, I would keep sending them "ups" so they could stay in business. Any notes that went bad were redeemed with a new note from a recent sale.

Now, not only was I laundering all this mortgage money, but I was making Julio prime plus 4 percent on every dollar. It wasn't long before over 600 resorts were using Zachary Marketing and Financing for all their marketing and financing needs. The second year, Zachary Marketing deposited over two billion dollars into their general account. Julio, Roberto and I quietly prepared to retire.

Tom married an Indian girl named Penwahee that June. Life was good for Tom and Penwahee.

Later that year, Tom's younger brother, who was in the Marine Corps, had an operation for lymph-node cancer and received a blood transfusion at the veterans' hospital. Due to his illness, he left the Marine Corps. Now a civilian, he continued to get weaker every day. No energy. Something else seemed wrong. Many tests later, nothing could be found. His white blood cell count seemed high. Everyone was worried.

Later that year, Tom sold Westover Park to a couple of men from Nashville. As part of the deal, Tom stayed on as an employee of the new owners. The corporation was titled "United Equities Corporation." Part of the sale was for this company to assume all obligations at all banks, including the construction loan for the new condo building under construction. The other part of the sale was for United Equities Corporation to pay Tom $465,000, in monthly installments, over the course of the next five years.

The first thing Unified Equities Corporation did was to fire Tom's sale manager and assign Tom to that post. All the accounting and tax payments were to be processed out of their Nashville office. They closed down the project for six weeks to bring in a new sales program that was going to double the closing percentage.

The new sales program, direct from some sales guru in California, was very impressive with lots of fancy printing. Actually it was incredible. The problem was that United Equities Corporation was now in trouble financially. Just months earlier they had millions in the bank, and now there was no money available for marketing. And without marketing money, there would be no future sales. I was too suspicious of these guys to offer them the Zachary Marketing and Financing deal I offered other resorts. Everything was going unpaid, even electric bills and phone bills, and Tom had never received the first payment on the $465,000 note owed to him. Meetings were scheduled for Tom to take the ownership of the project back. One of the two owners of United Equities Corporation had developed such a cocaine addiction, he was doing lines in the middle of the meetings and then carrying on conversations in space. The next month, United Equities Corporation filed bankruptcy in Nashville. That same month, the FBI arrived at Tom's office. The two men who owned United Equities Corporation were being charged for bank fraud in five states. They were part of the I-30 corridor scheme in Texas: the largest land-fraud scheme in the country's history. *60 Minutes,* a popular news program, had aired a scathing segment on this scam. One of the owners was a known drug dealer; the other was implicated in the murder of a previous partner. That same week, Tom received a letter from the IRS. No employee taxes had been paid by United Equities Corporation since the purchase of Westover Park. Everything was under lien by the IRS, including Tom personally, as he was the project director. At the end of the week, Tom's banker called. They were going to have to foreclose on his personal house. United Equities Corporation had not paid the construction note that they had assumed for Westover Park. But why foreclose on

Tom's house? Before UEC had purchased Westover Park, Tom's home was listed as additional collateral for the ongoing construction at Westover Park. Tom remembered seeing a release signed at closing, removing his home from the loan. "Sorry, we can't seem to locate that release, and you are now responsible for the outstanding debt of $245,000."

Tom got home that evening and told his wife, Penwahee, what was happening. They were going to lose their house. There was not going to be any payment on the $465,000 note owed to Tom. UEC was continuing to scam Westover Park by keeping all the note payments under the protection of the bankruptcy court. A very ignorant bankruptcy judge in Nashville was handling the case for the government, and didn't understand timeshare or the urgency to protect the assets. All Tom's accounts had been frozen or seized by the IRS to cover the United Equities Corporation's unpaid taxes, and Tom had $385 in his pocket.

Tom's wife looked deep into his eyes and said "I didn't marry you for your money, and we still have each other."

Tom didn't sleep that weekend. He just stared at the creek next to the house when outside, or the ceiling in his bedroom when inside. He just kept thinking of what he could do to once again pull Westover Park out of the jaws of failure.

What if? Two words everyone should learn the true meaning of when things are really desperate. What if this? What if that? What if we did this and they were willing to do that? Then what if they did this while the next person did that?

Build the chain of "what ifs" link by link. Soon you will have a chain long enough and strong enough to reach you and pull you out of the mud. The power of positive thinking. The desire to achieve a goal. The IQ to develop an achievable plan that will solve all the problems, and the ability to sell the program to all those affected. If one link in the chain breaks, the whole chain fails. A risky, all-or-nothing chain of "what ifs" would be required to salvage Westover Park.

By late Sunday night, Tom had a plan. Monday morning at 9:00 am, Tom and I started to build his chain by calling his end-loan mortgagor. Yes, it could happen if you could get this person to do such and such; then the banks, the old man Cap Paine who had the original underlying mortgage on the property, the IRS agent, the FBI. Everyone signed an agreement to let Tom take over. By week's end, Tom was in

Nashville, negotiating to purchase all assets of United Equities Corporation out of bankruptcy court. Sixty days later he was once again in charge – and he owned Westover Park.

It was in shambles, and Tom contacted three salespeople and purchased a handful of "ups" from another marketing firm. He needed cash flow. Over the next month, sales were made. IRS payments were being made on schedule and construction resumed. Through all these long, hard months, Tom was able to accomplish one thing no one could believe: not one person lost the use of one week's vacation at any point during this ordeal. Tom's secretary was also the maid. Tom himself cleaned the pool and weeded the gardens. He was going to make it. Westover Park was once again breathing. His plan had worked. But then it happened. Two negative forces came together: the old man Cap Paine's greed, and a lawyer willing to help him chase it.

Paine, the original landowner, had an underlying mortgage on the adjoining property, and he re-instated the foreclosure proceedings. Although he had a signed agreement with Tom not to, and Tom was current on his payments, he was proceeding with foreclosure anyway

Why? Tom was current on his note and all his payments with Cap Paine. All options for the adjoining property were current. Apparently the old man had a buyer for the remaining land Tom had optioned, and he would receive far more than he was going to get from his original agreement with Tom. It was greed, nothing more than pure greed. Tom talked with his lawyer. Yes, it was illegal for him to foreclose, but the docket is backed up for four years in Sevier County. It would take four years for Tom to clear up the flaw this would create on the title of the real estate. With no clear title, no end-loan mortgage could be sold. Who could last that long? Talk about justice delayed being justice denied. This went further than that. This was now the new judicial art form in the practice of law, by lawyers whose integrity was equal to that of shit dust. Tom's options were to let this old man steal his land back, or tie it up in court for years. He knew he would never get a local judge to give him an award for damages against an old, retired man even if he deserved them. Equal justice to all, my ass. So the state legislature passes laws to protect its citizens, and then the judges decide to enforce them unequally, depending on who knows them or whether or not they really like the law. If they give a ruling that interprets the legislative law in a manner that really is not what was met by the legislator, their ruling becomes "case law." This is the judge's way of really changing the interpretation of a law, created from the original bill, and passed by the legislator. This is legislation from the bench. Balance of power my ass. Then there is a court of law and a court of equity, but that changes to where all courts are supposed to give rulings by references. Some lawyers reference statute, and some lawyers reference case law. The judge can give an equitable judgment – in other words, forget all the law – this is how I feel, and I am the judge. Now that we have the playing field completely indefinable, let's open the door for lawyers with their smoke-and-mirrors show. People can say a few Hail Marys, and Mary had a little lamb, and hope that the lawyers can muddy the waters so badly that the judge will compromise and give each side something out of total confusion over the case in front of his court. The people who hired the lawyer clearly don't understand what is going on. This way each lawyer can claim some level of victory, with no winner, no loser, and large legal fees for both lawyers. And the Judge stands a chance of being re-elected, because he didn't really piss off either side too badly. After all, the judge knows that both lawyers are going to convince their clients they did better than their opponent, and the judge must really have liked them. The scariest part of all of this is that the people who hired the lawyers also have the right to vote when electing a judge. It's democracy at its best: the populace rules; morons can vote.

Tom decided there was a third alternative. He may not have personally been able to get the benefit of the equity from the optioned property, but he sure as hell could see that the old man and his slimeball lawyer didn't profit by this act either.

Tom filed bankruptcy, thereby giving all his assets to be dispersed by the bankruptcy court trustee to the IRS, the local creditors, and the local banks. If there was any money left, Tom would receive it, but there wasn't going to be anything left. After all that effort to resurrect the Westover Park development, a greedy old man had now broken the chain that had almost pulled him free of the mud. At least Cap Paine would not get one penny more than had originally been agreed for his land, as the bankruptcy court trumps the local court's jurisdiction. Westover Park was now over.

Tom and his wife were able to cut enough firewood off his mountain property to stay alive that year. He purchased a $1,500 used Pontiac Bonneville so he could commute to work in Maryville. They had saved almost $3,000 by year's end. Soon Tom's house and his land were sold by the bankruptcy court to repay the bank note that had been used to collateralize the condo construction note. Tom and Penwahee were now homeless. The only good that came out of any of this was that the bank was not going to be able to take Tom's parents' house, which had also been used as collateral for the note at Heritage Park. Tom had been successful in retiring all of the debt that was owed from the original loan for the construction of Westover Park prior to filing bankruptcy. His parents hadn't lost any money in the Westover Park investment and were able to retain their home. Then the most devastating blow of all came to Tom, Penwahee and his parents in a meeting at The University of Tennessee hospital. They all sat there in a room with Tom's brother's doctor. His brother had developed Pneumocystis pneumonia. He was also developing spots on the back of his eyes. This was common with people who were losing their immune systems. Although there were no tests at the time to confirm this, his symptoms were similar to those of a new disease that was showing up throughout the country called HIV2, and some months later renamed AIDS.

Tom and Penwahee visited his brother regularly at his home on White Oak Lane for the next nine months. His mom and dad were doing all they could, but the horror of what was happening caused them to drink more, and now they were barely functioning alcoholics. The whole family, Tom his wife and parents intentionally avoided all their friends as it was not yet known if or how the disease was transferred. It could be by casual contact, and any of them might be contagious. Tom's brother died a slow and painful death. Life was not good. If this wasn't bad enough, now the entire timeshare industry was under federal investigation. Because of Tom's affiliation with United Equities Corporation, he too was being investigated. As one of Tom's best friends, I knew I was getting closer to that place I didn't want to be.

Chapter 16

Regal Tower, every King needs to build a shrine.

Tom and Penwahee were able to stay in their mountain house for six months after it was sold. The purchasers, Daisy and Trish Wilhoit, were kind, and they displayed tremendous grace once they learned the whole story of what everyone was going through. These were two people who truly believed in giving forward and were a great example of how people should live their lives. It was in fact these six months of time that allowed Tom and Penwahee to pull themselves together and formulate a plan to move forward. The value of a six month reprieve to rest and recuperate from the last hellish two years may have been the difference in them ever being able to be successful again in the future. The Wilhoits could sense the need for this young couple to have some time to collect themselves. Although not their cross to bear, they insisted on Tom and Penwahee enjoy the home and remaining without the stress of an immediate move. During that time, Penwahee was pregnant with Tom's first child. Tom named him David. He was born two weeks before they had to move. They had both decided they wanted to stay in Townsend, so Tom went looking for a cheap lot where they could locate a trailer. Tom had given away all his hunting dogs to good homes, because he could not afford to feed them. He kept Penwahee's dog, a large male Rottweiler she had raised in their home to be her companion while Tom was at work.

I knew a developer by the name of Harold King who was looking for someone to head up the sales effort of a new condo high-rise he was in the process of building in Maryville, Tennessee. Although I felt Harold had hopelessly overbuilt the market, I did know that if these condos could be sold, Tom could sell them. Nobody was better at marketing and sales than Tom.

Harold hired Tom at their first meeting. Harold was an old, established real estate broker and CPA, and he believed Tom could really help him.

The building consisted of six floors, with eleven condominiums per floor. Regal Tower was very typical of a rental high-rise building. There was a pool on the main floor, but other than that, the building was uneventful and boring. No flash or flair; very clinical and stark.

Harold and his wife had joined two units together on the top floor, and the building was in its final phase of construction.

Tom was busy every day, cold-calling people in the Blount County phone book, asking if they would take a tour of the model that had been completed behind the main building. Not many takers. There were several obvious problems that were hampering his ability to get anyone else interested in looking at a unit.

First, they were overpriced. A two-bedroom, two-bathroom unit cost $118,000. To put that in context with the Maryville market at the time, a two-bedroom, two-bathroom house only cost $60,000 to $70,000 in some of the better neighborhoods, locations actually nicer than where the project was built.

The market for these condos was mostly "empty nesters" – those who had raised their family, retired from work, and grown tired of yard maintenance. To think that someone was going to pay on a mortgage for thirty years, finally get it paid off, and then go into another mortgage to purchase a condo was stupid. Harold was quite wealthy and really knew better; he just hadn't thought about it long enough before building the project.

Furthermore, in a move of incredible misjudgment, Harold let his wife take charge of the decorating. What a disaster that became. She decided she wanted to impress everyone with her sense of contemporary fashion. All the drab gray concrete hallways were covered with a drab gray carpet. No positive gain there. The entrance was a wild mix of tile and mountain stone. As you strolled through the lobby, a color scheme of drab concrete gray was blended with the color mauve, kind of a pinky purple. She had an art deco carpet custom made in mauve and gray for the lobby floor. Yeah, this made all the grandfathers and grandmothers want to buy; nothing like marketing to that large group of new wave, edgy punk rock, Maryville retirees. Of course, this was a plan that had to work because the boss's wife said so. After all she must have had lots of real estate marketing and sales experience in her previous job as a stewardess for the airlines that flew out of this dumpy Knoxville airport. I guess if one were to take the time to think about it, she was able to market her pussy to Harold, so she had to be able to market anything!

Tom mused in his mind how Harold's wife might have enjoyed visions of grandeur over the shrine she had created for herself. Maybe she would be discovered by some Hollywood producer. Imagine a show called "A Day in the Life of Regal Tower." Think how many people were going to be inspired with her decorating skills, and the amazing story one could write about the cool, trend-setting old people who lived there.

As if the design, price, and out-of-control wife weren't bad enough, Tom had to deal with the harlot that Harold had hired as a salesperson before Tom arrived at the condo project. Viney was her name, and blowjobs were her game. Trust me, when it comes to getting a good real estate listing, nothing works better than good, old-fashioned sex.

In Maryville, all the ugly, fat, middle-aged and old men liked Viney, and all their wives hated her. It was so obvious that it was totally embarrassing for Tom to have to work with her. She had blonde hair in a Farrah Fawcett shag, with heavy blue eyeliner and bright red lips. A young man's dick would get soft if it got anywhere near her face, but to an old, rich retiree she was eye candy. Better yet, she was no tease; she was willing to perform whenever a potential buyer called her out over her flirting.

Obviously, Tom couldn't compete with Viney's sales techniques. He couldn't do anything about Harold's wife's decorating failures. He could focus on doing something about the affordability of the unit. While brainstorming over ways to market the property, Tom came up with a sales program that would use a new form of financing. It would be like a backward mortgage. Tom called it the Regal Tower Life Estate.

What if? What if a mortgage could be designed that gave the owner a life estate that reduced in value until the person who purchased the condominium was deceased? What would need to happen that could allow this to happen? What yield would be necessary for an institution to purchase the note securing these Life Estates? How would one design a mortgage where the new owners never had to make a payment, but enjoyed the value they had accrued from their existing residence? How hard would it be to sell such a concept?

It took a few weeks, but Tom figured it out. The homeowner who wanted to move into the new condo would give the title to their house for a Life Estate in the new Regal Tower Condominium. Now, as a new condo owner, they would get a life estate deed to the condominium. The only adjustment necessary would be if the home was worth more than the number of years remaining in a person's life, or if they passed away soon after acquiring their condo. The solution was a life estate rebate chart. All you would need to know would be the age of the purchaser. A chart could be designed that reduced the value of the initial contribution (the house) of, let's say, 6 to 10 percent each year. If a person died unexpectedly before their normal mortality, the purchase of the mortgage would simply rebate some of the principal back to the heirs. Tom's research showed that 98 percent of the population dies within one year of their calculated mortality table. Not much risk here for an investment group.

I thought about the implications that this could have to society in general. What if a person could sell their home to an investor group, retain a life estate in their home, and take money from the sale to buy an annuity that would increase their cash flow? Those who were retired could enjoy an increase in income to offset the effect inflation was having on their fixed retirement income. At their death, their home's title would pass to that investor who purchased the house. This one program could salvage the entire federal Social Security Program without any cost to the government or future generations. After all, the future generations didn't have anything invested to lose after the present life estate owner died. Maybe the future generations would get off their lazy ass and start working harder, and buy a home of their own.

Harold King also loved the idea, yet he knew he needed a large financial institution to fund all these life estates. Harold decided to send Tom to Irvine, California in effort to sell the program to Metropolitan Life Insurance Company. Harold and Tom's plan was to try to be paid a quarter of a point with each closing of each life estate. At the time, Met Life had six billion dollars in liquid assets that were earning less than 4 percent. They also had just purchased Century 21, the largest national real estate franchise in the country. Their agents could arrange the purchase of the condo by selling the life estate, sell the owner an annuity for additional cash flow, and then list the home that was conveyed for the condo as collateral. Once the occupants died at some date in the future, Century 21 would immediately create another listing for the next person needing a life estate. Century 21 – a company whose business model was designed on the concept of two listings for one sale. This would generate more listings than imaginable. They might have to change this name to Century 31 or 41.

After meeting with the actuaries and returning to Tennessee, Tom received no response from their meetings. The actuary who earlier had been so engaging with Harold would no longer return Harold's phone calls. About four months later, I was reading in the Wall Street Journal how HUD and Met Life were going to try a new program with 200 families called a "Reverse Annuity Mortgage." I drove to Townsend to see Tom, thinking his deal had actually happened. As he read the article, it was clear he knew nothing about these new mortgages. Maybe they were already working on this concept before you contacted them," I said. I could tell Tom was devastated, as this was all he had been talking about for over a year. He told me he had a headache but thanks for letting him know about the article. He said he needed to take a nap.

I left and Tom went to bed. He fell into a deep sleep and began to dream.

...The dogs moved forward as a pair; one large and one small. Their noses twitched at every scent as they meandered without purpose across the earth. They were very healthy; obviously well fed and unworked. Although unused and no longer needed, their instincts were still trying to express themselves despite the dogs' kept lifestyles. The only purpose remaining in their uneventful life was to eat food and lick their masters while they wagged their tails. So sad was the fact that their lives were without any greater purpose. As I personalized these kept animals, I sensed that a great percentage of society bonded with their existence.

The idea that at some point in yesteryear these fine animals thrived from the hunt, the fight, the kill, and the birth of new members of their new pack was almost unimaginable...

While he was working at Regal Tower, Tom was still looking for a place to live. He only had a few more months of occupancy after the sale of his mountain house. He was urgently trying to relocate his pregnant wife before she gave birth. He went to the Blount County courthouse. It was the first time he had tried to research real estate title in a courthouse. Everyone who worked there was very helpful, especially a title attorney named Rob Goddard. Rob kindly took a few minutes to show him some basics. Tom was continuing to look for a place to put a trailer he wanted to purchase, when he bumped into a large tract of land owned by an attorney named J.D. Lee. It was a defunct development that might have a cheap lot.

The more Tom looked into the property, the more he understood all the problems.

It was like a déjà vu of Westover Park. The entire history of this property before him was being told to him, one document at a time. J.D. Lee, the developer, had made some of the exact same mistakes that Tom made at Westover Park. The only difference was that Lee had never realized what his mistakes were. Tom noticed that the entire file was still an active file in the Knoxville bankruptcy court. Still active after fifteen years? The more he researched the documents, at the courthouse and in bankruptcy court, the more certain he was he could come up with a business plan that would have a solution for all the problems. The power of positive thinking; the power of what if? Build the chain of what if's, and pull Laurel Valley out of the mud.

Tom was a different man now. He had learned some valuable lessons. You don't have to have the best cards in a poker game to win. You just need to play those cards well, and you can walk away with all the chips. The lessons learned from trying to sell the Regal Tower Life Estate still burned hot in Tom's mind. Maybe it was true Met Life had been working on the same concept for months before Tom came up with the Regal Tower life estate plan. But why didn't they tell Harold they were also working on a similar idea? Why not work together? Tom had so much to offer on the subject. Tom had thought of every angle and future problem imaginable. As an example, never should a reverse annuity mortgage be given to anyone living in any property that didn't have a real estate management company in place to make sure the property was properly maintained. Who is going to put money into a house to maintain it when they no longer own the house? This would create another financial opportunity for the Real Estate offices to generate revenue. Where is the money coming from for insurance and the upcoming funerals? Why not put aside monies for a funeral at the closing of the transaction? Imagine getting fees for managing the funeral escrow account? Tom could have really helped with the Reverse Annuity mortgage. Now the only thing certain is that the government, by insuring these mortgagees, is going to get stuck with a lot of decrepit old houses. Tom knew what to do to prevent this from happening, but no one was asking. Yes, Tom was a different man now and he had learned some valuable lessons in life. He had also learned some valuable lessons in business. He had advanced up another one of those proverbial steps in life that makes you a little smarter than before. There is really no way to hurry the process. You go through life, and all of a sudden there is another one of those steps in front of you. You can give up on advancing and stay the bottom of the stair, or you can figure out how to climb your way over it and take your life to the next level. Sometimes there is nothing wrong with doing nothing. The timing of the moment may not be right for you, and the smart move is to wait until you feel the moment is right. Lay low and strike when you are ready. But sometimes the moment is exactly right and this is when you need to plan carefully, work hard and work smart. Working hard may not be enough to be successful. Working smart may not have enough energy in it to be successful. But when you have a plan you have thought through from every angle, and you work hard and smart at executing that plan, you will almost always succeed.

Tom told his boss, Harold, about what he thought he could do to purchase the property well below market price, and Harold was excited. One of Harold's favorite expressions was "Bought right, half sold." The whole prospect of being able to straighten out a real estate development no one else could straighten out challenged Harold. Over the years everyone had tried – many developers, many law firms, and many government agencies – all to no avail. As he listened to Tom's plan to resurrect the defunct development, Harold would feed off the different ideas and approaches, often improving them or offering a better method or solution. It was very clear to both men that they could work together and do what no one else could do. They knew they could make Laurel Valley a viable community.

The plan was very involved, and timing at every stage was critical. It would be like a military invasion, or like a huge poker game with the contestants being the FDIC, the Resolution Trust Corporation, the bankruptcy court, the Blount County Planning Commission, the existing lot owners, the County Commission in charge of various bond monies held in escrow, and the bank that was going to lend Tom and

Harold the money to develop the project. There were survey issues and real estate title issues never before addressed in the State of Tennessee. Playing the cards perfectly through this stage of the game would only get them started. If successful, they had to build, totally create a new market, and then sell the new, soon-to-be-revitalized community previously called "The Smokies," located in the Laurel Valley area of Townsend. Participating and competing in an existing market is light years away from knowing how to create a market for a product that has no presence in that market. Harold and Tom were up for the challenge. Ten years later it became undisputable when it came to creating a market in real estate Harold and Tom were the masters of the game.

Chapter 17
Laurel Valley – The Beginning

…I was overlooking a large expanse of field. The grass was dead. Green onion sprouts were pushing their way toward the sun. A large cedar tree held a flock of doves, and a small covey of quail reluctantly stepped out from the edge of the wood line.

A male cardinal landed close to me, its blood-red breast gleaming in the morning sun. A large Cooper's hawk descended upon our environment, scattering all those peacefully enjoying the moment. One unfortunate dove was caught in its talons; crushed and bleeding, it was soon to be consumed…

It was Tom's first day, and his first assignment was to go to Laurel Valley and secure the border. This may sound simple enough, but this was no man's land. For decades, anyone could do whatever they wanted on this land, as no one was claiming it or exercising any right of ownership. Marijuana fields, dirt bike racetracks, bait stations for poaching; you name it and it was going on here. Furthermore, there would be no lifeline in this wilderness. No cell service, no companion, only Tom. Being able to survive as a lone wolf was Tom's only chance. He had no fear of the circumstances and enjoyed the thought of the challenge. Tom went to the Co-op and got some fence posts, barbed wire, and other such supplies and drove to the front of the property. It was a beautiful day; Tom took off his shirt and started installing the metal fence posts. Tom was the first employee at Laurel Valley. The problem was that neither Tom nor Harold really owned the property. While researching the title, Tom found a flaw in the Deed of Trust securing the promissory note held by the FDIC and subsequently the Resolution Trust Corporation. The government had a collateral position on all the lots from the previously failed developer, but failed to mention the common properties and the underlying road system in the subdivisions in its deed of trust. Further research showed that the roadways and the area for the golf course were labeled as common properties on the master deed, filed with HUD in Washington, D.C. As this was an active bankruptcy, Tom made an offer to the bankruptcy court for a quitclaim to the common properties. Tom had convinced the attorney who was in charge of the file to sign this quitclaim and get it approved, as Tom was trying to purchase a lot and needed a legal access to his lot. Tom offered the lawyer $5,000. The lawyer told Tom this was the first time in his life he felt he was selling something that was worth nothing, but he was going to make a nice paycheck of 10 percent, and agreed to the sale. Tom knew he had just acquired the key to the entire property. A bankruptcy judge had sold him the right-of-ways needed to develop the property further. All the previous lot owners could use the roads, but any new owner would have to go through Harold and Tom to acquire access. It was now time for the next move in their plans. They were going to exercise their rights to protect their property. At the same time, Tom was negotiating directly with the Resolution Trust Corporation to purchase the remaining land. There were about 2,200 acres in this tract of land. Tom offered the man in charge of the asset $200,000. The appraisal showed the property valued at $12 million, and the records in the Blount county courthouse valued the property at $900,000. Tom pointed out to everyone that they couldn't sell any of the property allowing anyone to use his easements without him agreeing to their use. Due to the mountainous nature of the area, there was no other access to the property.

People would occasionally drive by and ask Tom what he was doing. "Building a fence," was his reply. "One day this is going to be a beautiful mountain community." Most laughed and drove on. One day, a man asked if he needed any help. Tom said yes. This man became the second employee in Laurel Valley. His name was Eddy. After a few weeks, it became obvious that they were never going to be able to truly secure the boundary. Every Saturday or Sunday, someone would break down the fence or tear the posts out of the ground. It seemed like an endless effort of repairing fences every Monday morning before they could start the work they had to do for the day.

Tom and Eddy were tired of being punked by the four-wheel-drive club out of Alcoa. These were the people who were tearing down their boundary fences every weekend and tearing up the freshly graded roadways. This four-wheel-drive club would arrive in ten to twenty Jeeps and several four-wheel-drive trucks, with the occupants often quite drunk. After throwing a chain over a fence post and pulling it out of the ground, they would all charge through the hole, en route to the mountain logging roads that honeycombed the acreage. They would then exit in a different location, leaving another breach in the boundary fence. Tom drove to Maryville to meet Sheriff Avery Mills. After some brief conversation about the problem, Tom asked if he would please send a county patrol car up there next Saturday morning. The Sheriff horse-laughed at Tom. He said he wouldn't ever let the deputies go to Townsend. As a matter of fact, he forbade them to go past the Foothills Parkway Bridge in Walland. "Townsend is lawless. I am amazed you think people will buy property up there. No outsider has purchased property in Townsend in over ten years. There is no phone service in most of the district, and our police radios won't work in those deep hollers," said the Sheriff

Tom stared at the Sheriff, and said, "I live in Townsend and I am an outsider. No one bothers me." The Sheriff, somewhat taken back by Tom's remark and somewhat embarrassed, then said, "The last time we went to Townsend, your lawless neighbors cut trees down across the road and tried to steal the patrol car. The time before that, they blocked the road and rolled burning tires at my deputies, who were there trying to serve a warrant. You are going to have to take care of your own problem as there will be no help from us in Townsend."

Tom stared at the Sheriff for another five to ten seconds, and said in a low tone, "As you wish." He then got up and drove back to Townsend. When he got to Townsend, he and Eddy discussed some of the options he thought might work.

What really pissed Tom and Eddy off is the way the members of this four-wheel-drive club would parade around the breached fence, brandishing shotguns and pistols, as if daring someone to say anything to them.

That next Friday, one of Tom's bear-hunting friends whose name we'll not mention said to Tom, "Tomorrow morning, me find a weak place on their Jeeps, and me bring some friends."

As anticipated, the four-wheel-drive club arrived, and the leader of the club, a quintessential redneck, got out of his Jeep. Two of his lieutenants stepped out of the Jeep next to him, each holding a shotgun as if to protect their leader. The leader began to wrap a chain around the fence post, when the first shot ripped through his Jeep's radiator.

Just after the first shot was fired, lead started raining down upon all the Jeeps and trucks. Radiators and tires were the targets of choice, as people ran screaming from the vehicles. They hid behind the trucks, waving white tee shirts and screaming for mercy. The two lieutenants immediately dropped their shotguns and raised their hands, as they couldn't see where the volley of fire was coming from. The lead kept coming, and they then decided it would be safer if they jumped into the drainage ditch of the road.

Bear hunters stick together, and when one asks for help, dozens show up in support. Carefully hidden and in full camouflage, the bear hunters owned the high ground above the road, and the Jeep club didn't have a chance. They couldn't see the bear hunters and were too scared to shoot back out of fear the targets of choice would change from radiators and tires to humans. Quietly the bear hunters melted into the surrounding forests, leaving the entire club without one operable vehicle. The fence breaching by the four-wheel-drives stopped that day. The wind blew the news of the incident from the Townsend hollers all the way back to Alcoa, and there were very few trespassers in the future. It took about a year, but finally the government settled on a sales price of $300,000 and Harold and Tom now owned the entire 2,200 acres.

Approximately three months later, as workers were grading out the foundation for the future clubhouse, a brand-new four-wheel-drive Toyota came zooming over the hill. The two teenage boys in it had decided that the "No Trespassing" sign didn't apply to them. Seeing that they had inadvertently driven right into a construction site, they swung their truck around, and while speeding away, flung gravel on several of the construction workers. They drove over the hill to the future location of the first tee, to avoid capture by the irate construction crew. As they came to the bottom of the slope, their truck sank into the soft mud so far that they couldn't open the doors to get out of the vehicle.

The boys climbed out their windows and stood in the back of the truck for several long minutes.

Tom took off his nail belt, and he and Mick went to the edge of the hill. As the boys stared up at them, Tom pointed at them, then gestured for them to come up the hill.

As the boys approached the top of the hill where Tom and Mick were, the older one immediately started telling Tom he could call his father and his father would pay for all the damage he may have caused. Tom just stared at him, then turned to Mick and said, "Get the high lift and bury that truck." With that said, Tom just proceeded to walk back to the jobsite.

The boy started crying and grieving while he followed Tom, pleading for him to call his dad. Tom stopped, turned around, and said, "If I were you, I wouldn't keep following me back to that jobsite. The men you flung gravel on want to kick your ass."

Now the other boy also started crying, and Tom stopped and just stared at them. He then said, "Get in my truck; the blue Chevy over there. I am going to take you to the phone in Townsend so you can call your father." Tom told Mick, who was getting on the high lift, to wait until he returned before he did anything.

Tom drove the boys to the lone payphone, located at highway 321. He listened to the boy spin a tale to his father over what had happened. Eventually, the boy asked Tom if he would talk to his dad.

Tom turned the radio up in his truck and told the boys to sit in his truck while he talked to the father. This way, they couldn't hear what Tom was saying to the father. The father was falling all over himself trying to sound sorry, strong, non-threatening, but still bold all at the same time. He was obviously worried over his son and his son's friend's safety. After about a minute of his yammering, he paused and asked Tom if he was still on the phone.

Tom started by saying, "You can stop worrying. No one who works for me would ever hurt either of these children. The problem is that you keep enabling them to behave like this by always bailing them out. I can leave them here at this phone booth or pull their truck out and send them back to you at Farragut. You are the dad and it is your call, but let me warn you, if you don't hold them accountable for what they have done, one day someone is really going to hurt them. They may be young boys now, but soon they will be adult men, and you won't be able to help them. Now I have a son, and if you want some help from one father to another I have a suggestion for you."

The man paused a moment and then said, "What do you suggest?"

Tom said, "Tell them the only way I will let them go is if they come back at 8:00 tomorrow morning with rakes and shovels, and repair all the ruts they made. Of course, that is more than they could do in a day, and after a couple of hours I will let them go home. A couple hours of hard work, a few blisters, a few mosquito bites, and a little sunburn would go a long way in getting them to appreciate other people's property. I will be here all day, and I will watch them for the entire two hours, to make sure they are safe."

"Are you sure they will be safe?" asked the father.

"Judging from what I have just seen, they will be a lot safer than letting them drive around in that truck," said Tom.

Addresses and phone numbers were exchanged. The next morning, the two boys arrived and were put to work. Two hours later, Tom told them to go home. The next week, Tom received a letter of appreciation from the father. As Tom read the letter, he thought to himself, "That's how we do it in the South." Mountain justice – you sincerely apologize for your trespass, pay penance, and you are then forgiven.

It was midsummer, and Tom was bush hogging an area that had grown over since the previous developer had cleared part of the woods for the future back nine. Tom and Eddy had spent the first part of the summer removing all the trees, and identifying where the originally constructed nine-hole golf course had been. After removing the brush from the last fifteen years, they were going to need to plow and till everything to grade, and then start laying out the irrigation system. Tom was driving the tractor by the sixth hole, when he felt as if someone had taken an open hand and smacked him in the back of the head. Immediately the sensation changed to something like being stung by a hornet, followed by a dull, burning numbness. Tom had been shot. He stopped the tractor and lay behind the rear tractor wheel, not knowing if he should run or stay covered. This wasn't the first time Tom had been shot.

During one of his South Dakota pheasant hunts, when another hunter accidentally shot at a low-flying bird. Tom had caught a few pellets on the back of his coat, and a few on his head, but he was not hurt.

He had also taken a 9mm round through his left thumb in a fight in Sevierville, several years earlier.

The third time, he was shot while dove hunting with two friends. He had been hit by a careless hunter while crossing an open field, but sustained no injury.

This was the fourth time, but this time the intensity of the blast was much greater and his skin was broken by the pellets. He got up and jogged away from the tractor with his head ducked. It was late afternoon, and he was the only one who was still working. Upon arriving at his truck, he pulled his Remington 870 pump shotgun from the rack in his truck and got the binoculars from his dash. He scouted the surrounding woods, yet saw no one. Tom started to drive to the hospital, but by the time he got to Walland he turned around. The best he could tell was that he had two pellets under his scalp. There was no law in this end of Blount County, and he didn't have a clue who had done it, or why. His wife would be too scared if he told her, and he knew if he told Harold, he would not let Tom go back to work out of fear for his safety.

Laurel Valley was a great opportunity for Tom. He really needed this chance if he hoped to once again demonstrate his talents as a real estate developer. This situation would screw it up for sure. By the time he got back to Townsend, he had decided to go to Charlie Williams's house and have Charlie remove the pellets and dress his wound.

When Tom arrived, Charlie was inside drinking with another middle-aged gentleman. They cleaned off the blood, poured some of "Charles's Finest" homemade moonshine over his head, and carefully removed three pellets that had just broken the skin. Tom stripped down and showered off the scent of the moonshine in Charlie's bathroom. The place where the pellets had been was already starting to scab. The bleeding had stopped. Tom went home, showered again like he always did when he first got home, and ate dinner with Penwahee. Charlie and Tom agreed that it would never be discussed with anyone, as Tom's pregnant wife should never know of the incident.

And the winds in the mountains started to blow back to Tom over the course of the next week that the reason he'd been "dusted" was because he had inadvertently bush hogged over someone's pot plants.

From then on, Tom worked armed with a Smith and Wesson .357 revolver. This was the same gun that Tom used for bear and boar hunting when he ran his hounds. Tom was known for his accuracy with that pistol, from several incidents in which he had dispatched either of the two species under extreme conditions. Everyone knew that if you shot at Tom, he would shoot back. All the bear hunters also knew that if Tom could see the target, he could hit the target. Luckily there were no more firearm incidents.

The ground in Laurel Valley had a serious problem. All the fairways were covered with large numbers of softball-sized rocks that were clearly visible after Tom and Eddy had plowed and disked the earth. If a future golfer were to hit his club on one of these rocks, not only would the club be ruined, but the golfer's arm might also be harmed. They tried many mechanical methods of trying to remove the rock and debris. But there was too much trash and debris in the soil from the plowing, and every effort failed.

The only solution would be to hire a large number of people to pick up the rocks, and dump them in the creeks or adjoining wood line.

Tom called the Blount County unemployment office and asked how many of the workers were making over six dollars an hour when they went on the unemployment rolls. The lady said that over 90 percent were making less than that. He told her he needed twenty people for two months. She assured him she would have them in a couple of days. Only one person showed up, and worked for less than one hour.

The next week, Tom called the unemployment office again, and asked how many people were drawing unemployment in Blount County due to lack of work. She said approximately 1,800. He told her he wanted to hire all 1,800 unemployed persons for two months at six dollars an hour. That next week four workers showed, three quit before lunch, and one completed the first day and then quit.

Toward the end of that same week, Tom got a call from a woman on Carrs Creek who said for five dollars an hour – cash – she and two of her friends would come pick up the rocks. Being desperate, Tom hired them. Welcome to the black market economy. It is this underground economy that in later years would cause tens of millions of Mexican and Guatemalan workers to migrate to the United States. It is also the failure to understand the dynamics of this underground economy by political leaders that in later years would throw the country into a lengthy depression.

Over the next two months, the rocks were picked up, the clubhouse built, and Laurel Valley prepared for its grand opening. Congressman Jimmy Duncan brought Tom a flag that had been flown over the Nation's Capital, and attended the ceremony as the guest of honor. Tom hired a cook and everyone had a great barbeque. The Laurel Valley Country Club was officially open.

Staffing in Townsend during the late '80s was a challenge. Let's use the rock-picking girls as an example. They wanted to work, but only for cash so their "crazy checks" or disabled benefit checks from the federal government would keep coming. The week that the club was to open, Tom had sent the three rock-picking girls to Knoxville to pick out a matching outfit of skirts and blouses. He had decided to hire them as waitresses. His instructions were clear. They were to have a plaid Scottish accent to their uniforms. He gave them some money and sent them to Knoxville. They were also to go to a very upscale hair salon for a "makeover." After all, these girls had been picking up rocks all summer, and a little effort to tame the cavewoman hairdos seemed in order. A young lady Tom knew ran an upscale hair salon in Knoxville. It was known as Metz and Kerchner.

Upon arriving, one of the girls from the group blurted out to the receptionist, "We were sent here by Tom for a powder and a douche." Obviously, these were not Tom's instructions. The next day the girls were to meet Tom's wife to be trained in the proper method of waiting a table. Eating out to these girls meant going to the Shoney's breakfast bar. They all had brought their new outfits. They changed in the clubhouse ladies' room and presented themselves. Tom's wife just stared at him. The tops of the outfits were okay, but the bottoms... The girls had purchased pleated mini-skirts that were cut all the way up to their private parts. Trust me, no insult is intended to how good they looked – all three of them had fine figures. The problem was that they were dressed to work at a strip joint, not a country club. When Tom mentioned that the skirts would have to be longer, they said they would quit. They were in fact quite proud of their skirts, and how good they looked in them. Tom gave up, as the club needed waitresses, and the grand opening was only a few days away. Everything went fine with the uniforms, until one day one of the husbands came by and saw what his wife was wearing at work. He told the other husbands. The next day Tom had no waitresses. Staffing the kitchen wasn't any easier. Tom had hired a large Cherokee Indian named John to cook. He seemed like a very nice man. One evening Tom received a phone call from the club golf pro. The Cherokee had gotten drunk on the cooking wine and was holding a waitress hostage with a knife in the kitchen. Tom told the club golf pro to please ask all the patrons to leave, get them to sign a paper with their phone number, and say that we would treat them to a free dinner in the future.

Tom locked and loaded his pistol – the police still would not come to Townsend when called – and went to the club. He decided he would keep the pistol in his hand behind his back, enter the kitchen with authority, and shout at the waitress for not having served food to her tables yet. Hoping this would give her the opportunity to leave the kitchen, he would then ask the Cherokee why the place was such a mess. If the Cherokee attacked him or anyone else he was going to shoot him in the head.

When Tom entered the door, the cook immediately let the waitress go, walked two steps to the sink, and started washing dishes. The girl scurried out; Tom followed her and told everyone to go home. Tom returned to the kitchen and asked John the Cherokee why he was drunk, and his reply was, "Tom, I have been working my ass off." Tom told him to leave the kitchen and wait in the foyer while he called John's wife to drive him home. When she arrived, John quietly obeyed his wife as she helped him into the car. Now Tom no longer had a cook.

Laurel Valley opened the front nine holes that year, and they opened the back nine two years later. It was a fine course, and all the employees were well trained and a pure joy to work with. Each week, though, something would happen to force Tom to ban a player from the course for a year, or fire an employee, or deal with some other type of screwed-up situation. One week he had a player pull a gun over a golf bet, a waitress fired for giving a member a blowjob for fifty dollars (caught in the act), and another membership revoked because an adult male tried to molest a twelve-year-old girl at the pool. Every week there was some problem requiring a judgment call that would piss somebody off when Tom attempted to enforce some code of ethics or socially acceptable behavior. This continued for all nine years that Tom worked for Mr. King as Project Director in Laurel Valley.

Land sales were going well. Actually, Tom phased the entire development into a pre-sale style of presentation. Most of the inventory was sold before he was finished building each subdivision. In addition to real estate sales, Tom had started a home-construction division that stayed booked over a year out, all at cost plus 15 percent for the service. Over the next few years, Laurel Valley had grown into one of Blount County's finest communities. Many of the homes were in an overnight rental program with Tom's real estate agency, and he was able to generate substantial revenue for the homeowners. By default, Tom had been running the property owners' association for all of its eight years, as a favor to the owners. It seemed he could not get anyone to help with the task. But they were eight years of very positive meetings. Questions asked and answered. Problems politely discussed by everyone, until everyone unanimously agreed on a solution. It was a time of year that Tom looked forward to, as he enjoyed seeing all the people he had either sold property to or built homes for. The meetings were like a big neighborhood homecoming.

Throughout the year Tom would call board meetings, but seldom would anyone show. "Take care of it for us, Tom." Tom would do what he thought was best, and then the next year the membership would ratify his actions. Tom needed a break, as he had been working six days a week, and over twelve hours a day, for almost eight years. Then it happened. Tom apparently had his first stroke. He knew something had happened because his eyes started failing at an unbelievable rate, and he started constantly seeing double. Ultimately he would need two surgeries to correct the problem. After that, he decided to cut back to forty-to-fifty-hour weeks. It was at this point that he insisted, at the next annual meeting, that some of the other owners step forward to assume the responsibilities of a property-owners association. This was no easy task, nor was it a difficult one – it just required a lot of time, and it was a real nuisance. Tom picked a group of people he felt would take the responsibility seriously, as none of the previous groups really would help in any significant way.

One was a retired military officer. He seemed friendly enough, but he was obviously jealous of Tom's height. One was a retired surgeon. He seemed awfully young to have retired. One was a local contractor. There was a man from Louisiana who had moved to Laurel Valley with his new wife and her three kids. There were two other guys who volunteered themselves. Tom would remain on the board for a year with another previous board member, to keep the new people on track. Tom then took all the records and gave them to the surgeon, who became the president.

The Louisiana man, who was named Ricky, had been working for Tom as a sales agent. Ricky's wife had become good friends with Tom's wife Penwahee and her son was friends with Tom's son David. In the last year, however, this man's attitude had changed. Ricky was having some very serious problems with his young wife. It was alleged that she was having an affair with one of the local men, and that Ricky found out about it and started to beat her. He made her start carrying a cell phone everywhere she went as now Townsend just received its first cell tower. He would call every fifteen minutes to see where she was. It was never confirmed that she'd had an affair. In fact, over time, it was learned that it was just another nasty rumor started by a jealous woman in Townsend. Often Ricky would ask his wife where she was, tell her to pull over, and make her wait there. He would then race to that location to see if she was telling the truth. It was driving Ricky nuts, even though his wife wasn't doing anything wrong. Seeing the result of this rumor, other women, who were jealous of Ricky's wife, would start new rumors. She was now his slave, and he treated her like one. She had to accept the conditions, as she had no money and had signed a pre-nuptial agreement. While this was going on, Ricky was attending the local Catholic Church and donating large sums of money to buy forgiveness for his physical assaults on his wife. At the same time, he was being told lie after lie about his wife by some local thug named Jerry Grant.

Grant was an old cocaine dealer who had turned state's witness, or "snitch," as it was called locally. He enjoyed watching people suffer, and he would come up with some of the most unbelievable rumors about people. He would always start off the rumor "I heard in the wind yesterday…" He would always close with, "I really don't think it is true, and I think people should stop talking about it." Within an hour, the rumor would have circled all the way through Townsend, and if confronted, Grant could always say, "I told them I didn't believe it and told them to stop talking about it." Grant was driving Ricky crazy, and before long Ricky started acting as if everyone in town was having an affair with his wife. This attitude bled over into his work as a sales agent. He seemed as though he was becoming jealous of Tom, yet he would go to great extremes to act as if Tom was his best friend. It all came to a head when Ricky failed to disclose the entire truth about the sale of his brother's house.

Ricky's brother Andy had listed a house he owned in Laurel Valley with Tom's agency for $119,000. A newly hired employee at the pro shop named Jack Prior asked if Tom's agency had anything to rent. He offered to pay $1,200 a month for any two-bedroom house in Laurel Valley, and sign a two-year lease if the agency could find him a suitable property. Ricky called his brother Andy and offered him $110,000 for the house. Ricky also failed to tell Andy there was a potential tenant for his home, at $1,200 per month.

When Tom saw what was going on, he told Ricky that full disclosure was the law and that he would have to tell his brother Andy about the rental offer. Ricky became enraged – saying that things between his brother and him were none of Tom's business – and left the office for the rest of the week. Tom made Ricky call his brother and tell him the entire story. Knowing there was a rental offer at $1,200 dollars per month, Andy elected to keep the house and enjoy the income from the renter.

That next evening, there was a property owners' meeting at Dr. Garity's house. Ricky attempted to get a copy of the homeowners list from the president. Tom insisted that the property owners list could only be used for property owners' matters. Ricky resigned from the board, and opened a real estate office in a motel room on the road just in front of Tom's office. This was the beginning of Tom's troubles in Laurel Valley.

Now renting an office from Jerry Grant and Sue White, Ricky started reacting to everything they said. What happened over the next fifteen years is a story unto itself. In fact I have already written this story, but I have decided to wait to publish it until a few things happen.

Over the decades, I have written down what I know about what transpired. I have to wait for one more person to die off before I tell the story about why things are the way they are in Townsend. You see, you can't tell the Laurel Valley story without telling the City of Townsend story. You can't tell the city of Townsend that story without telling the story about District 15, or about Tuckaleechee Cove, as it is known in Blount County. And you can't tell the District 15 story without telling the Blount County story. Over the last couple of decades, I have been researching the relationship between all these groups. What an amazing cartel of people. I haven't been very noticeable over the last few decades. There was a reason for that. I purposely disappeared. Dropped off the radar. Things have gotten complicated. I can't keep up with the technology, and I have become concerned my identity may be compromised. There was a good reason for me to disappear, and I plan to keep it that way.

Chapter 18
Death Becomes Him

The stars express their last shards of light, only to be melted by the dawn. It has been a long, hot summer and even the night crickets sound tired. A lone coyote yowls an eerie howl to collect the clan. It is time to disappear, as daylight approaches.

Time marches forward, impervious to the reaction of the forest. It is time for day to arrive. The oaken masses of the canopy now become definable against the increasing light from Earth's eastern horizon. Two white oaks to my left, three hickorys to my right: a squirrel's buffet. The moment of birth of another day.

How more clued-in do we need to be? Clearly, this is a dress rehearsal to the next coming. Soon it will be the time of Man.

Life had been very good for Julio, Roberto, and me until Tom got involved with the guys from United Equities Corporation during his timeshare years. This brought in the F.B.I., as they were now investigating United Equities Corporation for mortgage fraud. Apparently, the two owners had a crooked loan officer or mortgage broker and a crooked appraiser on their payroll. One of the United Equities boys would look at homes for sale in the Gatlinburg area, and take one off the market with an escrow deposit. While the home was under contract, they would sell the home to their company, United Equities Corporation, at a highly inflated price. This markup would often be more than $100,000 higher than their purchase price for the home. The appraiser would issue an appraisal for the inflated price, and the loan officer would close the transaction using the higher appraisal. At closing, the original homeowner would be paid for the house with the borrowed funds. The rest of the borrowed funds would be given to the owners of United Equities Corporation. With each sale, a new market comparable would be created. After about twenty to thirty home purchases, they started buying timeshare resorts. Now Tom was in the middle of an F.B.I. investigation. Tom did all of his own marketing, so there was no business connection to me or Roberto. Having been on that side of the fence before, I knew it was just a matter of time before Tom would be asked if he knew me. It was time for me to disappear.

There was really more to my decision than just this connection. At this point we had "processed" over three billion, two hundred million dollars through various schemes over the last few years. The Treasury Department had infiltrated the Cayman Islands, and computers were connecting the dots between different banking institutions.

I had married a young girl from Maryville, Tennessee, and we had a beautiful daughter. My wife was still quite attractive, and she would easily be able to find another husband. I really didn't connect with my daughter, as I was considerably older than most fathers with young daughters.

I loved them both very much, and because of my love for them, I felt it would be best to disassociate myself from them in the event things went poorly in these F.B.I. investigations. I decided to fake my own death, and have one of the fake insurance companies I owned pay off handsomely on my life insurance policy. This way, my wife and daughter would be financially secure, and still be young enough to meet and enjoy life with another man to be their husband and father. I set up trusts for this transfer, so that no one could steal this financial security from them.

Faking a death is quite hard. You need several people to be actively involved. First there is a 911 call, where the fire department arrives and takes you to the emergency room of a local hospital. No problem there.

I had a history of heart trouble, and I'd even had a pacemaker installed a few years ago. All I needed to do was start jogging and get my heart rate above 160, and the damn thing would zap the shit out of me. I figured if I took a couple of ten-milligram hydrocodone pills, thirty minutes in advance, it wouldn't be too bad.

I knew which hospital each fire department used, and I knew when Dr. Morris was working in the emergency room.

Dr. Morris is our favorite coke and sex junkie. Roberto and I met him in a small bar in the Bahamas, on one of our trips. He was openly trying to score some coke at the bar, as he had a twenty-year-old coke slut hanging on his arm, wanting to trade sex for lines of coke. Roberto knew the bartender, and he also knew the girl. It was rumored that she had AIDS.

Roberto started some small talk with Dr. Morris, suggesting he could get him some blow. He pulled him aside and told him he would hook him up with some coke, but that he might want to find another girl, a clean one.

You should have seen the look on Dr. Morris's face when he learned that the girl was infected with HIV.

Roberto signaled me to come join them at a table, while he had the bartender remove the girl.

I couldn't figure out what Roberto was up to at first, and then it became obvious that he was cultivating this guy for some future need.

The three of us left this bar and went to a slightly nicer place on the east side of the island. It was a club that Roberto owned, and before long, each of us had a beautiful, "clean" lady hanging on our arm. The girl that Dr. Morris was with came equipped with her own coke supply. After a few small lines at the table, they left the club to go to the suite for the night.

The next morning, or really early afternoon, Dr. Morris surfaced at the club. Roberto and I were enjoying an umbrella drink, and Roberto asked him to join us. Within an hour, Roberto knew everything about Dr. Morris that he needed. Over the next few months, Roberto would have Dr. Morris join him on various excursions that always ended up with martinis, a beautiful woman, and coke in a room somewhere. A year later, Dr. Morris was working as the emergency room director at a small, eighty-bed hospital in one of the bedroom communities outside Miami, Florida. During the weekends, Roberto would set him up somewhere in the Bahamas as a "perk" for taking the job.

Obviously, the regulations and oversight were lax at this facility. Sometimes the police were not notified when a shooting victim needed medical help. Men arrived with fake IDs, and paid in cash, so no one at the hospital really cared. Why upset the applecart when everything is going so well? Over the years, Dr. Morris introduced Roberto to the hospital administrator and the male nurse who assisted Dr. Morris in the emergency room. What Dr. Morris didn't know was the hospital administrator had actually been hired by me. Every weekend, all three would arrive at the destination in the Bahamas that Roberto had given them. What was so funny was that Dr. Morris never knew I had purchased the hospital years earlier, with some of our money, as a long-term investment.

I contacted Roberto, and he assured me he would work out the details with Dr. Morris. This community was so small that the doctor at the hospital acted as the coroner, and pronounced people dead.

The funeral home was no problem. Actually, I owned this funeral home, along with about 130 others throughout the South. Some of them were named after local people who became my partners. One even used my proper name. I was to be cremated immediately upon arrival, as per the instructions from my will. I had discussed this over the years with my wife. I told her I had a hangup over people looking at dead people in funeral homes. I told her that if she loved me, she would agree to let the hospital where I die take me directly to the funeral home and cremate me. After a day or two, she could hold a memorial service for closure. Roberto would be there to see that my wife honored my wishes.

Of course, we needed a body for the employees of the funeral home to cremate. There would be some lackey from the insurance company sent out to investigate that there actually was a cremation. Because Roberto and I also owned the insurance company, it would be easy to choose our worst investigator to verify the death.

I picked a funeral home where I knew the administration very well. Actually, he partied with Dr. Morris, and about a dozen others, each weekend.

We did a photo shoot showing my naked body in a wooden box, starting to enter the crematory. These photos would be switched with the ones of the person who was really going to be cremated.

It took a few weeks before we found a homeless man, who had died of an overdose at the hospital during Dr. Morris's shift. The paperwork showed that he'd been given two aspirin, and sent back out onto the streets. That afternoon I kissed my wife and daughter, told them how great they were and how much I loved them, and went for a short jog in the park. My "death" went like clockwork.

I know it is kind of sick, but I had Roberto videotape my funeral. Tom and a couple other friends were clearly shaken. I felt very sad and guilty every time the video showed my wife and daughter. I knew they would be hurting, but it really tore me up to see them grieving and in such emotional pain.

The insurance check from my death annuity started arriving monthly. I was sent a video of the lawyer explaining it all to my wife. She couldn't believe she was going to be receiving so much money, every month, for the rest of her life. Whenever I would get melancholy, I would watch this video to cheer myself up and remind myself that I had done the right thing. Within a year my wife was remarried, to an optometrist who lived in Charleston, South Carolina.

I laid low in Belize with Roberto for about two years. I was getting quite homesick for East Tennessee and the beautiful mountains. I missed my "little brother," Tom, more than anything.

Prior to my "death," I had quietly purchased a reclusive cabin in the Dry Valley area of Townsend, Tennessee. This was close to where Tom was developing the golf course community called Laurel Valley. While in Belize, I underwent a series of surgeries to alter my appearance, and to make me look ugly and quite old. Usually, when people change their appearance, they are trying to look younger and more handsome. My appearance didn't matter to me, since whenever I wanted a Victoria's Secret-quality model for the weekend, I would dial one up through Roberto. Some weekends, I would have him send me two. We would all lie around my cabin and decks naked, enjoying the views and privacy. If I ever went anywhere with them, let's say Pigeon Forge or Gatlinburg, I would get a cane and act as though I was their grandfather. Sometimes the most obvious is the least obvious.

Townsend is a small community, and I was enjoying living vicariously, through Tom's success, in developing Laurel Valley. I felt as though I was going to work with him each day, as the whole town was constantly talking about Laurel Valley and what Tom was up to that week. As I blended into the old person's routines, I found myself able to get all the intelligence I needed. After breakfast, I would randomly drop by some of the merchants, or the Visitors Bureau, to catch up on the gossip. I was enjoying my retirement, playing this cat-and-mouse game of avoiding being anywhere Tom showed up in this peaceful little tourist town. Retirement was good. But then Tom moved to Maryville, and the town started to bore me. It wasn't entertaining anymore. There wasn't anyone doing or saying anything significant anymore. After Tom left Laurel Valley and started doing business in Knoxville, everything seemed to stop moving forward in Townsend. The growth seemed to dry up. In fact, it seemed as though Townsend was going backwards. The fact is that two other businessmen were also getting disenchanted with the stupid politics of Townsend. Pete Maples, who owned the largest motel and was not related to anyone in Townsend, was spending over $100,000 per year on marketing and advertising. Randy Jenkins, another non-local, was spending about the same amount on his cabin-rental business, and Tom was spending more than both of them combined in marketing his cabin rentals, golf course, real estate, and construction sales. That same year, the Smoky Mountain Visitors Bureau, which collected the hotel/motel taxes, spent less than $40,000 for their advertising of Townsend. The rest of the hundreds of thousands of dollars that they received in tax collections was spent on administrative costs for the Visitors Bureau and the Blount Chamber of Commerce. Jealous over their success, and frustrated over living off the "crumbs" left over from the approximately half-million marketing dollars spent by these three institutions, the locals did everything possible to make life miserable for these three businessmen. Within a few years, all three stopped doing business in Townsend. When they left, their marketing money left with them. Like a plump grape left in the sun, the commerce slowly dried up, and Townsend's economy became an old, shriveled-up raisin. At the same time, the adjoining Wears Valley area exploded with the opportunity lost in Townsend. Now, totally bored with the area, I decided I no longer wanted to stay there.

Chapter 19
A New Seed Will Sprout

...I dreamed that winter arrived last night. It was very late, and long overdue. The maples and beech trees were still cloaked in crimson and sunburst yellow. The wise old oaks were leafless, standing firm and still, having sent their life juices down into their deepest roots. The winter will be hard and severe this year, punishing the stark, gray forest. The survivors will again smell the warm spring air, and burst forward with another year's growth.

It is damp, windy and wet, yet an enthusiastic ray of sunlight has burst through the clouds, and it warms the back of my right hand. A shadow is cast on the paper under my pen, yet the rest of the white paper is bright and eager to participate. The clouds in the sky churn like fresh buttermilk, and the air is cold.

There are children in the loft of a new lodge, customizing the room with five bright colors. The pattern was previously finalized, and the entire sisterhood set forward, to put their signature on their part of the lodge.

They had started a "Little Sister of the Sun Adventure Club." In my dream, I see them take a voyage to the upper peninsula of Michigan for a two-week adventure. All of them learned the lyrics to "Candles in the Rain" by Melanie, an old early-'70s favorite. After hours of singing the song from Mackinaw Island to Knoxville, they designed a logo along with their membership cards. Born was the Charter Membership of the Little Sisters of the Sun Adventure Club. I awoke, feeling as though I knew who these children were.

In the fall of 2012, I was "letting" Roberto and my future replacement use my Townsend cabin. Roberto said he was grilling steaks, when a bear descended upon the grill and tipped it over. This caused a fire that burned my cabin to the ground. It didn't really matter; I had gotten bored with Townsend since Tom had left, and no longer spent any time there. Not much happens that is that interesting anymore. The cabin needed a lot of maintenance, and you could never get anyone in Townsend to show up as promised. Genetically speaking, there was a real problem with almost all the Townsend workforce. As the saying goes, "The acorn doesn't fall far from the tree."

I went by the location of the burned cabin on Rich Mountain for one last look. I figured I would just let the land be sold for back property taxes. The newspaper article about the fire said an unidentified recluse had lived at the cabin when it caught fire. As I ascended the mountain, I noticed how long it took me to hike up the path to the cabin. The trail was quite slick with the wet leaves covering the mountain shale. I felt cold, as it was the first rain of the fall. Unlike the summer storms, it was steady and continuous; settled in for the day.

The pewter skies kept a steady flow of medium-sized raindrops on the forest canopy. The remaining leaves on the trees glistened silver-gray in their welcomed bath.

I had awakened with dry, clogged sinuses and red, itchy eyes. But now that I am walking outside, the fall rain has made me well. The moisture in the cool, humid air has flushed my sinuses, and I breathe clean air. My eyes have been cleansed with nature's suspended fog, and they are now clear and crisp. I am healed, safe from the climate-controlled interior of my home, and I am challenged by the climb to the cabin.

The trees in the forest are so independent. Yes, they have to compete for nutrition in the soil; like humanity, their roots are intertwined from the constant struggle. But they stand strong and tall, independently adjusting to whatever the environment throws their way.

Another wonderful day at the lake
with the children and their friends.

When they get big enough, they will be chopped down and bled of their sap. They will be sliced into lumber, cut to a size to accommodate mankind, and crucified with metal spikes. Now naked and vulnerable from the loss of their bark, they will be coated in stain, paints, and chemicals to keep Mother Nature from reclaiming them into the forest floor.

And there they stand, shattered pieces of their previous self. Just like our welfare state, they are now completely reliant on civilization to keep them protected from the environment. Spray me or the bugs will eat me. Paint me or I will rot and disintegrate. Feed me with constant care and concern, as I am now completely reliant on you. I wonder, when we treat mankind the way we treat our forest, are we really doing them any favors? Then time passes, and sooner or later no one cares. The public concern and love will move on, and everything is left to decay. The decay may be slow, but it is as steady as the autumn rain.

I had still been monitoring Tom's communications. He had now built a cabin in an adjoining county, deep in the Cherokee National Forest. Most of his spare time was spent doting over his children and their friends. He had purchased a boat, and the children enjoyed the lake.

When I got home that evening, I interrupted one of his communications that he had sent to his own secret email account. There was no one at the other end to pick up his messages. He had set up the account years before to send his own letters, knowing they would never be read. He was still functioning day to day and working hard, but when I read the emails it was obvious he was developing a lone-wolf personality. Still, it was fun to follow the events he recorded and sent to himself.

We are now old. I had been with him his entire adult life, yet he had not seen me in decades.

I returned to Florida for a few months, trying to distance myself from my sadness.

After Christmas, I returned to Tennessee. I am going to get the last of my things from a storage locker, and give them to Habitat for Humanity. I still own a bass boat. After some thought, I decided to take it out one more time.

It was January, and I launched my boat at the Toqua launch in Tellico Lake. It may be winter, but I am going fishing. Fishing is an important part of everyone's personal development. For whatever reason, sometimes things just don't work. A perfect business plan, flawless execution, 100-percent effort and enthusiasm. Every leader or CEO should be required to fish.

Today I'm fishing for sauger. But for some reason, the fish don't want to bite. I have the ultimate boat. I put fresh line on my reel last night. As far as the presentation, I have green, silver, and red. And gold, green, with blue and silver, and about a few hundred other lures with every color under the rainbow. I am where all the fish should be spending their winter vacations. My depth finder can spot a fish hiding on the bottom or in a bush, up to three hundred feet deep. As this lake is nowhere near that deep, this may have been a little overkill. It is showing fish all over the place, but for some reason the fish don't want to bite.

I have a plain hook with the drab dog hair. I have one that is too dressed up, with pink feathers from a discarded boa, a failed attempt to "match the hatch." I have never seen a bug wearing a colorful feather, and my overstated color schemes could only be described as hooks dressed in drag. Big fish, little fish, happy fish, sad fish, we have a color for you. Maybe I overdid it in the fly-tying category.

Sauger is kind of a southern walleye found in the Tennessee Valley, and yes, they have a little orange on them mixed in with a marbled green and brown pattern. They say the worst, most miserable days are when you catch sauger. They taste like walleye, and that is why I fish for them.

As far as a miserable day to be out on the lake, today is perfect. It is somewhere between thirty and thirty-four degrees; it is snowing; the wind is blowing hard from the west. Most people have never eaten a sauger at home, enjoying the comforts offered to them by the Tennessee Valley Authority. A heat pump warming a house. Coffee freshly brewed. Grandma's cookies. But I am enjoying the lake created by TVA off

Tellico Point. Even though I have the whole lake to myself, the fish don't want to bite.

For some reason, when it snows, people think things turn white. They don't turn white; they turn gray, kind of a cold steel gray. The sky is gray, the green pinecones look gray, and the white snowflakes melt when they hit the cold, blue-gray water. The gray rocks along the shore look grayer. Everything is gray. On Tellico Point, a state park, they have built a fort to replicate a settlers' village. The perimeter fence looks like it was made of identical-length pine poles run through a large pencil sharpener. I am sure that all the settlers had these large pencil sharpeners with them wherever they went. I am really convinced they built fences that looked like this. Very authentic.

There isn't much area to grow crops inside the fence. Sooner than later someone was going to have to go outside to get something to eat. I also noticed that the enclosure is reasonably far from the water. During the summer, when it is really hot, someone is going to want to drink. The flag flying inside the fort is British, so let's break it down. A British fort that can't grow food and has no water, and it's surrounded by the art deco fence of its time in the middle of the Cherokee Nation. Maybe they would have done better if they had just tried to get along with the Indians.

In the distance, I hear heavy traffic crossing the 411 bridge. I have no idea where everyone could be going on such a miserable day. I think all the local people have poured out of the hollers and are driving as fast as they can in an effort to get to Kroger. It seems to be somewhat of a cultural thing in East Tennessee. Whenever it snows, go to Kroger. I think Kroger owns the local cable channel that carries a twenty-four-hour weather broadcast format. It never snows half of what they say.

It had just dawned on me that I am fishing where and when all the locals fish, and that the locals are not here. For some odd reason, none of the locals made it out to fish today. They must have gone to Kroger.

Well, there is always an ending to everything. There are lots of beginnings, but always endings. Time marches on. I have buried friends, family, and family friends; employees, employees' family, and employees' friends. Thirty years ago, almost to the day, I saw Tom bury his brother. That was hard. I hope that when I die they bury me that same day. Call and tell my friends, after it is too late to inconvenience them, to come to my funeral. Of course, everyone thinks I am already dead. But it was a nice thought. This should have been my last act of courtesy. At least no one will have to attend my real funeral. I am sure it was an inconvenience to everyone I knew, by having them attend my funeral years ago. What a waste of time. After all, we all know sooner or later that life will have to end.

It is getting late. This day is about to end. Despite all my best-made plans, I have caught no fish. The ice peels off my line as I retrieve my bait and place myself into the driver's seat of the boat. I move as though I am 100 years old, but I feel very alive. For some reason, the fish won't bite. But this moment defines me. For with every ending there will be a new beginning, and tomorrow, maybe, I will try again.

I returned to my motel room and lay on the bed. I placed a blanket over my legs, as they were quite cold. I opened my laptop and scanned through Tom's ghost email account for a warm story or happy letter. I came upon his last entry. It was about Laurel Valley and Townsend and he had just downloaded the entire file. He had obviously been writing it for years, as it was hundreds of pages long. Now fully engulfed into his lone-wolf personality, it was obvious he was anticipating a nearing end.

It was spring before I made another trip to Tellico Lake. I went to the Chota Memorial for the displaced Cherokee nation. This was close to a beach that Tom fished when the walleye made their spawn run each year. I was hoping I might notice Tom on the lake fishing, but he was not there. As I looked over the lake, and thought of all the lost time and missed opportunities, I stared into my soul. All I saw was an empty space.

I went one more time to Tellico Lake in fall, 2013, hoping to see Tom from a distance. He was not on the lake. A train meanders in the next valley, causing the mountain to echo of distant thunder. The sad, slow whistle of yesteryear sounds at every road crossing. It must be 9:02 am. The railroad is an institution that clearly understands the importance of time.

An adolescent squirrel starts to bark. So much to do, now that the nuts are ripe. How he loathes the deer. The more acorns he buries, the more they nuzzle and paw them out of the ground. He barks at the deer as they raid his winter provisions. If only the hunters would pay attention to him, he would help them kill every last deer in the woods. But he knows too well that you can't trust a predator if you are, in fact, prey.

The warming air causes the trees to pinch the acorns and nuts off their limbs. They have grown and nurtured them through the hot summer, and it is now time for them to go. The trees look pale and tired now. They will soon blanket the fallen acorns with millions of leaves, protecting them from winter's cold mornings.

Tomorrow's trees, the next generation of forests. Mother Nature's period. And yes, time marches forward, impervious to the reaction of the forest.

I kept thinking about Tom's last entry into his ghost email account. It was so interesting and well documented. I just couldn't let it go. I realized that my job as his mentor and guardian was over. Soon we will be together and live our dreams again, surrounded by the songs of the whippoorwills and the cries of the hounds. But I still feel restless. I still feel the need to tell the story about Townsend, and Laurel Valley. Unbeknown to Tom, over the years, I had intervened with some of the personalities in his life who needed a little correction from their poor behavior. I realized I still needed closure over what happened to Tom and why he left Townsend. As I lay there reading his years of emails, I knew his story needed to be told.

In fact it is time to tell the story of Tuckaleechee Cove, or District 15, as it is known. I am ready to start telling all: all the truth about everyone's lies and misdeeds. It is all here on my laptop. Tom's ghost emails need to come to life. I just don't want anyone to figure out that I am the one who is telling the story.

History demands that everyone know the pain and suffering of Tuckaleechee Cove. Between my research, and Tom's ghost email account, I realized that I now have a complete history.

Remember the bear hunters? They see all. If you are hearing a hound in the night, they are in the woods. They hunt, and they witness. They are always watching from the shadows. And when they see things, those moments travel in the wind through the mountains. It is an old expression: "I heard it in the wind that..." No one ever knows where the story started; they just know the story.

I know a story. I know many stories, because I knew the bear hunters, and I now have the emails written by Tom about Townsend's history as told by the bear hunters. I am going to write these stories down. Stories that were heard in the wind. The untold stories of the mountain men's lost souls. The Tuckaleechee tears.

Townsend was the last stop on the road at the edge of true wilderness. It was also humanity's last stop in more ways than one. There are some good people in Townsend, along with a lot of bad people. Every holler has a pack of hounds, and everyone knows what everyone else is doing.

Tom was a young man when he first moved to Townsend. My "Tuckaleechee Tears" story will start out in a holler at the end of Carrs Creek Road. I think the holler was called Swampy Branch. What happened that year, on the upper end of Townsend, is why Townsend is not the size of Gatlinburg or Pigeon Forge today.

Little mountain children, Alyssa and Nathan,
ready to take on the world.

Epilogue

I am awake, yet I feel as though I am asleep.

Last night the sun set hard, with the clouds smothering the western sky. Bad weather will soon be upon us.

In the East, the full moon crept over the horizon, bold yet apprehensive. Scattered clouds occasionally touched the pale halo, tickling the moon up the ridgeline. It finally broke clear, into the pale blue atmosphere blanketing the mountains.

I walked into the forest. Trees of white and pink glowed, their blossoms reflecting the moon's rays. Unorganized and happenchance they grew in groups of three, seven, twelve – and occasionally they stood as one.

I lay on the forest floor, a soft carpet of yesterday. And the moon continued to rise new, proud, and without hesitation. Time passed, and like metal to a magnet, I felt my body being pulled by the forest floor.

I looked at the pale light on the back of my hand. Blood pumped through the veins; they swelled, quite pronounced under my thin, aging skin. The flow of life, so contained and regulated, yet so vulnerable and exposed. Deep in my soul I feel the need to stare at the moon. Now in the early morning of the next day, it turned bright red, like fresh blood. I watched the bright red turn to a red brown, the color of old blood. Is this a message, a warning, or just the passing of another moment in time?

As I gazed at the blood moon, one became three, and I knew I would be exposed to all in a short period of time. There would be the passing of three seasons, twice, and after the fourth blood moon rises in the East, all in Tuckaleechee Cove will fully understand their failed dreams – and why they will cry their tears for generations to come.

About the Author

The author was born in Knoxville, Tennessee, raised in Stamford, Connecticut, and then returned home to attend the University of Tennessee Knoxville.

He is an avid outdoorsman and hunter who has the greatest respect for the beauty of East Tennessee and all the wildlife that lives here. His philosophy is, if you kill it you eat it, take out what you take in the woods, and it is our responsibility to be good stewards of God's creations.

He became a licensed contractor and has been building custom homes for over thirty-seven years and restoration work for insurance companies for fourteen years.

During his early years he lived in Townsend, Tennessee. While living there, he and his partner developed a 1,800 acre golf course community known as Laurel Valley Resort. He is also a licensed real estate broker and has developed numerous subdivisions.

After having three children, he and his wife, Penni, moved to Maryville, Tennessee for the superb school systems.

Together with Pastor Jeremy Graham, they have been working with a men's ministry called True Purpose Ministries, helping to train young men in the construction trades, helping with job placement once they graduate, and assisting with the men's housing and needs.